A BOLT FROM THE BLUE

A BOLT FROM THE BLUE

a Bennett Sisters Mystery

LISE MCCLENDON

THALIA PRESS

A BOLT FROM THE BLUE

A Bennett Sisters Mystery
© 2019, by Lise McClendon

CHAPTER ONE

FRANCE

The morning light dimmed as Francie Bennett maneuvered her rental car through the narrow lanes of the backwoods of the Dordogne and into Lot-et-Garonne to the south. The trees grew thick, arching over the road. Where once the skies were fierce and blue, the sun warm on the side of her face, now the oppressive greens and browns of the woods blotted all that out. Was it some kind of omen? She doubted it. But nothing about this estate had been ordinary.

She wound her way on the ever-smaller roads, following the directions from her phone. Otherwise she'd have been lost for days, driving in circles down shaded lanes, far from civilization. She'd once marveled that cosmopolitan France, land of manners and fashion and cuisine and sophistication, could still have such neglected backwaters. Where were the house-flippers and Brits on the prowl? These places seemed untouched by modernization, neglected and gone to rot.

The mission, to find this old house, had sounded delicious, even mysterious, evoking a girlish curiosity that Francie was glad to discover she hadn't outgrown. To outlive curiosity, to be jaded about the unknown and undiscovered, would be tragic. So here she was, deep in rural Aquitaine, far from vineyards and goats and, well, people. To open an old woman's manse that no one had cared about for nearly forty years.

There was no village, no town square, post office, or store. Not much of anything but overgrown lots, cows, and sparse stands of trees. The destination was approached carefully, with intention, winding around hummocks and along streams. It was on no maps, just a blip on an unnamed road. A hamlet, something she somehow associated with small ham sandwiches—ridiculous, yes—that's what it was. A collection of a few houses of varying sizes, on acreages with falling-down barns and grass up to your knees.

She slowed to a crawl, phone in hand, looking at directions. This must be the place. She turned off the car and stepped into the weeds. Putting aside visions of rats and pigeons, she stood outside the stone house, dangling the keys. Of course she was curious. She'd read about apartments in Paris that had been boarded up during the war and never touched for sixty years, museums of a long-gone time. Would this old house be fabulous, or simply disgusting? Merle's cottage had been more filthy than delightful at first.

The house was much larger than her sister's. Not a château like she fantasized but a good sized villa. The old lady apparently came from a family of aristocrats, what was left of them in secular, socialist, post-Revolution, postwar France. A lapsed duke, a long-ago count: they remained, their wealth often tied up in land and houses no one wanted, or their fortunes gone forever along with their heads.

Two stories of weathered gray stone, the mansion had a roof that sported fancy gables with odd-shaped windows, indicating a third floor under the slates. Windows were shuttered, a soft, peeling rose color, or smothered by vines. The yard was flat cream-colored gravel overrun with weeds. Dry, prickly thistles scratched those who dared to enter. A half-dead tree stood guard, its leaves yellow and black.

Villa Pardoux was not quite a mansion, not anymore.

The first padlock, on the door shutters, was awkward and rusty. But with a few trials it popped open. The shutters creaked and one hinge fell apart. Now, key in the door lock, she wiggled it for two minutes before she felt it give. The house didn't want to give up its secrets, that was obvious. Then it turned, a loud, metallic click, just as her cell phone rang.

It was Dylan. "Did you find it?"

"I think so." He read off the address again, which didn't help. "There are no street signs. No numbers, no signs of any kind."

"Well, if the key works, there's your answer."

"I'm unlocking the door right now. The padlock on the shutters opened."

"What's it like?"

"On the outside, about what you'd expect: dirty and weedy. Pretty big, but in the middle of serious French nowhere. Not another house or person in sight. All the shutters seem intact though, and the roof looks good from the front at least. Nothing growing through the slates."

"Call me later? I'm hoping to come down next weekend. I'll be waiting for your call."

She slipped her phone back in her pocket and pushed open the double doors. The stale stench of dust, mold, and animal droppings swept past her as if glad to be free. But there was something else, flowery, powdery. Her eyes blinked against the darkness.

She paused, pulled out a small flashlight, and stepped inside.

CHAPTER TWO

Oklahoma: Two Weeks Earlier

On the day the letter arrived, Axelle Fourcier was preparing for what she hoped was the last move of her life. She sighed, feeling the ache in her back. She was old; she couldn't move at the drop of a hat anymore. She'd retired three years before from the university and found herself bored to tears at least once a week. She wished she could go back to teaching. That was impossible. The dean had said as much, a glassy horror in his eyes at the thought. So she now had all the time she wanted to read history and keep up on her native French. That was excellent, she tried to persuade herself. Keep the brain active. She did read for hours each day, but mostly in English. For the French she watched France 24 news on their website and found it dry as toast.

The letter at least added a minor frisson to her thrilling day of packing boxes. She gave them a stare, piled haphazardly in the hallway. Who knew if she'd be happier, healthier, more engaged in life in North Carolina than in Oklahoma? She certainly didn't, although she'd decided she'd rather be blown off the earth by a hurricane than die a moldering death in the flatlands of America. The little beach house had called to her. At least hurricanes weren't boring.

The letter was from an attorney's office. In Paris. That gave her a slight chill. *Paris.* Flashbacks of her youth, burning cars in the streets, sitting crosslegged, arm in arm with thousands of classmates under the Arc de Triomphe, then marching, chanting: *"Adieu,* de Gaulle!" So long ago and yet she could still smell the asphalt of the streets and the melting rubber tires of the cars.

She walked out onto the porch of her house, just blocks from the university campus, carrying the unopened letter and shaking the images from her head. The past still haunted her. She thought she'd put it to bed years ago, but it was obvious she had not.

She stared at the ornate handwriting on the envelope, in blue ink and very French. She sighed, squared her shoulders, and tore open the flap. A single sheet of fine ivory stationery was folded inside.

The name of the law firm rang a distant bell in her mind. Where had she heard it? The letter was in French, which seemed presumptuous after all these years.

> Madame:
>
> It is with the greatest sympathy that we must inform you that your great-aunt, Mathilde Fourcier, has died. Her long and ebullient life must be a consolation to you and all her relatives. She died without issue. As her closest family members she leaves her estate to you and her nephew, your cousin, Lucien Daucourt, of Paris.
>
> Monsieur Daucourt has personally examined the estate papers and informed us of your address. This took some time, as apparently you have not recently corresponded. Madame Fourcier passed away on May 3 of this year, four months ago. M. Daucourt took charge of arranging her effects and has placed the urn with her remains in the family crypt in the Passy Cemetery here in Paris. We pray that this is satisfactory with you.
>
> It is imperative that we meet with you at the earliest possible time to discuss the disposition of the estate. Madame Fourcier did not deplete her estate, despite being 104 years of age. There is much to examine.

Therefore, we request your presence in Paris at your earliest convenience. Please call us at the number above.

Regards . . .

AXELLE SAT down on a dusty porch chair and reread the letter. Several of the French legal terms made her squint into the dry lawn, trying to dredge up their meanings. The main message was clear: Tante Mathilde was dead, at 104.

Axelle closed her eyes, memories of her family struggling to surface. She'd last seen her aunt in 1969, when they were both young. Feisty and independent, Mathilde had hair like Brigitte Bardot and a string of high-society boyfriends, none of whom she liked well enough to marry. She was so charming and exciting, a light in the stratosphere of Axelle's unsophisticated teenage world. Axelle could hear her aunt's laugh now, head thrown back, crimson lipstick, full throated as a lark. A champagne glass breaking, a sparkling bracelet on a slender wrist.

A sadness for the past washed over her. The French curse, this pitiful nostalgia for things that will never be again. This melancholy for *temps perdu,* as Proust called it. He couldn't find his lost time, and the search for it crippled him. She would not let nostalgia cripple her. She was as American, as modern, as optimistic as anyone. She'd lived here since her twenties, nearly fifty years. She'd worked so hard to cleanse herself from the eroding pessimism of her countrymen.

But it was still with her. *Her* curse. Because, try as she might, she was still French.

She took a deep breath and stared at the letter in her lap. Her dear *tantine* had not forgotten her. And also this cousin. Who was he? She had no memory of any cousin named Lucien. Their correspondence was nonexistent. Still, he apparently helped track her down. There couldn't be much left of the estate, despite what the attorneys said, not after 104 years of extravagance as only a woman who was rich, wild, and French could live. The question was, was there enough left to warrant a trip back to the past?

She would call the lawyers. It might be nothing. Surely it was nothing.

Going back to France was, after all, against everything she stood for, as she'd told everyone who'd listen all these years. *Never!* she crowed when they asked if she would return. The looks in their eyes, the confusion over her adamant statements—no one understood, because she never explained. Keeping her hurt inside made it precious, and real.

And yet. A twinge of regret stung her. She had missed seeing her aunt one last time, kissing her dusty cheeks, catching her orange-vanilla scent. Missed easing her into her last comforts. Missed feeding her pink macarons and jasmine tea from Mariage Frères, tucking a cashmere shawl around her thin shoulders.

Axelle sighed deeply, frustrated and tired. She felt every day of her many years. Her stubborn pride was a burden.

Did she still, after all this time, despise *la république*?

CHAPTER THREE

New York

Francie Bennett stretched her legs on the back porch, catching the September sunshine before it went behind the line of trees at the end of the lot. Dylan Hardy's house, a tidy, gray cottage with white trim, agreed with her. In occasional moments of insanity she saw herself living here, cozy and content, baking cookies and growing tomatoes. Autumn lingered in the Northeast, warm and colorful. She smiled, leaning back, closing her eyes, and feeling the relaxation of a Sunday afternoon flow through her.

It had been another hectic week at the law firm. Renamed after the departure of the original partners, Scott Lyons McFall was just as mad as Ward & Bailee had ever been. Brenda McFall had been named a full partner, along with the two men who had angled relentlessly to take over the firm. Despite their competitiveness, the three seemed to be a pretty good fit. Having Brenda, her mentor, as a full, named partner definitely made Francie's life better. In the midsummer shake-up she had been promoted to managing partner, and now had underlings to do the dirty work she despised. No more spanking hands, wiping noses, and listening to whining for this Bennett sister.

But definitely a crazy year. In one week she and Dylan would take off for Paris for a working holiday. He claimed it wouldn't be much work on his end. She knew for a fact she was doing no work for Scott Lyons. Her summer had been full of long weeks and weekends at the office. She had earned this vacation.

Dylan pushed open the back door. He carried two glasses of wine.

"Sancerre?" Francie said, sitting up and taking one goblet. It looked like their favorite white, buttery in the sunlight.

"Nope." He sat down beside her on the old redwood furniture. "Had to raid the cellar. You drank all the Sancerre."

"I seem to recall you helped."

He clinked his glass against hers. "It's not even French. An Australian sauv blanc."

They tasted the wine and declared it *buvable*. It was Francie's favorite French term: drinkable. No raving compliments among blasé Europeans.

Francie had been spending her non-working weekends here in White Plains—that is, when Dylan's daughter wasn't staying over. He had Phoebe, now nine, every other weekend but the schedule sometimes changed. Two weeks before Francie had been settling in on a Friday night. Dylan was cooking something fabulously French and garlicky. Then the phone rang, his ex on the line. Half an hour later Phoebe was eating dinner with them, glowering at them both. She hated changes, Dylan said, and life as the only child of divorced parents was all about changes.

They'd made it through that weekend just fine, although Phoebe gave Francie the silent treatment. Dylan finally made her speak to Francie on Sunday afternoon just before she was picked up by her mother. Her "Nice seeing you, Miss Bennett" sounded as sincere as you'd expect from a sullen preteen.

This weekend had been blissfully child-free. Francie felt a little guilty about enjoying Dylan Hardy solo. She'd be mad if she were Phoebe, cut off from her father most of the time. Her own father, Jack Bennett, adored, and was adored by, his five daughters. The upcoming vacation would probably be difficult for Dylan's ex. She tried to put it out of her mind. It wasn't her problem, was it?

She sighed and sipped the wine. Dylan set down his glass on the table and turned toward her. She squinted. "What?"

"I just had a call from Paris."

"You don't have to work after all? We can go straight to the Dordogne?"

He smiled. "I wish. No, I have to go early. We'll still have the same time together. I think."

"When?"

"Tomorrow. I take the red-eye."

Francie pouted for a moment then smiled. "Well, I have a thousand things to do so I can take a vacation. But I do hate to fly by myself."

"Maybe Merle can fly with you."

Her older sister was visiting in the States. She lived in France now, but she'd been home to see her son and the family. "I think she's got a couple more weeks, but I'll check." She smiled at him. "It's no big deal."

"You squeezed the blood out of my arm last time."

She laughed. She was a bit of a nervous flyer. "I'll drink more wine." He looked thoughtful, gazing out onto his expansive, velvety green lawn, his pride and joy. Such a man. "What's going on in Paris then?"

"I'm not sure really. So far I've just had the summons from the firm. Something about a longtime client." He smiled at her. "I'll tell you as soon as I know."

"They won't want me to really *do* anything, will they? Because I'd rather swan around Paris and buy cute shoes and chocolates."

He frowned. "We did get you cleared for a little work, Francie, remember."

"Oh, I know." She waved her wineglass in a circle. "But not real legal work. I don't have a license to practice law in France."

"So bring some sensible shoes this time."

"Of course, Monsieur. I will be prepared. There will be lots of sightseeing?"

"And bring some business suits. The firm is pretty formal over there."

"Seriously?" Francie sipped her wine. She had been hoping he was just being nice about work in Paris. "I'll have to come in to the office?"

He tipped his head and said in a mock patronizing voice: "Yes, Francine."

She rolled her eyes. "What exactly will I be doing?"

"Probably not much. Legal assistant stuff. Go to lunch with the English-speaking clients, stuff like that. We always have a shortage of English speakers."

"To discuss widgets? Do you know me?"

"I know you like to eat French food."

"You do know me." She reached over to kiss his cheek. "What's for dinner?"

By Wednesday Francie was so busy putting out fires at the firm, handling personnel issues, negotiating salary bumps, and handling grievances that when Merle returned her call late in the afternoon she'd forgotten that she'd called her sister.

"Tonight's the night? Sorry, things are chaotic around here." Francie sat down and took a sip of cold coffee, wincing at the taste. "So we're on?"

"This is the only night I've got free before you leave," Merle said. "If it still works for you?"

Francie checked her wristwatch. Nearly six. "I'll go straight to the restaurant. Are you there already?"

"Just about to leave Mom and Dad's. I'll see you there in fifteen."

Francie had picked a restaurant halfway between their parents' house, where Merle was staying while in the US, and her own Greenwich apartment. It would actually take Francie more than fifteen minutes to get there, but Merle could have a nice glass of wine while she waited. Francie threw on her coat, barked at her secretary, and rushed out the door.

As busy as her life was at the law firm, it was easier now. Alice was no longer her assistant, having taken a year off to get her paralegal training. The firm had given her a nice settlement due to her harassment, which she was using for tuition. Greg Leonard, the junior associate who had made her life hell last year, had been let go in July. Rumor was he had moved away. Learning to play with the big shots in the law firm was challenging, but Francie was up for it. She actually enjoyed the maneuvering and sparring, likening it to a never-ending chess match.

But she was worn out, ready for vacation. That she could go back to Paris with Dylan was a huge bonus, but regardless, she needed a break. She drove into the setting sun, lowering her visor against the autumn glare, feeling the fatigue in her neck and shoulders.

Paris couldn't come soon enough.

Merle was halfway through a glass of rosé when Francie bustled in and found her at a table near a window, her favorite position. They hugged, ordered, and settled in. Then Francie asked if there was any chance Merle could fly back to Paris with her on the weekend.

"Dylan had to go ahead," Francie explained. "It's not a big thing, if you can't."

Merle eyed her younger sister. "You still get nervous? Still want to breathalyze all the pilots?" She smiled. "Annie told me."

Francie grimaced, shrugging. This was an emotional carryover from her marriage to a pilot who drank. "Not so much. But, yeah, a little."

"I wish I could fly with you." Merle sighed. "But Pascal is coming here on Saturday."

"He is? I'm going to miss him."

"I know. Sorry. But we'll be back in France in about a week. I think we fly on Friday. You'll still be there, right?"

"Oh, yes. Definitely."

Merle sipped her wine. "You look tired, honey."

Francie slumped in her chair. "I can't wait for this time off. But, guess what? Dylan says I might have to do some legwork for him over there."

"Private eye again?"

"Oh, I don't think so." Francie grinned. "Just take clients out to lunch. I may need a list of Michelin-starred restaurants, the really good ones. The firm will be paying."

Merle held up a finger and grabbed the strap of her purse, hanging on her chair. "I already have one!" She pulled out her phone, scrolled around, then tapped a button. "Sent." She touched Francie's hand. "Have fun, okay?"

FRANCIE TOOK Friday afternoon off to pack. Her flight left early Saturday morning. She went to the office early, ran to the dry cleaner's to pick up her suits, got her hair trimmed, and was headed home from the hairdresser when Dylan called. He wanted her to pick up a pair of his shoes at his house and bring them with her.

"That means more bags for me, Dylan," Francie warned. "Extra charges."

"The firm will reimburse you. You know which shoes I'm talking about?"

"I think so. I'll call you from your closet if I can't figure it out."

She was sitting in his walk-in closet at four that afternoon, staring at vast lineup of men's shoes, when his telephone rang at his bedside. It was weird, like Dylan knew she was staring at his oxfords. She listened idly as it stopped after four rings. No message. His closet was tidy, much more organized than hers, all color-coordinated. He didn't have as many shoes as she did, but several pairs matched his description of "golden-brown brogues." Which pair? She snapped a photo of them and texted it to him.

The phone rang again. This time Francie stood up and walked into his bedroom. Should she answer? Was it something she shouldn't hear? She waited for the answering machine to pick up. Dylan's voice asked for a message. Then a beep, then sobbing.

Francie stepped closer. More crying. Then: "Daddy?" Should she pick up? Phoebe's voice was soft, almost too low to hear. She sounded scared and upset. What was wrong? "Daddy, where are you?"

Francie snatched up the phone. "Phoebe? It's Francie Bennett. I'm over at your dad's house to pick up some shoes for him. He's out of town."

A groan then more sobbing.

"Phoebe, talk to me. Are you okay? Can I help?" Where was the girl's mother?

"He's not home?" she croaked.

"No, he went to Paris early. Did you try his cell phone?"

"He didn't answer."

"I'm sorry, Phoebe. Are you hurt? Is it an emergency?"

"Huh? Ah, no. I'm okay." She sniffed and stopped crying.

"Where are you, honey?" It was the first time she'd called her "honey" but it seemed appropriate. Something was going on.

"At home."

"Is your mother there?"

"Yes."

Okay, that was good. Francie knew nothing about Rebecca, Dylan's ex, but at least she didn't leave her kid alone. "So, what's going on? Why were you crying?"

"Sometimes I—I hate her," she said with bitterness.

"Who? Your mom? I know the feeling." Francie hadn't ever really hated her mother. Bernadette Bennett was a taskmaster at times though, and she had run a tight ship with five daughters. Francie tried to imagine how it would have been on her own, without her sisters to give her advice and wipe her tears and give her that "case of courage—bucket of balls" pep talk. She sat down on Dylan's bed, cradling his phone in both hands.

"You do?" the girl whispered.

"Oh, yeah. We had all sorts of rules when I was your age. You're nine, right? Let's see. When I was nine I had to take out the trash, empty the dishwasher, and make my bed, every day. And get my homework done by dinnertime. I always had to share a room with my little sister. We fought sometimes."

Phoebe whispered: "I wish I had a sister." She sniffed again then gasped: "I have to go," and hung up.

Francie stared at the phone for a moment and replaced the receiver. Was it just teenage angst come early? Phoebe might be lonely, but she was safe at home. It wasn't Francie's place to get into the daughter's stuff with her boyfriend's ex. Besides, Phoebe would call

Dylan again on his cell phone and tell him all about it. It was probably nothing.

She stalked into the closet, scooped up all three pairs of brogues, and drove home. She wouldn't be nervous on the plane, she told herself.

No, not at all.

CHAPTER FOUR

PARIS

The moment the huge jet bumped onto the tarmac at Charles de Gaulle Airport outside of Paris, Francie shut her eyes and said a silent "thank-you" to whoever was the patron saint of air travel. She'd made it across the big, wide ocean again. Without drowning. Without using the life preserver under her seat. Without hyperventilating. Somehow it was worse this time, alone. Maybe because her expectation was she'd be half of a vacationing couple and that hadn't happened. She was still a single girl, the airlines reminded her, although a single girl with a business-class seat and free champagne was pretty nice. *Thank you, Dylan's law firm.*

He was waiting for her outside security, looking tanned and happy. His hug was warm and worth the nerves. They pulled the bags into a taxi and were inside the City of Light within an hour. It was already evening, and the lights on the Eiffel Tower twinkled against the purple sky.

"Are you hungry? The food's not great on that airline," Dylan said, squeezing her hand.

"You're right about that. I only ate enough to keep drinking. Of course I'm hungry."

"Good, because I made dinner at the apartment. Just a little something."

Dylan Hardy's version of "a little something" was a knockout French feast: chicken *paillard* with lemon and pasta and a salad and a sweet fruit tart for dessert. Francie oohed and ahed over it, eating every last morsel.

His apartment was one the law firm had rented for him. It wasn't as fancy as his last place she'd seen, and wasn't in the first *arrondissement,* but it was still amazing to look out on the balcony and see the geraniums blooming across the way on other balconies, to stretch out in a bed in an elegant 1920s room with elaborate crown molding and gilt.

"It's lovely, Dylan," she said, wiping her mouth. "The apartment."

"I thought we deserved the best, of course."

"How did you find it?"

"Someone at the law firm is in charge of that. I just told her, make it a four-star experience, just this once, for my *petite amie.* Normally I crash at Leo's flat, but he's in town. Or they rent me something shifty. The last one had bugs."

"Ick." Francie glanced in the corners.

"Don't worry," he said. "I've already cleaned once."

She stared at him. "You cleaned for me?" She put a hand on her forehead. "Am I hallucinating?"

"I saved the dishes for you."

They settled into the lumpy sitting room chairs, which were upholstered in a silvery blue velvet. Dylan topped off their wineglasses, and they sat watching the sky out the tall glass doors to the balcony. The dishes could wait, she thought, listening to the quiet of the breeze and birdsong and the occasional roar of a motorcycle down on the street. Up here, three stories up in the air, it felt impossibly peaceful.

"Oh, Paris," Francie said, sighing. "How do you get any work done here?"

As if on cue a gust of wind blew in off the roofs, rattling the doors. Dylan rose and closed them. He turned back to her. "Do you want to hear about it, or have one blissful day without discussing legal?"

"I want to have one blissful week without discussing legal, but I can see that's out of the question." She clinked a fingernail against the wineglass. "Okay, give it to me."

He sat down next to her. "I wish I had more free time. Both of us really. But it's all starting to pop so we have to get cracking, as the Brits say."

She set down her glass. "Is it interesting, at least?"

Dylan smiled his mysterious smile. "Not a widget in sight."

He told her the story as he'd been told it, from the start. The founding partner at the law firm had been an aristocrat, a bit of a dandy who was brilliant at law but even more brilliant at bringing in wealthy clients. The firm prospered after the war. He had a reputation as a rake that he enjoyed immensely, especially the rumors that he'd bedded each of the society women he signed up to represent.

"So basically, a Frenchman." Francie raised her eyebrows.

"Right. Gaston Bozonnet was his name. He built the law firm from scratch, so we can't say anything bad about him, ever."

Francie mimed zipping her lips.

"Plus he's long dead, so whatever he did doesn't matter anymore."

"Wait, this is a lost son thing, like my case with Reese Pugh?"

Dylan shook his head. "He might have had some illegitimate heirs, but that's not what we're dealing with. He died twenty-five years ago. So all that's sorted by now."

"Did you know him? Wait, you wouldn't have."

"He died when I was twenty."

Francie grabbed her glass. "More wine? I think this is going to take a while."

The dandy/lawyer, Gaston, had a coterie of female admirers: rich socialites, exiled princesses, dowagers, and starlets. Many of them eventually became clients of the firm as they got older and needed advice about wills, banks, money, and all that. One of these women was a Mathilde Fourcier, by all counts a headstrong party girl with a lot of francs.

"That would be back in the thirties and forties. She had salons, met Hemingway, all that. By the fifties, she became an upstanding patron of the arts. She still threw fabulous parties though. The clip file is stuffed. Every fashion designer, artist, and random royal was there."

"They never married, of course, she and Gaston."

"No. He had a wife somewhere along the line. She remained single until she died this spring at the age of one hundred and four."

"Wow. And still a client?"

He nodded. "Her estate is a mess. Initially the estate partner thought things were in good shape. He's an older guy, he's known her for decades. He'd seen her bank statements, paid her bills for her, all that. She didn't have a load of cash or investments, so he thought things were fine. But he's only entered her apartment once or twice since about 1995. She preferred the telephone."

Francie grimaced. "Rats?"

"I haven't seen it yet. We're scheduled for a tour on Monday if you want to come."

"I'm guessing it's not going to be, like, pristine from some random day in 1942."

"She's been living there. Not sure about pristine, but I'm doubtful. I guess she only lived in one or two rooms."

"How did she manage? Did she have relatives to help her?"

The law firm, Dylan explained, had found her a live-in helper. Part of the apartment was closed off. The partner—his name was Cédric Corne—was unsure what was in there. "Could be bad, could be good, could be dust bunnies, could be nothing."

"But probably something."

"We'll find out on Monday."

"So who inherits?"

"Two cousins. One is a male cousin who has already been involved in the estate since he's here in Paris. The other is a woman who has been living in Canada and the US for the last fifty years. She hasn't been back to France since she was a teenager apparently. But she arrives tomorrow. That's where you come in, Francie."

"I—what? Escort her about?"

"If she'll have you. Apparently she doesn't like men—or Paris."

CHAPTER FIVE

PARIS

*A*xelle Fourcier woke up on the airplane with a throbbing headache. *A French headache, how apropos,* she mused, as she checked into the small, family run hotel on the Left Bank. Her aunt's law firm had reserved the room. It was early, not yet noon. The room probably wouldn't be ready. Somehow, thankfully, it was. The clerk was a foreign student, possibly Middle Eastern. She could barely understand his French as he explained the elevator, set her luggage in it, and handed her the pass-card that worked as a key. It had been a while since she'd stayed in a hotel. Five years? Maybe longer. She'd become a homebody, preferring her own bed.

Now she was thousands of miles from home. She sat on the low mattress, the pain in her head pounding. The room was ridiculously small, like the miniature replica of a hotel room. It occurred to her she'd never stayed in a hotel in Paris. Maybe all the rooms were the size of a postage stamp. She turned sideways to get into the bathroom, took a pill for her headache, and lay down on the bed.

All the way over on the plane the past had come to her in images and flashes. Her parents, strict and cold, raised on deprivation and war, expecting her to be sensible, practical, to attend the *Grande École* of their choice. Her friends, none of whom she'd seen again. Some wrote to her in Canada, but she'd lost most of them when she'd moved on to America. What had they seen in her, in their friendship anyway? She was different. She hadn't acquiesced to the powers that be, bowed down to society, to the government, to her family. She had stood up, she had fought as all good socialist revolutionaries should fight. Until she had no fight left, and flight seemed the only solution.

She didn't have many friends in the US either. She'd told only her elderly neighbor, Marvin, that she was leaving, and would he please mow her lawn. "Elderly"—he was younger than she was. It was, after all, an appalling small life she had. It made her a bit sad.

But no, she wouldn't give in to that feeling. She still had years left, years to find new friends, to walk on the beach, to drink her favorite wines, to—a picture in her head of two old people, holding hands as they walked on the sand. Her eyes opened. Who was that? Was she suddenly going to find a lover at her age?

The memory of her friend Vivienne flooded her mind. She had been in love with pretty, petite Vivienne in high school, but she wasn't interested in Axelle. The rejection had crushed her for a while, and led to a series of questionable decisions, male and female, career and private life. She couldn't blame Vivienne for those. Axelle's decisions, good and bad, had formed her, pushed her to new heights. She took full credit for them.

And now, France had pulled her back. She took credit for that decision too, as Mathilde would want her to take over now that she was gone. To be the matriarch, if necessary. Axelle's parents had died years ago, in quick succession. She had not come home for their services, or to receive any inheritance that did not come. She assumed they had cut her off, as she had cut them off. They had been furious with her. Why would she keep up a relationship that was neither beneficial nor benign? It was all right, all that had happened, she told herself, even as a walnut of melancholy rolled around in her gut. Was it possible to accept the past and all its terrifying regrets, and remain optimistic? She would try to find out.

Because France now had her full attention.

• • •

SHE JERKED AWAKE. It took a moment for her vision to clear, to remember she was in a small Paris hotel room that was unnaturally warm. She was perspiring. A phone was ringing, that annoying artificial sound of a mobile phone.

Fumbling in her bag, she hit the button. "Axelle Fourcier," she announced, clearing her throat. "Who's that?"

"Hello! My name is Francine Bennett. I'm working with Bozonnet Patroni, the law firm? For your aunt's estate."

Axelle sat up and smoothed her skirt. "Ah. What is your name? I missed it."

"You can call me Francie. I'm American. I live outside New York City, but I'm working in Paris for a bit. To help you out, if you need me."

For a moment Axelle felt relieved. She wasn't entirely alone. And she wouldn't have to deal with arrogant, starched-cuff Frenchmen, at least for a while. "I see. Well, I've arrived. That's all I can tell you right now. I have a raging headache, but some pills and a nap you interrupted have helped."

"Oh—I'm sorry."

"How could you have known?" She paused, trying to decide what to say next. "Francie. I would like to have a decent meal tonight. Somewhere close by my hotel. Do you have a recommendation?"

Francie, it appeared, had more than a recommendation. She was some sort of travel agent. She would make a reservation, pick up Axelle at seven thirty, and take her to dinner. "With pleasure, Miss Fourcier. Looking forward to meeting you."

"You may call me Doctor Fourcier."

"Oh, of course. You taught at the university there in Oklahoma. French history, right?"

The woman sounded like an overly cheerful child. Axelle sighed. She was so done with teenage students. "I'll be in the lobby at seven thirty."

THE RESTAURANT, Axelle had to admit, was very nice. Traditional white-tablecloth place with deep red walls, elderly waiters, and candles.

The smell of French food brought back another flood of memories. Apparently she was going to be deluged with the past. She might as well get used to it.

The travel agent was older than she'd expected. And chatty. Very chatty. Axelle glowered at her across the table, hoping her mighty visage would be enough to get her to stop talking. It worked temporarily. Or maybe it was the waiter, come to take their order.

Axelle told him they were not ready. Her French came back to her, like a pop-up on her computer, unwelcome and brash. "*Ne sommes pas prêts.*" He nodded reverentially and backed away.

Francie held the huge menu at arm's length, staring at it through reading glasses. Much older, at least forty, Axelle reckoned. "What are you having?" Francie asked. "I am not good at ordering in French."

Axelle told her she was having a steak. Francie declared herself hungry as a horse and said she'd have one too. "Can you order us wine? I'm afraid my skills are bad in that department too."

The older woman sighed and did all the ordering when the waiter returned, stepping up at the wave of her hand. It was different being old in France, Axelle realized. People respected you, especially if you gave off that typically French air of self-importance.

The food arrived, and the travel agent had to go silent to eat. A blessing. Axelle had ordered an expensive bottle of Bordeaux from Pauillac, assuming—rightly as it turned out—that the law firm was paying. She sipped one glass and poured herself another. Maybe Paris wouldn't be so horrible. She eyed her companion.

"What exactly is your role here, Francie? Are you my tour guide? I can't figure it out."

Francie dabbed her mouth with her napkin. "Well, that's two of us. I just got this assignment. I'm a lawyer, back in the States. My friend is a lawyer here in Paris and also in the US. He is working on the estate for the law firm."

"You're just along for the ride?"

"So far I'm to take care of you, find you anything you want. Bozonnet is very concerned that you'll be happy with the settlement."

Axelle narrowed her eyes. "Have you seen the will?"

Francie grimaced. "I'm not sure there is one. At least not one less than forty years old. Your aunt had such a long life. So impressive to make it to a hundred and four."

"A will is a will, is it not?"

"Sure. But if all the assets are not spelled out in the will, there is a lot of work to be done to document them, split them up, all that."

"What assets? The apartment?"

Francie nodded. "And anything else. She had some investments: stocks and bonds, I hear."

"That should only take a few days."

"For you, yes, probably. Do you need to get home?"

"I'm moving in two weeks' time. Cross country. Lots to do to get the house cleared out."

"How exciting! Where to?" Francie had a very toothy grin.

"North Carolina. The Outer Banks."

"Nice. That'll be a lot different from Oklahoma, won't it?"

Axelle felt bad when people from the coasts disparaged places like Oklahoma. "The state has been good to me. It's been my home for thirty-five years."

"Of course," Francie said, chastened. "But it has no beaches, right?" She sipped her wine. "Tomorrow morning we can go through Mathilde's apartment. It's scheduled for ten. Is that good for you?" Axelle nodded. "You remember her apartment?"

"Naturally." In fact it was a vague memory, full of martini glasses and slick men and diamond necklaces. A blur of decadence without focus. "It's in the fifth."

Francie looked away. "The ninth actually. North of here, Right Bank."

"Yes. Of course I knew that. The ninth. *L'Opéra*." The knowledge came back, rolling off her tongue. How stupid. The Haussmann building, the wrought iron balconies, the mosaic tiles in the foyer. "I have not been to Paris for many years, Miss Bennett."

"You haven't lost your French at all, I see." Francie said. "And your accent in English is nearly perfect."

"Fifty years in another country will do that."

Francie raised her eyebrows at that: *fifty years.* A lifetime. "Do you feel French still?"

Axelle sat back in her chair, swirling the wine in her glass. It was a good question. If she'd been asked that last week, before the letter, she'd have said, *No way, Jose.* Just like an American. But now, back in Paris? There was something so seductive about this city, so enfolding, so enchanting. It was as if Paris had not forgotten her, had forgiven her faults, her dirty deeds, her betrayals. Paris still cared.

The question then was, did she still care about Paris?

"That remains to be seen, Miss Bennett."

CHAPTER SIX

Francie stepped out of the taxi the next morning as it paused in front of Axelle Fourcier's hotel on the Left Bank. She waved at the tall woman who stood on the sidewalk in a long khaki trench coat, hands in pockets, her cap of gray hair blowing in the slight breeze. As usual she had a fierce expression on her face, like she would rather rip your head off than speak to you.

"Good morning!" Francie stood by the curb. Axelle stalked toward her then into the cab, pulling the door shut behind her. Francie blinked, left behind on the curb. She saw Dylan's face inside the car, then he opened his door.

"Come around," he said, waving her around the cab. "I'll sit in front."

They brushed hands as they passed, giving each other a look that said, *Let's humor her for now.* Francie slid in next to Axelle. Dylan got in next to the middle-aged driver, who ignored him and drove out into traffic.

Dylan turned in the seat and introduced himself to Axelle. They shook hands awkwardly. Dylan glanced at Francie, her cue to take up the conversation.

"Did you sleep well, Doctor Fourcier?"

She made a *harrumph* sound. "The room was very warm and there is no way to turn it down or open a window."

"I'm sorry. I'll speak to the manager, if you like."

"I've done it myself." The older woman glanced at Francie. "I don't travel well. I've discovered I like being home."

Dylan turned again. "Francie tells me you're moving to a beach in North Carolina."

"That is correct."

They had discussed Axelle Fourcier at length in their hotel room the night before. Her gruff nature, her imperious attitude, it was all dissected. Dylan said he was relieved Francie was on the case as he had no idea how to handle a client like Axelle. This surprised Francie, but she didn't tell Dylan that. She had the notion he was a smooth operator, charming women and cajoling men into signing this and that. But maybe he knew his limitations with older women.

They were silent then until the taxi pulled up across from the address. Dylan paid the driver as the women exited and looked up at the classic stone facade, the short wrought iron railings across tall windows, the bump of a bay window on the fourth floor. Was that Mathilde's apartment? Francie was eager to see it.

The door facing the street was green and battered, with an arched top. It was the sort of old-style Paris door that promised lovely secrets if you managed to get inside. As they approached across the street the door opened, revealing a young woman with a tired face and stringy blond hair, wearing a blue jumpsuit and pink cleaning gloves.

Dylan spoke to her. "Bonjour, Margot." He turned to Axelle. They had all stepped over the wooden doorjamb into an open stone court-yard lined with bicycles. "Madame Fourcier—*pardon*, Doctor Fourcier—this is Margot. She has been cleaning the apartment for us. Getting it ready for us to tour."

Margot smiled at them.

"What?" Axelle cried. "You've let a stranger in to rearrange, to steal?"

Francie startled. The cleaner spoke rapidly in French to Dylan.

"I understand what you're saying, Margot," Axelle barked again. "*Je parle français.*"

Dylan turned to the older woman. "She has worked for us before, Doctor. She comes with high recommendations. Someone from the law firm has been with her all the time. No need to upset yourself."

"Upset myself?" Axelle began, but Dylan turned and walked away, taking Margot with him. "Of all the nerve," she muttered.

"Shall we?" Francie asked quietly. As they mounted the stairs she said to Axelle, "Are you excited to see the place? I know I am."

The change of topic had no effect on Axelle. She grunted, pulling herself up with the bannister, a lovely wooden fixture. "Does the elevator not work?"

Dylan, walking ahead, turned back. "It's not helped getting the apartment ready. They tell me it will be fixed next week."

They reached the fourth floor and stood panting for a moment. Margot got out her keys and unlocked an unmarked cream-colored door, newly scrubbed but in need of a fresh coat of paint. There was only one door leading off the hallway, Francie realized. The apartment must be the entire floor. She looked up the stairs. At least one more floor above them.

The door opened and the smell of cleaning fluids wafted over them, mixed with staleness and mildew. Dylan waved Axelle in after the cleaner then did the same with Francie. She grimaced at him. The apartment better be good or they'd never hear the end of it.

Last night Dylan said he'd only seen a few snapshots of the apartment. The older partner, Cédric Corne, was the only one who'd really been inside, and he didn't have any good words to describe the place. After Mathilde died he'd been here once to check on things and took a couple photos with his phone. But no one had a real idea what the apartment held in store. Monsieur Corne hadn't wanted to begin snooping around until the heirs were all found. Francie thought either his restraint was admirable or he was allergic to filth.

Because even though Margot had been tidying up for a couple days, the odor of the unwashed was heavy on the upholstered furniture, the thick drapes, the oriental rugs. The apartment's windows were open now. That helped alleviate some of the distress of the smell of decay. Francie blinked, trying to keep her composure with the overwhelming odors.

Axelle had her hand over her nose and mouth. "*Mon Dieu*," she whispered.

Monsieur Corne met them wearing a perfect gray suit, a purple tie, and a crisp white shirt. His gray hair was thick and neatly swept back. He smiled slightly at the tall, older woman and held out a hand. "Madame Fourcier, it is with great pleasure that we meet at last."

Axelle had to remove her hand from her face to shake his hand. "Monsieur." She nodded and glanced around the sitting room. In one corner sat a plump green velvet chaise, well-worn, stained with some-thing dark, blankets and sheets folded at the foot, a pile of pillows stripped of their cases on the floor nearby. Corne followed her eye.

"That is where your aunt spent her last days, Madame. It was her wish to live—and die—here at home."

Axelle swallowed hard. "I understand that sentiment." She straight-ened, apparently inured to the smells by now. "Shall we take the tour then? Or are we waiting for Cousin Lucien?"

"He could not attend this morning. His patients were scheduled," Corne said.

"He's a physician then?"

Corne gave her a look. "In the southern suburbs. It is a distance."

Dylan had told Francie that he doubted Axelle knew this cousin. The word at the law firm was that they had never met. She had been gone for fifty years. Francie wondered what sort of family rift had taken place. And, optimistically, she hoped having some family left in France would be some kind of solace for Axelle. She seemed like the sort of lonely old person who needed a caring friend to smooth out the rough edges that life tended to give you. *Well, we all need a friend.*

The apartment was indeed the entire floor of the building, some nine rooms including an enormous library full of dusty books, four bedrooms set up with brass and wrought iron beds plus dressers, mirrors, and fireplaces, a huge oak-paneled dining room with a table and chairs for twelve, and a kitchen with a butler's pantry. A fabulously large space by the standards of today in Paris, New York, probably anywhere. By the style of the interiors it had been fitted out around the turn of the twentieth century—the 1890s, the Belle Époque—

complete with gilded everything, frosted glass globes, and tassels galore.

Two of the bedrooms had doubled as storage spaces, stacked with furniture, crates, wooden boxes, piles of clothing, odd trunks and armoires, and who knew what. The dining room had a fabulous view, but the long table was lined with dishes, huge tureens, punch bowls, and cut-glass this and silver-plated that. Mathilde, Corne explained, had lived her last thirty years in the first salon they entered, a smallish room compared to the others. It was next to the only bathroom and the kitchen. The cooking space was a jumbled mess: dishes and pots everywhere in all states of crusty, food rotting on countertops, a tiny refrigerator that let out hideous smells, and an overflowing trash can. Had the cleaner done anything? Not here.

They wound their way back through the apartment to the salon. Francie tugged Dylan's sleeve and whispered, "It's huge! And gorgeous underneath the junk."

"Worth a small fortune," he whispered back. "Stench or no stench."

They regrouped, chatting about the flat: its antiques and valuables, its marble bathroom and ornate plasterwork, all rather mercenary. Even Monsieur Corne, who had known Mathilde the best—or most recently—of all of them, talked as if her presence was just an impediment to the disposal of a lifetime. The money the apartment would bring would be substantial. Axelle was silent, lips pinched together, as they listed items: artwork, crystal, silver, furnishings, rugs. Dylan had begun a list in his notebook and scribbled away.

"Many of the furnishings have negligent value in the state they're in," Corne reminded her. "The moths and the mice have seen to that. But if there is anything of sentimental value, I will try to see what we can work out with Monsieur Daucourt."

Axelle narrowed her eyes. "I would ask *him* for items then? He had a relationship with Tante Mathilde, did he?"

"I—I really can't say," Corne stuttered.

"Can't or won't?" she parried.

"*Pardon?*" Monsieur Corne straightened defensively. "He is a reasonable man, Madame. We can come to amicable terms, I'm sure."

Francie had heard this sort of legal sweet talk before, right before the other side screwed you to the wall and stripped you bare. What were the men up to? Surely they couldn't steal Axelle's inheritance—could they? She said to Axelle, "Is there anything you can identify now, something with sentimental value as monsieur said? I'm sure that would be helpful to the lawyers."

Axelle surveyed the room, ending with a long stare at the artwork hanging prominently over the marble fireplace. She walked up to it, clasping her hands behind her back. The painting looked like something blown up out of a comic book, very graphic but catchy. It looked odd in this room, Francie thought. Almost tacky amid the glitter of the 1890s.

"This piece. I've always loved it and it was my aunt's favorite. She was quite a collector." She looked around the salon. "Where are all her other pieces?"

Dylan and Francie looked at each other. Maybe the apartment wasn't where the value was after all. Corne said, "You mean the ones hanging on the walls?"

They took a second walk-through of the apartment then to look at the art on the walls. Axelle unhooked a couple large canvases and examined their backs. "This one is a Rothko," she said, setting a colorful painting of red-orange and gold blocks against the wall on the floor. "You know the art scene? How much do you think it's worth, Monsieur Corne?"

"Rothko?" He blinked, baffled.

"The pop artist?" Francie said, seeing a signature in the lower right corner, with a date. Was this an original or just a good print?

"Mark Rothko. Nineteen-sixty-six. Right there," said Axelle, pointing at the signature. "Probably worth a million euros today. I think Mathilde got it for a song. She had quite an eye."

After Axelle identified three other paintings as from the same time period, all pop artists whose names Francie vaguely recalled, they returned to the salon. The fresh air through the windows was doing its job. The rank odor was dissipating. Dylan's list was getting long. He and Francie exchanged another silent glance. This could get dicey. The more money in the estate, the more trouble between heirs.

Axelle pointed to the cartoonish painting over the mantel, the tacky one she'd said she liked. It featured a woman with blond hair, tears on her cheeks, and a speech bubble that read: *If only I'd known what sort of man he was.*

"This one is not worth anything. It's some sort of copy. I just like it."

Her tone of voice had changed, become girlish and false. She was obviously lying about that painting.

"Well," Monsieur Corne said with a huff, "we must get an appraiser in here. I have two others set up for later in the week. One for the apartment itself, a real estate man. He will know what must be done, how it will sell. And another for the furnishings. So we add on an art appraiser."

"We used Geiger last year on the Guillaume estate," Dylan said.

"Yes. Call him, Hardy," Corne said.

"I will just take this painting with me," Axelle said, reaching for it on the wall.

"Wait, Madame!" Corne bellowed. She froze, halfway to the frame. "You cannot take anything from the apartment. Not a handkerchief nor a teaspoon. Everything will be appraised then decisions will be made."

"But this is what I want. You said to identify anything that had sentimental value."

Monsieur Corne put on his charming face and stepped over to her, extending his elbow as if he was going to escort her into a ball. "All in good time, Madame. This is France, you remember? We make note of your request. The estate must be sifted and sorted. There is much work to be done. There is your cousin to think of. Mathilde did not leave you that painting, or any other particular thing. *Dommage,* Madame."

Axelle stared at his arm, a curl on her lip. "What is truly sad is that you are the lawyer in charge, Monsieur."

CHAPTER SEVEN

*D*ylan and Francie sat across the table from each other outside at the bistro. It was one of their favorites, a big, traditional, old-school café on Boulevard Saint-Germain, bustling at all hours. A place to people watch and meditate over a café crème or a nice Sancerre. On this Monday afternoon it was full of tourists and locals, eating, drinking, and being Parisian.

"Well, what do you think of her?" Francie asked. "Did I describe her right?"

"To a T," Dylan said, sipping tea. He had taken to ordering herbal tea with lunch, and Francie followed his lead. They had work to do in the afternoon, after all.

They had dropped Axelle Fourcier off at her hotel when she claimed she had another headache and wanted to lie down. She was silent but seething in the cab. Francie couldn't really blame her. That slick French lawyer, Monsieur Corne, was obnoxious.

"I do sort of feel for her," Francie said. "Your guy, Corne, sounds like he's out to screw her out of—something."

Dylan frowned. "Why do you say that?"

Francie shrugged. Maybe she shouldn't bad-mouth the boss. "Just women's intuition."

"No, really." He sat back, waiting.

"He doesn't like her. Hell, nobody *likes* her. She's abrasive and arrogant. Maybe she should get her own lawyer to negotiate the settlement of the estate."

"I'm supposed to do that for her. I'm her advocate here. And I don't dislike her, Francie. Not any more than any other client."

She smiled. "Right."

"What does that matter anyway? I have plenty of arrogant, abrasive clients. I will fight for her. You can count on that. *She* can count on it."

"I know you will." She waved a hand. "Never mind. There was something about Corne that set me off. I'm—you know, touchy."

Their soup arrived. It was creamy asparagus, despite being out of season, and delicious. Dylan was halfway through when he set down his spoon.

"I'm glad you said something, Francie. Sometimes I get too into the details to see what's going on."

"Like what?"

"It occurs to me that Corne is representing the other cousin himself. Lucien Daucourt."

"Oh yeah?" This was what she meant. Corne was going to screw Axelle, somehow. He was going to help the man, the elite, the true Frenchman.

Dylan bent to his soup bowl again. "France is pretty much a fully functioning patriarchy, as far as I can tell." He lowered his voice. "They have no harassment laws with any teeth in them, even now. They're afraid it will stifle the bit-on-the-side tradition."

"So I've heard. Flirting is a national sport."

"No more catcalls on the street though. They outlawed that."

"Well, that's very important." She rolled her eyes. "Let's not talk about harassment. It's a sore subject after this year." Her trials and tribulations at the Greenwich law firm were a painful memory, but at least they were over now.

Dylan nodded and finished his soup. A cheese plate arrived, overloaded with selections. Francie always liked to try new cheeses. Cheese was her spirit animal, her sisters proclaimed hilariously. But they were right. She nibbled on something with an ashy coating.

"What about this art? How does that fit into the plan for the estate? A Mark Rothko could be worth millions, I looked it up in the cab."

"There will probably have to be an auction. There's no way to appraise the market value of high-end stuff like that without it. Then they can split the proceeds evenly."

"Can't you just give Axelle the one she wants, and her cousin the Rothko or some other one?"

Dylan shook his head. "Corne is going to insist on an auction. That's why he's hiring the appraiser. We used him last year. Norbert Geiger. He's a big deal in the art world, I guess. He'll want the publicity. She's not going to like selling, is she?"

"It's her aunt's collection. She's got a sentimental attachment to it."

"Maybe she can get the silver." Dylan grinned. "Will that help?"

"No, silly. What about that piece over the mantel? I think she was fibbing about it being worthless."

"I took a photo of it with my phone and sent it to a lawyer in my New York office who knows art. Let me see if she's answered." He took out his phone and scrolled to his messages. "Roy Lichtenstein, she says. You know him?"

Francie thought she'd seen his pieces at the Museum of Modern Art in New York. "I think he's famous, Dylan. All those artists seemed that way to me. Google his name."

Dylan took a slice of brie and worked his phone while Francie tasted her way through the cheese plate. After a few minutes he said, "Wow."

"How much?"

"Nearly eight million bucks." He looked up at her. "This is going to be a royal pain in the ass, Miss Bennett. Just warning you."

The Lichtenstein piece Dylan had found online was similar to the one in the apartment, a comic book blow-up but with a wartime theme of bombs and planes. It had been auctioned before the economy crashed in 2008 and was larger than the one in Mathilde's apartment. They discussed whether the Fourcier piece could be a print, but Dylan thought it looked painted. He didn't really know art. Neither did she. But his instincts about the mess that would ensue if the heirs got to squabbling over millions of dollars, or euros, in artwork were no doubt spot-on.

"What if—?" Dylan began. She waited as he was deep in thought. "What if you do the cataloging of the apartment, at least the stuff the appraisers don't do? Then you'd be on the scene and can look out for her interests. There may be some other hidden gems, I mean, real jewels there. You never know. Unless you have some serious shopping to do in Paris."

Francie's initial thought: *Hell no. I am not a secretary.* But then she remembered she was basically a hand-holding assistant and arm-candy sidekick of Dylan on this gig. And she did like bossing people around, something the terrible cleaner Margot badly required.

"I do have some shopping that is begging to be done. But I guess I could do some cataloging. If I have resources."

He raised his eyebrows. She added: "I can hire people to do the actual work."

He laughed. "I think that can be arranged, General Bennett."

They stood up, folding their napkins on the table. Francie said, "The good news? All the lawyers will get paid."

He took her arm. "And it won't be peanuts, Madame."

DYLAN RETURNED to the law firm after lunch. Francie felt energized by the events of the day, the exploration of the old woman's apartment and what lay in store for the heirs. She took off walking along the Seine, visited her favorite bridges, and ended up staring up at the weird industrial architecture of the Centre Pompidou. The modern art museum certainly advertised its difference to Parisians. In a huge open area that sat below street level, the plaza currently sported a giant screen showing a talking Mona Lisa about thirty feet tall. People were lined up, asking the moving, sentient painted lady questions she answered with humor. Francie watched for a few minutes before making her way inside the museum. She was curious now about some of the artists they'd discussed this morning, ones in Mathilde Fourcier's collection. The Pompidou had a well-known modern art collection that must include at least some of those artists.

Dylan had given her his notebook from this morning's apartment tour, to begin her cataloging. She opened it as she rode the museum escalators up to the fifth floor. Mark Rothko, Andy Warhol, Ellsworth Kelly, Robert Indiana, he'd written. She pencilled in Roy Lichtenstein, the one last identified. That one, if found to be authentic, was a major score. But several of the others were no doubt valuable too. Dylan had cajoled the appraiser into an early appointment. He was scheduled for the next day. The firm was eager to get on with the disposition of the estate. The heirs too, of course.

The Pompidou had some Lichtensteins in their collection, according to signs. Wandering, she only found one, a geometric abstract. She glanced at room after room of colorful pieces by all the big names, from Warhol and Miró and Picasso to wild and crazy Fauvists and those who favored simple blocks of color. In the museum shop she found an exhibition catalog of a Roy Lichtenstein show the museum had mounted five years before. On the cover was a comic book painting of a blonde with tears on her face. So similar to Mathilde's it gave her chills. She paid for the catalog and went back outside, where poor Mona Lisa was being barraged by questions from nitwits. "Why do you smile?" "Because I have a secret." "What is your secret?" "If I tell you it won't be a secret."

The afternoon had warmed, a golden sunlight piercing through the buildings. Piles of fallen leaves rustled on the pavement. A comfortable chatter rose from groups of high school girls and boys. Francie found a table in the sun next to the plaza but far enough to not hear the talking painting. She ordered coffee and read her exhibition catalog.

By the time she finished the last drop she knew: the Lichtenstein piece was either going to break their hearts or make somebody extremely wealthy.

CHAPTER EIGHT

*D*ylan arrived back at their apartment late that evening, after dark. Francie had made arrangements to take Axelle to dinner again, at a simpler place this time, a hole-in-the-wall bistro from Merle's list. Francie made the reservation for three, hoping Dylan might join them. But as soon as he entered the flat she could see something was on his mind.

He threw his briefcase onto a chair and loosened his tie.

"What is it?" Francie asked, crossing her arms. "Axelle?"

He stalked over to the kitchen and popped open the cork from yesterday's wine. He poured himself a large glass and stood in front of the French doors, staring at the lights. He didn't offer to pour her one, so she did it herself. Then she sat in one of the velvet chairs and waited. He seemed angry. She didn't really deal that well with angry. He would tell her eventually.

It took longer than she thought, nearly his whole glass of wine. Finally he turned away from the windows and set down his goblet. He glanced at her and said, "Sorry." Then he sat down in the other chair.

"What's going on?" she asked, keeping her voice light.

"It's Phoebe."

Francie blinked, remembering that teary phone call before she left the States. She forgot to tell Dylan about it. And now—?

"Is she all right?"

He nodded. "Well, not completely. She's getting bullied at school. Or something—who knows. Anyway she's very unhappy there."

Francie opened her mouth to tell him about the call, but he continued.

"Rebecca isn't being helpful, or sympathetic." He glanced at her. "She's had problems in the past. Emotional stuff. I'm not sure what's going on now."

"Oh, dear."

"And here I am, halfway around the world. When my little girl needs me."

Francie reached out and squeezed his hand. He held onto hers. He looked worried and sad. "Can I do anything?" she whispered.

"I don't know. What can *I* do from here?"

"Dylan, I talked to her, to Phoebe. That day you asked me to pick up your shoes. I forgot to tell you. She called your house, looking for you. I picked up the phone. It was wrong. I shouldn't have gotten involved. But she sounded very upset."

He squinted. "What day was that?"

"Friday?"

He nodded. "She called me on my cell. I was in meetings all afternoon."

"Did you talk then?"

"We never could find a time that worked. All weekend. You arrived and I—" He rubbed his face with his free hand. "What did she say?"

"That she hated her mom sometimes. I assured her that was normal."

"Was she crying?" Francie nodded. He groaned. "We finally talked today. Rebecca kept her home from school for some goddamn reason."

"How was she?"

"Rebecca? Cold as ice."

That was interesting. "No, Phoebe."

"She was quiet. She gets that way when she's upset sometimes. Like a volcano about to erupt."

Francie sipped her wine. That did not sound good. But, as he said, what could they do from here?

Dylan said, "I think we may have to change schools. She's going to this public school near home but maybe it's time for private school."

"Is she getting bullied? What did she say happened?"

"She wouldn't tell me. That's what got me so worked up. What if it's something worse than being bullied?"

"What does Rebecca say?"

"She was very hands-off about it, like it was just some 'mean girl' thing. But then let her stay home today."

"Even a mean girl thing can be devastating at nine."

He nodded. "I know. Rebecca is kind of useless."

Francie looked at her watch. "Look, I'm supposed to meet Axelle in fifteen minutes but I can cancel. Or if you're hungry I made a reservation for three?"

"No, no. You go on. I told them I would call back at three their time." He looked at his watch. "That will be in the middle of dinner. Besides, I need some quiet time to get my head on straight. Figure out what to do."

They stood and Francie pulled him into her arms. She wished there was something she could do for him, for Phoebe, but there wasn't. So she squeezed him tight.

FRANCIE STEPPED down the stairwell onto the sidewalk. The purple had left the sky, making the streetlights more dramatic against the dark. She'd decided to walk to the restaurant tonight. Whether Axelle would walk or cab it was her own business.

The restaurant was tucked into a side street just off one of the busy streets along the Seine, on the Right Bank. Francie looked it up on her phone's map for a moment then shut it off and struck out. If she got lost, well, so be it. She wasn't going to announce her tourist status every time she walked around Paris.

As it happened she walked straight to the little bistro. It was barely wide enough for two rows of tables but crowded with customers, including a few waiting on the sidewalk. Francie peered inside for

Axelle and spotted her in the back, near the kitchen. Not the best spot but maybe she wouldn't complain.

Francie explained to the woman who handed her a menu that their third person wasn't coming. This caused a frown and gathering of utensils. Francie sat down and shrugged off her trench. Axelle sat rigidly on the bench seat against the wall, nostrils flaring.

"Did you not tell them to seat us in the front? The clatter is deafening back here."

"I'm sorry. I didn't know." Francie let it go, examining the menu. She would definitely order for herself this time. English translations were jotted in under the French names for the dishes. *Thank you, thank you, merci.* She glanced at Axelle. She was rosy-cheeked, her hair freshly washed, and wearing what appeared to be a man's wool cardigan with the gray knit cuffs rolled up. An un-chic choice for Paris.

"Feeling better?" Francie asked.

"Yes. I got some rest." Axelle peered through half glasses at the menu. "I like this place, Francie. I should have started with that rather than a complaint about the noise."

She smiled at the older woman. That was the nicest thing she'd said. "You might like to know I've been assigned to help catalog Mathilde's belongings. Mr. Hardy thought it would be good if someone on our side was around."

Axelle listened, nodded. "You mean, versus Team Lucien?" She sighed. "When will I meet this mystery cousin, do you know?"

"Tomorrow night, I believe. The law firm sent out an email about a *soirée* at a wine bar near their office. Lucien and his wife are supposedly coming. Seven o'clock."

"Oh, he has a wife, does he?"

"Apparently. Have you met him?"

"If I did he was a toddler. How old a person is he?"

"Mid to late fifties? Something like that. I guess he would have been a child when you left France."

They ordered wine and a small plate to share. Francie felt they were on better terms tonight, almost like friends. "What are you having?"

"Lamb. Do you want me to—?"

"I've decided on my own. Well, the translations help. I'm having scallops."

"*Coquilles Saint-Jacques*. One of my childhood favorites. My mother wasn't a great cook, but she could make that dish."

Francie straightened her napkin in her lap and took a bite of the appetizer, a small tureen of duck pâté with baguette slices. Then she asked quietly, "Can you tell me about her? About your parents?"

Axelle blinked. "Why?"

"Just curious. If you don't want to talk about them, that's fine."

The older woman gazed toward the plate-glass window and into the street. "They were ordinary French. My father was a bureaucrat in the government. Something to do with dairy products. My mother worked as a seamstress in a small couture firm."

Francie smiled. "What were their names?"

"Hubert and Murielle. Tante Mathilde was my father's aunt, my great-aunt. She was the youngest in that family. My grandfather was the oldest. He would be—oof—a hundred and twenty or something, if he lived today."

"Oh, interesting. How many siblings were there?"

"In Mathilde's family? Five, I think. But the brothers died young, in the wars. There's always a war to kill the young men, isn't there?"

"Sadly. So just Mathilde and a sister were left? Who is Lucien related to?"

"It had to be a brother. The sister never married either and died ages ago. I remember she lived in the South somewhere. Maybe his grandfather is the brother who made it through the Great War. I never met him."

Francie wanted to ask more questions, like if Axelle was an only child. But if she wasn't then her siblings had died as well. Best to let her volunteer that. Francie didn't want to push her luck. At least she'd gotten Axelle to open up a little. "I did a little research about some of the artworks. They could be quite valuable. But we'll let the appraiser tell us more."

"The Rothko certainly is."

"And the Lichtenstein over the mantel. The one you like."

She blinked. "It's just a print. A good one but a—what do you call it—a serigraph."

"Okay. But still valuable according to recent auctions." She sipped her wine. "Axelle, they might have to auction the art. To split it up between you and Lucien. It hasn't been decided yet, but I just want to warn you."

The older woman straightened then, the color rising up her neck. "No. Never. I will not allow it. That is my piece. If I have to buy it from Lucien, I will do that."

Francie sat back, trying to think how to calm her. "So you remember it from the sixties?"

"Of course I do. Tante and I discussed it all the time. That line in it: *If only I'd known what sort of man he was.* That was our motto, our standard bearer, our words to live by. She didn't speak much English, but we translated that, and loved it. I can't—I will not—let someone else own that piece, Miss Bennett. Mark my words. Do not get between me and the Roy."

THE NEXT DAY Dylan left early, leaving Francie to begin her cataloging duties. She decided to go early as well, to get a jump start before the art appraiser came, but found she wasn't alone. The cleaner was there, as expected, but also some others. She spotted a business card on the entry table, the name of a real estate agent. This would be the appraiser then. As the cleaner ushered her in, she could hear rapid-fire French from another part of the flat. The housekeeper, Margot, wearing a plastic apron, rubber gloves, and old black slacks spotted with debris, disappeared into the kitchen. One could only hope she was getting that space under control.

Pulling the notebook, her phone, and a pen from her purse, Francie draped her trench coat over a chair and got to work. She began with photographs of each and every valuable she could spot: art, dishes, rugs, silver. Then she began writing down descriptions, trying to keep them in some semblance of order. Why hadn't she brought stickers or tags to identify pieces? Well, the appraiser would probably do that.

She had finished the salon and was ready to move down the hall toward the bedrooms when the other group came through a door, laughing. They spotted her and quieted. The French lawyer straightened then seemed to recognize her.

"Miss Bennett, yes?" Cédric Corne was cordial, but formal as usual. "I see you've started cataloging already."

"Yes, I—" She had been about to profess her virgin status in this duty but instead squared her shoulders. "Our client, Doctor Fourcier, is keen to get this going. She's got to go home soon. She's moving cross-country."

The real estate man, a short, impeccable type with a large nose, gave a knowing glance to Corne. Had she misspoken? Given away some secret? Why would it matter if Axelle was moving? *Oh, dear.* Francie gulped then smiled at the three of them. "This place is so amazing. It shouldn't be difficult to sell, right?"

Corne turned to the short man and his female assistant, a haggard middle-aged woman who looked like she worked too hard and slept too little. He rattled off something in French and they nodded, aahing. So they just didn't understand her? Was that it? She hated not knowing French. It was becoming a handicap.

Before Corne could interpret for her a knock came at the door. He excused himself and made for the salon. Yet another man entered, this one in an expensive suit, starched collar, and gold silk tie. The two men shook hands, muttering between themselves until Corne ushered him over to the rest of the group.

"Madame Bennett, this is Lucien Daucourt, Madame Fourcier's cousin and also an heir to the estate." He turned to Daucourt. "Miss Bennett is helping the law firm catalog the contents of the apartment. To move the events in question along *plus rapidement.*"

"Ah, *très bien.* Very good." He reached out his hand, they shook. He was about the age she'd estimated, midfifties, hair mostly gone except around the sides, but immaculate in the way of successful Frenchmen. He smoothed his suit coat with the hand he shook with, as if to wipe off her germs, then turned to the others. Corne introduced them. He hadn't bothered to introduce them to Francie, she noted. She and the assistant exchanged womanly looks, but about what, Francie wasn't sure.

Monsieur Corne proposed a tour of the apartment to the cousin, or so she inferred from his gestures. The real estate people said goodbye as they left.

Francie went back to work in the library. So many books! *Mon Dieu.*

An hour passed as she counted the number of volumes—a staggering three thousand seven hundred and ten. Whether any were worth anything was someone else's call. Some titles she recognized: Marcel Proust, Ernest Hemingway, *The French Lieutenant's Woman, The Great Gatsby* in a French translation. She pulled out the Hemingway, a brown leather cover. It was a copy of *The Sun Also Rises* and appeared to be signed by the author.

She looked carefully at the books near the Hemingway, looking for signed copies and what might be a valuable first edition. She stacked them on a side table for the appraiser and took some photos for her growing archive of notes. Straightening, she sighed, looking around the library for anything else to catalog. The furniture was sparse in here. The desk was a writing table with all supplies gone, no pens or inks or papers. Its chair sagged, a spindle broken.

Over the mantel a few small framed pieces leaned against a gilt mirror. Francie moved closer to examine them. One was an old sepia-tone photograph, a woman at a beach somewhere, in an old-fashioned swimsuit that hung to her knees. She held a small parasol and laughed at something. Was this Mathilde, young and vibrant? Her hair hung in a long braid over one shoulder. So happy, it made you smile.

The next was also a photograph, a stern, unsmiling couple, man and wife apparently, with a small girl sitting on the man's knee. They all wore dark clothing and looked miserable. Francie picked up the frame and looked at the back. In a spidery hand it read: "Hubert and wife, Axelle, age four."

Here was Axelle! Francie flipped it back, peering at the child with cropped blond hair, fair eyes, and a rather annoyed look on her face. One of her feet was a blur as if she'd been swinging it. She wore a drab shapeless dress and patent leather shoes.

Francie looked around for other photographs. Were Monsieurs Corne and Daucourt still in the apartment? She poked her head into the hallway. Finding it empty, she tiptoed to the salon and slipped the framed photograph into her purse. There. Something at least for Axelle.

She stared at the Roy Lichtenstein over the mantel again. She'd only photographed it earlier. Now she lifted it to the floor and examined it carefully. There were numbers on the lower left as if it was a print, as Axelle had said. "14/20," it read. Did that mean print fourteen out of a total of twenty? The signature was original, it appeared, although a squiggle. The back was blank, papered in craft paper glued to the frame. She propped it up against the marble fireplace surround for the appraiser. He would no doubt sell it for many euros. Axelle would be heartbroken about her "Roy." Unless there was some wiggle room in negotiations. Wasn't there always? Well, no.

Monsieur Corne and Lucien Daucourt appeared suddenly from the hallway, pausing to take in the salon. Corne tipped his head. "It is a beautiful piece, is it not?" He moved closer as if to protect it from Francie. If only he knew about the photograph she'd lifted.

She smiled. "Is the art appraiser coming today?" She glanced at her watch. It was lunchtime.

"In one hour. We were going to take some lunch. Then come back."

Lucien Daucourt spoke: "Would you care to join us, Madame? A very short meal, I assure you."

Without hesitation she said, "Yes." Nothing better than a meal behind enemy lines.

CHAPTER NINE

$\mathcal{L}$unch was pleasant enough with the two sophisticated Parisian gentlemen. They asked her no personal or professional questions, but Lucien snuck in a few glimpses at her breasts. She wasn't flattered; he appeared to have no real interest. Maybe he was a gynecologist. Had they invited her to lunch to keep her away from the apartment? Did they suspect her of something? Her purse was large enough to hide the photograph, and why would they care about that? No, it was all the valuable art. The race was on to keep it, sell it, or fight over it.

They both spoke excellent English and were kind enough to continue that way in her presence, only lapsing briefly into French. No long, wine-soaked lunches for these two. They had soup, a small glass of red each, and a crust of bread, then paid the bill.

Axelle called Francie while they were walking back from the neighborhood bistro. She seemed relaxed and actually happy. "I've received a phone call from an old friend. She and I went to school together. Did you give her my number?"

"No," Francie said, following the two men who walked briskly toward Mathilde's building. "I don't know any of your friends, Axelle —Doctor Fourcier."

"Oh, well, it doesn't matter. It was so good to hear from her. We've made arrangements for dinner tomorrow. I said I couldn't tonight because of the law firm *soirée*. It is tonight, correct?"

"Yes, at seven. Can I pick you up about six forty-five? See you then."

Francie skipped to catch up with the men, now stepping through the green door. Corne held the door and closed it behind her. Before they could get across the cobbled courtyard with the bicycles, a knock came from the street. Corne turned on his heel and unlatched the door.

On the street stood a tall, thin man with a regimental air, carrying a slender leather briefcase close to his chest. He wore a jacket with leather elbow patches and a German felt hat, green, with a feather in the brim. Francie almost laughed out loud at his appearance, so very Bavarian.

His name was Norbert Geiger, appropriately enough. The firm, Dylan had explained, had used him for a company whose assets were being sold to some international conglomerate. The CEO's art was part of the deal and had to be assessed and given a value. The same here for Mathilde, although they might need Geiger's connections in the auction world where he worked as a consultant. Francie had no experience in this high-flying art world and hoped to glean a little knowledge from him.

He was by all appearances a cold customer. All business, he listened briefly to Monsieur Corne and waved them away to get started. He was made to tolerate Francie because Corne told him she would assist, but he obviously would rather she would not. He removed his little hat and his patched jacket, setting them carefully on one chair then moving them to another. Then he got to work.

Unlike Francie's old-school pen and paper, Mr. Geiger pulled an iPad out of his briefcase, turned it on, and began madly typing in details about the artworks. He would do evaluations later, he explained, when he could research. He took photos with his iPad too. The Lichtenstein, Axelle's "Roy," intrigued him greatly, although he tried to keep his enthusiasm under wraps.

"That's a nice one, isn't it?" Francie said. "One of the heirs would like to keep it in the family."

He didn't reply. After a few more smaller pieces he demanded: "Show me the next room if you please."

Francie led him through the kitchen into the dining room. Two large canvases there grabbed his attention. On to the first bedroom, then the second, then the library. He spied the third small frame on the mantel, one Francie hadn't examined yet.

"What's that one?" It was a small oil, about twelve by eighteen inches.

Geiger put his nose close to the canvas and muttered something. Then he turned the piece over, turning it at angles to examine it with the window light. He made another noise and set it reverently back on the mantel, giving the frame a love pat.

"Something good?" she asked.

"Small Matisse," he said.

"Oh. Very nice." She wrote that down in her notebook. What other little treasures would he find?

After that tidbit Geiger went silent again, grunting occasionally while tapping on his tablet but otherwise mum. The number of pieces rose to eighteen, of which twelve were large ones, the rest small like the Matisse. Not a huge collection, but a valuable one. The more Francie examined the pieces, the more impressed she was with Mathilde's eye for color and form. The pop artists she favored were mostly American. Francie glanced at her list: Rothko, Lichtenstein, Jasper Johns, Robert Rauschenberg, Indiana, Rosenquist, Kelly. She'd even gotten her hands on a Warhol print of Marilyn Monroe, from a series of four dated 1962. Even art-illiterates like Francie knew that was something.

"Have you looked in all the armoires and such?" Geiger asked as they finished the last bedroom. "The hiding places?"

"Ah, no. Should I—?"

"Go to the next room. Call to me if you find artwork."

In the bedroom she'd been assigned to, an armoire stood behind a dresser and chair. She pulled them out of the way and tried to pry open the armoire. It wouldn't budge. She opened the drawers of the dresser: empty. She opened the drawer on the bottom of the armoire and—*voilà*—there was the key, on a faded red ribbon. She unlocked the armoire and swung open both doors.

One side of the piece contained a stack of drawers, while hanging space took up the other side. A jumble of hat boxes sat on the floor of the hanging side. She rummaged through them quickly, finding—surprise!—hats. The drawers were mostly empty. A single gray glove with pearl buttons. A rhinestone brooch. No art.

The rooms had no closets, only freestanding armoires, trunks, and dressers. She moved to the next bedroom and found Geiger already there, his head inside an old upright steamer trunk, pulling out corsets and bloomers and piling them on the floor.

"Any luck?"

"Move on. Next room!" He was a bossy little Prussian. When he barked his odd accent sounded even more German.

The last bedroom hadn't been used for storage. The bed was made with a navy brocade spread with gold tassels; matching drapes were held back with gold rope. Everything smelled dusty and full of mildew. Francie leaned down to peer under the bed and found another trunk.

A small one, this trunk was utilitarian metal and unlocked. This was like a treasure hunt, she thought, eagerly flipping up the latch. Disappointment again; the trunk was empty. She shoved it back under the bed. The armoire opened easily here but had little to offer. A few fake flowers, old silk stockings, a man's hat.

When she found Norbert Geiger he was putting on his own hat in the salon, slipping back into his jacket. "Nothing in the last bedroom," she said, closing her notebook. "You find anything?"

"Nothing more." He picked up his briefcase. "Tell Monsieur Corne I will have the appraisals in two or three days. Good day, Madame."

He slammed the door as he left. "And a *guten tag* to you too, *Herr* Geiger," she whispered.

Francie looked at her watch. It was nearly five. She suddenly felt so tired. Her feet were killing her. Why had she worn her cute shoes today? Idiot.

Margot was still banging away in the kitchen, washing pots and silver and crystal. Someone must have told her to clean everything.

Bags of trash were lined up under the window. Francie cleared her throat.

"Margot? I'm leaving now." She made walking gestures with her fingers. The cleaner stared at her then nodded.

"*Au revoir*, Madame," she muttered, her hands back in the soapy water.

"Um . . . *tout*—all the men are gone too. *Les hommes?* Poof!" Francie mimed a disappearing act with her hands. This was ridiculous. She had to take some French lessons.

Margot wiped her hands on a towel now. A smile crept over her lips. "*Ah, oui. Merci*, Madame."

"*Au revoir!*"

Margot gave her a get-out-of-here wave and began stacking plates. Francie gathered her purse and coat, tucked away the notebook and phone, and made her way down the stairs to the street. It was still light, a golden glow off the west-facing buildings rendering the scene magical as only Paris could be. That special light made her smile, remembering last spring with Dylan here, and forgetting that her feet hurt, she walked back to the apartment.

She unlocked the door on the third floor and called his name. Where was he? It was nearly six now. Francie kicked off her shoes and fell into a velvet chair with her phone. A quick text to Dylan and a quick answer: he would meet her at the wine bar. Working late again.

After a shower and a change into something a little fancier than her daytime jeans and sweater, Francie caught a cab and was only five minutes late picking up Axelle. She leaned over and opened the door for her.

"*Bonsoir, Docteur*," Francie trilled.

Axelle slid into the cab and adjusted her coat. "*Bonsoir*, Francie. How are you this evening?"

"Looking forward to this *soirée* in the *soir*. I get it now, why we call it a *soirée*. Something in the evening."

Axelle gave her a side glance and pursed her lips, silent. Francie smiled to herself. The woman was so easy to annoy, it was almost criminal.

"I met your cousin today. He came by the apartment while I was working there."

The older woman turned back toward her, straightening her scarf, something new in splashes of red and yellow. "Oh?"

Traffic was heavy. The cab pulled out and immediately stopped behind a line of cars. It was almost full dark now. Somewhere the Eiffel Tower was probably sparkling, but they couldn't see it from here.

"Monsieur Corne gave him a tour like he gave you."

"And what is Cousin Lucien like, may I ask?"

"Like? Probably exactly as you picture him: well-dressed, slightly bald, not very tall but not super short. French and proper."

Axelle nodded. "Well, we meet soon enough."

"Did you even know about Lucien? That he existed?"

"I'm afraid not. The last letter I got from anyone here was in the 1990s. And that was Mathilde, telling me about her health. She knew better than to mention family."

"Your parents died before that?"

She nodded. "In one six-month period."

"I'm sorry. That must have been hard for you."

"Not particularly."

And a topic dies. Francie cast about for something else. She remembered the framed photograph in her bag. "I found this in the apartment." She lowered her voice. "I pilfered it for you."

Axelle took the picture frame in her hands, running her fingertips around the old wood and onto the faces of her family. "This is from the fifties, I think."

"On the back."

Axelle flipped it over and held it up to the streetlight to read the words scribbled there. "Age four." She turned it back to look closer at the faces. "So long ago. I've forgotten the frown of my mother and the half smile of my father." She sighed, letting it fall into her lap. "So many years ago."

A long pause as another topic was retired. Francie asked then: "Who is the friend you talked to?"

The cab jerked forward as the traffic began to move. "Her name is

Blandine Baudet. She was married for many years. Her husband has passed. I guess I'll find out all the details tomorrow."

"That's a pretty name. I like your name too. I've never known an 'Axelle.'"

"It is typically French. Like Blandine."

Blandine sounded so . . . bland. "What was she like in school?"

"Just like me. Passionate, political, full of fight. We were arrested together, in 1968."

"Arrested? For what?"

Axelle looked at her coldly. "May 1968. You might have heard of the protests. Before your time?"

"Oh, right. The student riots. You were there?"

"More than that. I helped organize my entire high school. They weren't 'riots.' They were protests against the government. They started in the schools then spread to universities, laborers, unions. People forget that. It was us, teenagers, who started the movement. France came to a halt. *We* did that. An exciting time, for a while."

She sounded wistful. Even—especially—with an arrest, it must have been heady times. Changing history. Suddenly the cab swerved to the left curb and stopped.

"*Voilà, mesdames. Chez Pierre.*"

CHAPTER TEN

The bar was an old, traditional one with blue-painted wooden panels across the front, a few curtained windows, and the smell of stale cigarette smoke permeating the interior. They were pointed toward a stair and descended into a stone-vaulted room that looked like a place to age wine in barrels. The space was large, and dark, with a few small table lamps and sconces against the walls. At one side was a long bar set up with wineglasses and sample bottles. Francie made her way in that direction, her calm roiled by incomprehensible French conversations all around.

Heads turned toward the tall, gray-haired woman in the red-and-yellow scarf. Axelle dropped her gaze and let Francie pull her toward the bar.

"Shall we take off our coats?" Francie ordered a glass of Sancerre. "What would you like?"

Axelle slipped out of her trench and handed it to Francie. "*Un verre de Côtes du Rhône,*" she asked the bartender.

Holding the coats, somewhat annoyed to again be the woman's slave-assistant, Francie looked around for somewhere to set them down. There was Dylan, coming through the door. Francie excused herself and went to greet him with kisses on both cheeks.

He looked tired, with circles under his eyes and a patch of beard that hadn't been completely shaved in the morning and now was coming in dark along his jawline. He loosened his top shirt button and sighed. "How's it going?" He glanced around. "Is she here?"

Francie tipped her head toward Axelle, who was sipping red wine at the bar. "I'm just throwing the coats somewhere. Go get a glass of wine and talk to her for a second."

He nodded, and she skipped through the crowd of suits to find a coatroom in the back. She quickly hung their coats then returned to the throng. It was a throng—that was odd. How many people worked at Bozonnet Patroni, and how many were involved in the estate negotiations? A lot apparently.

Dylan handed her the glass of Sancerre and clinked his own glass with both hers and Axelle's. He didn't have a toast to inspire them though. Axelle muttered something under her breath, took another sip, and squinted around the room.

"Is he here then? Let's get on with it," she growled.

Dylan ran a hand over his hair anxiously and set down his glass. "Let me find him." He disappeared into the crowd.

At that moment the kitchen doors opened in the back, and two waiters arrived with large charcuterie platters full of salami, sausages, and other meats, many cheeses, fruit, olives, and sliced vegetables. One was set down next to them at the bar. Immediately a rush of hungry lawyers pounced on it, pushing them ever so slightly off to the right. Axelle was bumped by a young woman in a navy-blue suit who apologized profusely then dove toward the cheese and meat. We all have our priorities.

"Well," Axelle harrumphed as she turned back toward Francie. "I see why everyone's here now. A free meal on the law firm."

Francie raised her eyebrows at the scene then tried to look cool and collected. "Come on," she told Axelle. "Let's go sit down somewhere."

They found a small round table and drank their wine in silence. Where was Dylan? Where was Lucien Daucourt, for that matter? Or Monsieur Corne, the head of the firm? No one from the law firm bothered to introduce themselves or say hello to Axelle. It was a bit shocking to Francie since she'd had good experiences with most French men and women. They were polite to a fault, at least to your face. She watched the crowd at the two charcuterie platters and realized they were all young, most not even thirty. Did they all work at the law firm?

Dylan appeared. "Guess what, ladies? We're at the wrong party."

He led the way out into the stairwell and across a hallway. He pushed open a door and stood aside to let them go in first. Axelle put her head up high and clasped her hands in front of her, having abandoned her wine glass at Party #1. Francie gave him a sly look, clutching the rest of her Sancerre in one fist. He replied with a smile.

In this much smaller room the crowd was subdued and dignified. Definitely the law firm party. About fifteen people, mostly men but a few women, stood in small groups, holding wine glasses and chatting in low tones. There was Corne, with Lucien. Axelle paused and Monsieur Corne immediately rescued her, taking her arm and leading her over to Lucien Daucourt. Their introduction appeared friendly but cool. They were adversaries in this ordeal after all. They shook hands instead of cheek-kissing. Perhaps more cool than friendly, especially for relatives.

"Who were those people over there?" Francie asked Dylan as they got more wine. "At the wild party."

"Some dot-com company. The manager was embarrassed that you'd wandered into the wrong room. He should have escorted you downstairs."

"No harm done. Free wine." Francie tried to make him relax, but she wasn't successful. Two worry lines etched his brow. "How was your day?"

He hitched a shoulder and winced. "Let's talk about it later. How was yours?"

"Lots of cataloging. I met Lucien with Corne, we went to lunch, then in the afternoon the art appraiser worked for several hours." She leaned closer. "There's some very nice stuff in there. Warhol. Oh, and a Matisse," she whispered hoarsely, wiggling her eyebrows.

"Really."

"A small one. And those pop art things are super hot right now. I did a little checking around. I told Axelle we'd probably have to auction everything and she was pissed. She really wants that one over the fireplace. I mean, she is set on it. She calls it 'the Roy.'"

"Well, maybe she'll get enough money to buy it."

"Maybe." Francie doubted that Axelle would put out millions for a piece she thought was legitimately hers. She'd probably sue Lucien first. She frowned. Could you sue a fellow heir in France? She opened her mouth to ask Dylan, when the cousins and Corne arrived in front of them, tense smiles plastered on their faces.

Cédric Corne did quick introductions and excused himself. Apparently he'd had enough of the cousins. Dylan didn't jump at the chance to keep the conversation going, such as it was, so Francie began.

"Lucien—may I call you Lucien? Monsieur Daucourt? Docteur Daucourt?"

He looked pained but said, "Lucien is fine."

"Good. You're family, right?" She beamed at Axelle, who stared at her hands. "Dylan, get Axelle and Lucien something to drink. What will you have, Monsieur, Madame?"

When everyone was nursing a glass of wine, she nudged Dylan to get him to talk. His mind was somewhere else tonight. "Ah—I hear you've seen the apartment, Lucien?"

The doctor nodded. "Yes. It is quite a lovely flat. So large, with all the original fittings."

Axelle was staring at him now. "You'd never seen it then."

"Perhaps when I was very small. I don't really remember it. My grandmother knew Mathilde quite well though. And my mother, of course. Unfortunately my mother passed many years ago, at quite a young age."

"I spent many happy hours in that apartment," Axelle said pointedly. "Many."

Lucien gave a rueful smile. "Family is very important, is it not?"

Now Axelle got bothered. "Is it? You never got in touch with Tante Mathilde? All these years?"

"To my regret," he said sadly, or mock-sadly. "Can I apologize to you, Axelle, for that oversight?"

"You can, but it won't make a difference to Mathilde. Your neglect cannot be changed. And please, call me Docteur Fourcier. I don't really know you well enough."

Lucien bit his lip then and said no more. He was wearing the same suit and tie from earlier in the day, not quite as well-pressed anymore but still sharp. He was an attractive man, Francie thought, probably a nice one who didn't deserve Axelle's caustic wit. But then, who did?

Francie and Dylan watched a trim middle-aged woman in a green sheath dress coming toward them. Lucien turned toward her gratefully, taking her arm. "Ah, my wife, Severine. This is Docteur Axelle Fourci-er"—he couldn't help himself using her given name—"my cousin, and also some of the lawyers in the firm working on the estate."

The wife shook Axelle's hand briefly and said she was so pleased to meet her. No response from Axelle. Dylan shook her slender hand and introduced himself, then Francie. "You are Americans?" she said, a look of wide-eyed wonder on her expertly made-up face. She had shiny, dark hair in an attractive wave, small dark eyes, and a pale complexion. "American lawyers?"

"We are," Dylan said. "I work in both Paris and New York for the firm. Francie is a US attorney but is helping out on the estate."

Severine glanced at her husband then said, "I see something here. You two?" She waggled a finger between Francie and Dylan. "You are *petits amis*?"

"*Chérie*," Lucien cried good-naturedly. To the rest of the group he explained, "She thinks she has special powers to perceive romance. My apologies."

Francie laughed. "But she's right." She squeezed Dylan's arm. "I'm here because of him."

Axelle made a noise. "What?"

"And because of you too, Doctor Fourcier," Francie continued quickly. "Because of the estate."

The older woman squinted at Francie suspiciously. Severine and Lucien watched all this with intense interest. Lucien said, "We are all here because of Mathilde. What a long and fabulous life she lived." He raised his glass. "To Mathilde."

They all murmured "To Mathilde" and sipped wine. Apparently when you toasted to a dead person—as opposed to someone's health—

you didn't need to confirm it with eye contact all around because nobody bothered. Lucien and Dylan both drained their glasses.

"A hundred and four years. Wow," Francie said, just to keep the conversation going.

"If you could have seen her in the fifties and sixties," Axelle said softly. "So beautiful, and so talented. So many glamorous parties and fabulous friends. She was so good to me. I loved her so."

Lucien and Severine looked uncomfortable. Here they were, inheriting what would probably be millions of euros from a relative they never bothered to meet. Even though she lived within a few miles of them. They at least had the grace to look sheepish. But they'd probably get over it quickly.

The *soirée* broke up early as everyone went on their merry Parisian way. Fashionably late dinners, children to tuck in, a nightclub, or legal paperwork—whatever was next, they drank and said their *à bientôts* and took off down the street. Dylan, Francie, and Axelle waited on the sidewalk for a cab to arrive. At the last minute Francie pigeonholed Dylan.

"Let's send Axelle home and go get some dinner," she whispered. He kissed her and nodded. When the taxi arrived he told Axelle they'd decided to walk home and gave the driver her hotel's address. She didn't seem to care, lost in the sour flavor of the evening, meeting the dreadful cousin.

It was nine o'clock by the time Dylan and Francie slipped into the banquette seating at the restaurant. This bistro was one of Dylan's standbys, he told her, for nights when even making a decision about food seemed too overwhelming. She smiled at him on the walk over, holding his arm. What had made this day so difficult? Was it something to do with Mathilde's estate?

But she didn't ask. She watched him over her water glass as he fidgeted with his reading glasses, ordered for them both, and leaned back into the leather booth. He slipped his glasses back in his jacket and sighed. Francie reached out and took his hand.

"So," he said tentatively, as if embarking on a journey into the unknown. His eyes looked worried, darting to her face and away. He said no more.

"So," she repeated carefully. "More wine?"

He shook his head. "This day." He pulled his hand away and rubbed his eyes. Finally he took a big breath and said, "I have to go home."

"Right now? We just ordered."

"No, I mean back to the States." He leaned in then and took her hand again across the table. "It's Phoebe. She needs me. I have to go."

"Oh. Of course." Francie frowned. "What's happening?"

"That's the thing. All I get is crying, no details. Something is wrong, and Rebecca isn't dealing with it for whatever reason. I have to see it for myself, I guess. Talk to both of them. You would think that my ex-wife could deal with things for a few days but she—" He bit his lip and shook his head.

"It's all right. You shouldn't make assumptions. You just need to go and figure it out."

He looked so relieved, she knew she'd said the right thing. Even though she was a little ticked off at his ex. Making him fly all the way home from Europe for a crying jag seemed excessive. Or was it something worse, something he wasn't telling her? What was the problem anyway?

"And Phoebe. Are you worried?"

"Worried, yes, but I'm not really sure what's going on. Rebecca has her eye on a couple private schools, I guess, both of which are not cheap. But I guess you don't really want a cheap private school, do you? That's not the point."

Francie shrugged. "I went to public school, all my sisters did. My mother taught in a public junior high." She smiled and tried to dial back her tone. She did dislike snooty private institutions, but not all of them were snooty. "But I don't have kids. What do I know?"

"I went to public schools too," he said. "But times have changed. What about your sisters? Do their kids go to public schools?"

Francie frowned again, trying to think. "Actually no. Most went to private. My nephew, Merle's son, went to public school but only when the money ran out."

"Yeah." Dylan sighed again, raised a finger to the waiter. "I changed my mind about wine."

Their meal was simple but delectable. Dylan had ordered himself a duck dish, *magret de canard,* and for her, chicken roulade stuffed with Gruyère cheese and fresh sage. They ate and paused, sipped wine, ate some more, talked very little.

Dylan was leaving, going home. So far their working vacation had been all work and no vacation. Now it might be already over for good. Who knew how long the mess with his kid and his ex would last? Maybe he wouldn't come back at all. Maybe his ex would find a way to keep him away from her. Francie looked around the bistro and sighed. All this wouldn't be the same without Dylan.

But it would still be France, still the City of Light. And plenty of cheese to discover. Somehow, with or without him, she would try to enjoy it.

THE NEXT MORNING WAS BITTERSWEET. Francie was hoping for a little parting romp in the saggy but beautiful bed, but Dylan was pensive like the night before. Distracted, worried, and not in the mood. She wondered if this was his real personality, a mopey middle-aged dad, depressed about the way his life had turned out. He was normally so attentive and loving.

On the sidewalk, as they waited for his taxi, with the morning light picking out the orange of the geraniums on the balconies, he held her close. "I'm so sorry," he whispered. "This didn't turn out the way I planned. The way we planned."

She squeezed him to her. "It's okay. You can't plan for everything, can you?"

He kissed him, still looking for reassurance in her eyes. Then the taxi arrived. They said goodbye. He promised to try to be back by Monday but, really, how could he promise that? For all Francie knew he wouldn't be back for weeks, if at all. The law firm here needed him for the estate work, but no doubt they could send over that Lucy what's-her-name, who was also bilingual. Maybe you could never recapture the magic of Paris in springtime, rediscovering the love you thought was lost forever.

Back in the apartment Francie flopped down in a velvet chair with an espresso and pondered her day. Or her fate, if she was being melodramatic, and, face it, she usually was. She wasn't practical like Merle, or creative like Annie, or domestic like Stasia. What was Elise? The coddled child, the youngest? That seemed unfair. All the sisters were different, but each had a dominant trait. Francie's was a flair for the dramatic. Which was letting her down right now.

She would not wallow in this disappointment, she told herself. Dylan had no choice. Of course he would pick his sweet daughter over her. *Be practical like Merle.* Francie got to Europe thanks to Dylan, and at least got to spend half a week with him. No, it was fine. She would explore Paris, research art, swan around with the grumpy Axelle. A daunting prospect, that.

Wait—Merle was coming back to France this weekend! With her dishy Pascal. With Merle she would figure this out, how to tackle the problems, how to enjoy the hell out of this mess. If Merle had any special powers, it was how to make the worst situation into something dreamy and wonderful. Francie jumped out of her chair, threw on her trench coat, and ran down the stairs to meet her short but oh-so-sweet Paris life.

CHAPTER ELEVEN

*T*en minutes later Francie was standing in line at a boulangerie, picking up a mini quiche for breakfast, when her phone rang. It was Bozonnet Patroni, Dylan's law firm. She winced, wondering if she was fired now. That would upset her plans to stay busy and happy. But she had to answer.

"*Allo*, Francine Bennett *ici*." She was quite proud of her accent. Wrongly, but she wasn't aware, so it didn't matter.

"*Allo,* Madame. Cédric Corne." He rattled away in French, making Francie freeze for a moment and stare at the baguettes, eclairs, and tarts in the case with horror. Then he chuckled nervously. "Oh, I am sorry. You don't speak French. What am I doing? So. Madame. You can arrive at the Fourcier apartment today? We will be on the spot at ten in the morning."

"Of course, yes." She wasn't fired, huzzah. It was just nine. It would give her time to walk there and get some exercise while she ate her breakfast. Quiche in hand, Francie made her way to Pont Neuf, her favorite bridge, and found a bench in the morning sun. After inhaling the quiche she made her way down the steps to the island in the center of the river, Île de la Cité, and walked the perimeter until she was on the very tip, looking downstream toward the ocean. This was where she'd first spotted flowering trees, cherry or plum or something, in the spring. That was a memorable hunt. She looked around but didn't really know her trees well enough to identify them without flowers. Their leaves were fading to yellow as September crept into October.

Her river and bridge meditation over, Francie walked briskly to the far side of the bridge toward the ninth arrondissement. Had Mathilde always lived there? Maybe the lawyer knew.

Cédric Corne met her on the street, swinging the huge green door aside and waving her inside. "Perfect time," he said in his swishy accent. "I have only just arrived myself."

Upstairs in the apartment there was conversation again. This time from the kitchen, women talking. Corne headed in that direction through the salon, pushing through the tall, ornate door. The doors throughout the apartment were white, decorated with plaster wreaths and flowers, the sort of thing that cost a fortune today. The apartment smelled better today, more like ammonia and less like mold. Paintings lined the floor of the long hallway, ready for the next phase, whatever it was.

In the kitchen Margot was stacking plates again. She looked up at Francie, hair falling in her tired eyes, but made no greeting. Poor thing, they were working her ragged. On the other side of the kitchen stood a slender French woman in a classic tailored suit, dark hose, and heels. Her ice-blond hair was pulled into a chignon. She had a pinched mouth with bright red lipstick and was obviously giving Margot some sort of lecture. She paused as Monsieur Corne entered and straightened, attempting a smile.

"*Bonjour,* Monsieur." She glanced at Francie. "*Bonjour,* Madame.*"*

Corne introduced her in French to the woman. Then he turned to Francie. "This is Madame Élodie Maitre. She works at Bozonnet as well. She is taking over for Monsieur Hardy today."

Francie nodded at her. "She speaks English then?"

He turned to the French lawyer. "*Vous parlez anglais?*"

Élodie blinked and attempted a laugh. "*Un petit peu.*"

"So, a little," Corne said to Francie. "I'm sure you can figure out how to get along. I will translate for you for a moment here then I must be on my way." He said something in French then. The lawyer replied. "She would like the china and crystal cataloged, all the plates and bowls and glassware. Also the silver, the spoons, and so on. We hope to join a household goods sale coming soon at Hotel Drouot. A large auction house."

"Of course." There were stacks and stacks of china. Cupboards of glassware set out along the length of the twelve-foot dining table in the next room, visible through the doorway. If only Merle or Stasia were here. They knew china from everyday plates. Francie would have to do some research and look at imprints on every piece. She sighed. It could take days.

Élodie continued to expound in French. Monsieur was inching toward the door but paused. "She says the auction house wants a good photograph of each different type of glass or plate or bowl or whatever. *C'est possible,* Madame?"

"I guess. On my phone?" She held up her cell phone.

"*C'est bon,*" Élodie said, adding something incomprehensible.

"Just be sure to email them to the law firm every hour or so, so nothing gets lost on your phone," Corne said. "Madame Maitre will provide you the address. Now I must go." He turned and ran toward the door.

Francie set down her purse and pulled out her notebook. *Here we go again.* This cataloging wasn't exactly what she had imagined. Hadn't she asked for helpers? Now she was barely above the cleaner on the labor scale. But she wouldn't make a scene: she repeated that on a loop. *Make no scene, drama queen.* She took a deep breath, straightening with her supplies. "All right. Let's go."

The two French women frowned at her, exchanged a glance, and shrugged.

FRANCIE WORKED SOLIDLY for two hours as Margot and the lawyer chattered, rearranged dishes, and brought her new items they'd discovered somewhere in the apartment. It wasn't difficult work but tedious. By the time noon rolled around, Élodie announced *dejeuner* and left. Lunchtime was not to be ignored. Margot peeled off her cleaning gloves and disappeared. Francie set down her notebook on the last stack of small tea plates she'd cataloged to remind herself where she stopped. Then she picked up her phone and saw a message from Axelle.

"Must talk. I am very upset about the artworks."

Francie called her and proposed lunch. "Give me fifteen minutes." She directed Axelle to the bistro on Saint-Germain that she and Dylan liked. After a brisk walk Francie found Axelle sitting rigidly against the windows, just inside the door.

Axelle wore her old man's sweater today, with black slacks, no scarf. Her eyes looked bloodshot and her hair was matted on one side. She growled as Francie sat down.

"How are you today, Doctor Fourcier?"

"Not well. That room is suffocating and all I can do is think about poor *tantine*, suffering these last years with no one coming to her aid but some—some person hired by the lawyers. No family. I should have come back. I blame myself."

"What's done is done. We can't go back."

"I know that! That's why I want the Roy to remind me of all the good things, the good times I had with my aunt. Cousin Lucien has no memory of her at all, never met the woman, never set foot in the apartment, and yet he gets half of everything."

"I understand that is French inheritance law," Francie said quietly. "I guess you should be glad there are no more cousins."

Axelle's eyes flashed. "You are assuming it's all about the money! Everyone assumes that. All you greedy lawyers, that's all you understand. There is history in that apartment. Lives lived, meals shared, wine poured, tears and laughter, good times and bad, under the eye of that painting and the others." She shook her head. "You'll never understand."

Francie did understand but kept silent. It was important for Axelle to get her grievances out, to air her rage, but there wasn't an answer. They would have to follow the law, and the law said that heirs get equal shares. The only real solution for both the artworks and the apartment itself was to sell them and split the proceeds. What else could they do? No one knew what the art was worth. The only way to appraise it, to get market value, was to auction it. Unless Lucien Daucourt suddenly became generous and kind, all must be sold.

After they ate their soup silently and sipped a glass of white, Francie sat back in the chair. "Would you like to visit the Roy this afternoon? I'm working over there. I'm sure it would be fine."

The cab dropped them off at the corner and they walked to the green door. It stood ajar, so they pushed it open and walked up the stairs. "Still no elevator then," Axelle complained, wheezing.

Margot opened the door. She eyed Axelle then disappeared into the kitchen.

"The art is down. All lined up in the hallway." Francie pointed Axelle in that direction as she took off her coat. "I'll be in the kitchen."

Margot was mopping the kitchen floor with an old string mop. Francie stepped around the wet spots and went back to her notebook which was sitting on the stack of delicate china plates. She moved to the next stack, a cluster of tiny bowls—salt bowls? Next to them sat their tiny spoons, as if waiting for a doll's party. She snapped a few photographs of the salt bowls and their identifiers and jotted down the number in the notebook. She picked up a miniature spoon and held it up to the window light. If there were markings on it, a microscope would be required.

Voices rose in the hallway. Francie looked at Margot, who was still mopping. Where was Élodie? Now there was shouting. Francie put down her notebook and went through the dining room to the hall.

Axelle and Élodie faced off in the long, narrow hallway, each yelling loudly in French. They waved their hands angrily, pointing at the art and each other. What was happening? Had Axelle done something? Should she not have brought her here? And, wait, wasn't Élodie supposed to be representing Axelle's interests in the estate? Had they even met?

Francie stepped up next to Axelle and held up both hands: "Stop. Wait. Please."

Both women immediately went silent and looked at her. They didn't seem particularly angry when not shouting, their expressions mild. "Doctor Fourcier, did you meet your new lawyer?"

"Unfortunately," Axelle muttered, looking up and down the severe figure of Élodie in her black suit. "She's my lawyer now?"

"Élodie Maitre," Francie began, gesturing to Axelle, "Doctor Axelle Fourcier. Your client."

The lawyer nodded at Axelle warily. She said something in French. Axelle nodded in return and muttered something else.

Francie said, "Okay? Is there something you need to translate for me, Doctor? What's the problem?"

"We were discussing the art. The Roy," Axelle said. "She told me it was all to be auctioned. She says a museum is interested in it and I told her absolutely not."

"And she—disagreed?"

Axelle nodded. "She's not really my lawyer, is she? What about Mr. Hardy? Is he your boyfriend? Is that what you said?"

"He's gone home, to the US. Family emergency. I'm sorry no one told you."

Élodie spoke in French. Axelle listened, eyes squinted, then said, "She says the law firm and the art appraiser are decided that the art must be sold. The heirs must agree, and Cousin Lucien is on board. Without my consent the entire estate could be held in—what is the word, limbo? escrow?—for months, even years. She reminds me of the bureaucracy of France, as if I need another reminder. She says I could die before I see a *sous*. Which is a very unkind thing to say." She focused her formidable glare on the lawyer.

Élodie raised an eyebrow and squinted at her client. She said something more.

"She says it is only the truth. That I am not a young person. I may not have years to wait." Axelle then spoke harshly to the lawyer. "I tell her she is a cold-hearted witch."

This was going well. Francie sighed. "Maybe you should leave, Doctor. Can I call you a taxi? I have more work to do."

Axelle straightened her shoulders. "No. I want to look around. Maybe there are some personal items no one else wants. Tante Mathilde was my own aunt, my soul mate. I must have something from her, something personal and meaningful. Have you looked in every nook and cranny?"

They left the lawyer standing with her hands on her hips in the hallway. The library was the best bet for personal items, Francie figured. They stood in the middle of the room and eyed the stacks of books on the library table, the many more still on the elegant wood shelves that stretched up to the twelve-foot ceiling.

"I'm sorry about that. She's—"

"A bitch. That's obvious," Axelle said. "I used a nicer word because I need to get along."

Francie chuckled. This was her version of "getting along," exchanging insults with everyone who might help her. "Well, maybe there's something in here she won't care about." She walked up to the bookshelves and ran her finger down the book titles. "Maybe a book?"

They spent a quiet half hour pulling out books, leafing through them, setting a few on a pile to peruse further, rejecting most. Many were irreparably damaged, eaten through by worms and moths and mildew. Axelle worked one side of the room while Francie sneezed on the other side. Then Axelle made a discovery.

"This is not a book. Look." She held out what appeared to be a book. It was a thick, hard cover with dusty pink boards. Axelle delicately opened the front to reveal that it was a box, not a book.

"A secret box." Francie looked inside. "Letters."

Axelle pulled out the chair from the desk and sat down, the box in her lap. "You continue. I will have a look."

Francie returned to her side of the shelves, pulling out books, leafing through them, and returning them to the shelves. She'd already identified most of the important first editions. Unless there were more secret boxes, this was a waste of time. She should be back in the kitchen, cataloging tiny spoons.

She looked at Axelle, holding brittle, yellowed stationery up to the light, squinting at faded ink. It would take her some time.

"I have to go work on the china and crystal, Doctor. I'll be in the dining room if you need me."

Axelle glanced up and returned to the letter she was deciphering. Francie went back to the dining room table and picked up her notebook and phone. Margot and Élodie had disappeared. The quiet was peaceful but a little bit creepy. So she spoke aloud to herself: "All right, tiny spoons. How many are you?"

It was almost an hour later when Axelle burst into the dining room, her face flushed. She marched up to Francie, who had moved on to grapefruit spoons and butter knives. Axelle thrust the box at her. "Take it," she demanded.

"What's wrong?"

"Just take it!" Axelle's shoulders slumped. "Please."

Francie took the box from her. "Is there a problem?"

"The letters. They're from me." Her eyes began to water.

"Oh." Francie wasn't sure why that made her upset. "Is that a bad thing?"

Axelle shook her head violently. "Keep them for me. I just can't—" She turned on her heel and was gone.

CHAPTER TWELVE

*A*xelle Fourcier was late, on purpose, which was typically French. She had worked hard to lose that aspect of her culture in the Western Hemisphere but now it sprang back in all its impolite glory, and she was glad. She'd needed those extra moments to gather her thoughts, her memories, her emotions. It had been a trying day.

She walked to the brasserie her friend Blandine had chosen for their reunion. The walking, while tiring, had served its purpose as a meditation to clear her head.

The letters she'd read at her aunt's apartment had sent her back into a dark place. The first was one she'd written at twelve while she was on a trip to the beach in Normandy with her parents. Her father liked to visit World War II sites and recall all the horrors. It was a strange obsession of his, one his wife seemed to tolerate but his daughter did not. Axelle found it morbid and depressing: the bunkers left by the Germans, the endless headstones of the cemeteries, the memorial markers that must be read with solemn gratitude. She understood now, as an adult, that she should feel grateful to all those who had fought and died for France. But as a child it weighed heavily on her, a witness to everything old and dated and dead about her parents.

The letter was full of complaining and descriptions of the hatred she felt for her mother and father. Why would she hate them so much when they took her to the beach? They had asked that question then, and she asked herself now. She was a petulant child, an ungrateful one with a sour attitude. That was perfectly clear from the letters.

The Paris evening was mild with a light breeze, and somewhere in the vast purple sky stars popped out. Most of this was lost on Axelle as she stared at her large feet, clopping along the sidewalk in run-down loafers. Even the prospect of meeting her old friend felt like a burden today. They would be so old. She wouldn't even recognize Blabla, as she had called her friend years ago. When had they last spoken? Fifty years before. She had been so excited when Blabla tracked her down. But it was oppressive to think of all those years gone by.

Suddenly she stood at the golden windows of the brasserie, a bustling family restaurant with full tables, dogs on laps, children racing around. Axelle remembered the place, where she and her parents had dined once in a while. They rarely ate in restaurants, but this place was cheap back then. She looked up at the sign and didn't recognize the name. Now it was called Le Rendezvous, which had a sensual connotation that didn't bear out in the interior. Inside it looked the same: noisy and bright, with scuffed wood floors, a high tin ceiling with chandeliers, round tables full of customers eating and drinking and talking loudly. She shuddered.

"*Mon amie!*"

She turned to find an old woman with white hair pulled back from her cheerful, lined face. She was nearly as tall as Axelle, and that was the detail that brought Blandine back to her. They were the "tall girls" in school, and proud they were of it. But she had aged horribly, dear god. Her face was lined with wrinkles. Poor thing, her thin shoulders barely held up the heavy wool coat she wore.

"*C'est moi*—Blandine. Blabla!" She laughed and held out her hands for a hug. Axelle hesitated then fell into the hug, accepting and giving kisses on both cheeks plus one more for an old friend. She let her friend pull her inside the restaurant. Their table was in the back, away from the more boisterous guests.

"Do you remember this place?" Blandine asked. "We came here

once, all of us. Your family and mine and maybe someone else? After a choral concert, I think. I loved singing back then. Do you still sing?"

"No," Axelle said, already regretting the dinner with her friend. She was too talkative, with too good a memory. They ordered soup and risotto with mushrooms and decided to split a half pitcher of red wine. Axelle gulped down her wine and poured herself more. Blandine didn't seem to notice.

"So tell me everything," her friend began, a huge smile on her face. "I can't believe you're back! You always said you'd never come back."

"And I didn't until now. You heard about my *tantine*?"

Blabla tipped her head sympathetically. "Yes. In the newspaper. I'm so sorry."

"There was a death notice?"

"*Oui.* That's how I knew you might be here. Such a long, celebrated life. I went to the service but you weren't there. I called the lawyers mentioned in the notice."

"I wasn't informed until recently. I'm her heir, along with a cousin I never met." She set down her fork. "I've had no contact with my family for years, Blandine. No one told me she died. But it was my mistake. I cut off everyone. I should have kept up a correspondence with her. With someone."

"Like me perhaps?" Blandine smiled, softening her criticism. "No one writes letters anymore."

Axelle thought of the box of letters. Why had her aunt kept them all these years? Maybe she'd put them away and forgotten them.

Blandine said softly, "I went to your parents' services too, Axelle."

"Bless you."

"It was hard without you there. There were a number of people there, but I never understood what happened." She smiled again. "I mean I know what happened. But why were they so strict, so unbending?"

"What did your parents do?" Axelle wanted the conversation off her parents. So much heartache. "After we were arrested. Did they punish you? I forget."

"Oh, there was a huge shout. That lasted for two days or so. Then everyone calmed down. Especially when they could see I had really done nothing—*we* had done nothing—that was truly awful. Just exercised our rights as citizens."

"And then you just went off to the university, right? They paid for expenses, didn't they? Your parents were very liberal. They are gone, I suppose."

"Not my papa. He is ninety-five, can you believe it?"

Axelle shook her head. "Give him my best."

"They were very kind. He and mama helped me so much. University wasn't free back then, remember? I'm sorry your parents were so—"

"Heartless? Stingy? Cold?"

Blandine frowned. The waiter arrived with their food. Blandine changed the subject. She filled in her old friend about her life during the past fifty years. Her dead husband who she had loved but not so much that her life ended when his did. Her children, two daughters who lived in Paris and Nice and had given her five grandchildren, some friends of theirs she ran into once in a while, her job until she retired, teaching in an *école maternelle,* a preschool. She managed to get Axelle to talk generally about America and Canada, Oklahoma and her move to the beach.

Then, mid-question, Blandine straightened, frozen for a moment. She stared out the windows at the street. Her lips pursed as if she was trying not to say something. Axelle frowned at her. She seemed agitated. Axelle looked around the room to see if someone was looking at them. But it was the same scene: happy families, dogs, old women. She glanced out the front windows, but the sidewalk was empty. When the meal ended Blabla grabbed her coat, said she had to go check on her father, and left Axelle at the table. It was a bit startling, the abrupt way she left Axelle sitting there alone. Had she said something offensive? Axelle was usually the rude one. She didn't like it on the other side.

She sipped the remainder of the wine and paid for their dinners. Blandine had left a twenty-euro note on her placemat for her dinner. Her abrupt departure only cemented Axelle's conviction that there was nothing left for her in France. Everyone had moved on from 1968. The time to live in the past, to be one of those nostalgic French women who never give up on memories, was over. She was not her parents, living in old times, pining for what would never be again. All she had to do now was get this inheritance worked out and go home.

My home is in America. It gave her some comfort to think that this would all be over soon and she would finish packing her books and baubles and move to the house on the sand.

The waiter returned to pick up the money. Behind him another man turned to squeeze through and caught Axelle's eye. He was gray-haired, dapper, and wore glasses. He paused as if caught by her beauty, smiled, and moved on. *Just a moment with an amorous Frenchman*, she thought, reminding herself that she was back in Paris where her life had been dark and painful. But a little flirtation made the end of the evening a bit less depressing.

When she arrived back at her tiny hotel with her impossibly small room, the phone was blinking. She had a message.

"Axelle! *Ma cousine.* It is Lucien. I feel we got off on the wrong foot. I am eager to get to know you better while you are here in Paris. I have been so busy, my wife barely knows my name. But this is very important. Please allow me to buy you a coffee tomorrow?"

Lucien mentioned a café that she knew was just a half block from her hotel, on the corner. She'd passed it many times already. He said ten o'clock tomorrow. He left his phone number but said she didn't need to reply. "Please just come."

BLANDINE BAUDET UNLOCKED the door to her town house, looking nervously over her shoulder. She had taken a taxi home tonight, an extravagance, and told the driver to wait for her to enter her house. Her street was quiet, a breath of breeze rattling leaves hanging on trees, a garbage can tipped over by cats, a car alarm beeping in the distance. Quiet and safe, that's what Richard had always said about this street. Too far from everything interesting, he meant, but she wanted quiet and safe always. And he had agreed with her, and gone along, as he always did, dear thing.

She swung open the door and flipped on the lights. To the driver she held up one finger for him to wait as she went through and turned on lights and looked around. What was she doing? Surely no one had broken into her home while she was at dinner. She was being crazy.

She returned to the front door and flickered the porch light to signal to the driver that all was well. He pulled away as she locked the front door and collapsed into a chair in the hall. It took a good three minutes for her heart to stop clattering.

Seeing him again, that vile man, had nearly caused her to have a stroke. She had heard tales of him from classmates, whispers, rumors, and once in a while his antics made the newspapers, on a back page where most of the petty criminalities were written up. He had been in prison, she was sure of that. He was *persona non grata* amongst their classmates.

Why did it have to be tonight? Why did their paths have to cross at all? But this was Paris, where she lived, and had lived for her whole life. Eventually it was bound to happen, that two old classmates would run into each other. Did he recognize her? Surely not. He hadn't changed so much. Still a *séducteur*, he had actually winked at her in the brasserie! Of all the nerve. He did know her, he must—or maybe he just winked at every woman. Yes, hold onto that.

Blandine took a deep breath and tried to relax. At least she had gotten him away from Axelle. It was important, in case he recognized her. He wouldn't, would he? It had been too long. Axelle hadn't even recognized her. She probably hadn't given him a second thought in all her years in America. Their whole lives had passed between 1968 and today, years and years and children and grandchildren. So much had changed in France.

She stood, feeling wobbly, and shrugged off her coat. So much had changed and yet—had it?

CHAPTER THIRTEEN

The next morning Francie took her time walking back to Mathilde's apartment after her coffee break. The air was brisk today; a cool wind blew dry leaves around in the gutters. She was bored with cataloging a zillion teacups and their matching saucers. If she never saw another gravy boat she would die happy. How many serving dishes did a family need? Her busywork didn't really seem like a good use of time in beautiful Paris, but she felt she owed it to Dylan to finish out the week. He had enough on his plate. He'd only sent her the briefest of texts since he left.

She double-checked on the packet of letters in her purse. She'd tucked Axelle's old letters from the book box into a manila envelope and tried to read a few in the coffee shop. Technically she hadn't been given permission, but she figured Axelle wouldn't care. She'd given them to Francie after all. And the older woman was so freaked about her past she'd probably never get around to reading them. Francie couldn't get much out of them though. Her French was not improving, although she'd started doing fifteen minutes of lessons a day online to improve her pronunciation at least.

Maybe Dylan could translate them when, and if, he returned to Paris. Axelle was making noises about a return flight. She needed to get back to her moving duties in the US. And she hated Paris. How could someone hate the place they were from so vehemently? There was a story there, but whether Francie would ever hear it was doubtful.

She pushed open the apartment door and took off her coat. She could hear Élodie talking in the hall. Before she went into the kitchen she paused to see what was happening there.

Élodie stood with the art appraiser, jotting down notes on a pad as he rattled off something, pointing to each piece. Francie caught artists' names and little else. Élodie's eyebrows raised and she blinked hard at various times, presumably when he mentioned auction estimates. She saw Francie watching them and frowned, tipping her head toward the kitchen. *Back to work, scullery maid.*

Margot scrubbed the sink, trying to work out a century of stains. Talk about indentured servitude. Francie went through to the dining room where she had her notebook set up for the next round of cataloging, an enormous number of champagne flutes of all sizes and types. She worked for a half hour, counting, taking photos, making notes, until Élodie pushed through from the hallway.

"*Ça va*, Francie?" she said, eyeing the overloaded table.

At least she knew this term. "Yes, all right. *Ça va.*" She pointed to the hallway. "And out there? Has the art been priced?"

Élodie squinted then understood. "Yes. Many good numbers."

"Is a museum, ah, *musée*, interested in the Lichtenstein?"

"*Oui.* Centre Pompidou. But the number is high. Maybe madame will donate it?"

Francie shrugged. "How high is the number?"

"*Trois à cinq*—three to five million euros." She pursed her lips in surprise.

"That is high. And it must be sold? Because Madame Fourcier would like to keep it to remember her aunt."

Élodie shook her head. "*C'est impossible.*" She went into a long explanation in French then caught herself. "The estate must be broken in half. Madame must understand that. Can you help her understand?"

"I can try."

The lawyer smoothed back her platinum hair. "Madame *et moi* —we do not agree, *tant pis*. Too bad."

"Madame is in mourning for her aunt, remember. For a life she once had in Paris."

Élodie looked puzzled, blinked a few times, and disappeared. What would Axelle do about the Roy? There seemed to be an impasse. Francie let the problem roll around in her head as she went back to work on the crystal.

Lucien and Axelle sat across from each other at the small, round café table next to the window, feeling the sunshine warm them as they fingered their demitasse cups of espresso. It had surprised them both that their preference was identical, a dry type of coffee, very strong, called *café serré*. It was generally called ristretto in the US, the Italian term for the bitter, half-water espresso. She ordered it that way and the barista knew what she meant. When Lucien ordered the French version, he told her it was the same and they had a pause. To find someone with the same taste in exotic coffee was—unique. To be related to them, perhaps not unusual.

They were second cousins, he had explained. Their grandfathers were older brothers of Mathilde. Both had been gone for many years. Her grandfather died in the '30s. Lucien's grandfather had died during the Second World War, leaving behind two small children. He'd never known him. When his mother, a Fourcier, also died young, the family connection frayed. It was a common story, and Axelle found herself warming to the man. It wasn't his fault that he forgot about his great-aunt, a woman with fifty years on him. It was unfortunate though, and she still thought he could have tried a little harder.

But if he had kept up the acquaintance, been attentive and solicitous of Mathilde over the years, wouldn't she be suspicious? Think he was being kind because of the inheritance? He had after all helped the lawyers find her, tracking her down in the US. He didn't have to do that. He could have claimed the whole inheritance. So she had to soften her stance toward her cousin, although she didn't want to like him. He was fancy, in the French manner, with slick manners, soft hands, and a very Parisian accent.

"And so," he said in English, smiling beguilingly, "tell me about your life in America. You have many university degrees, I hear."

"Several. But mainly European history with an emphasis, of course, on the French. I taught history for many years in universities."

"And where did you teach?" He would ask this. The French could be so classist about education. He wanted to hear "Harvard" or "Yale," no doubt.

"Nowhere you've heard of, I'm sure. I retired a few years ago from a large university in Oklahoma."

"Oklahoma?" He looked puzzled, which made her smile.

"Near Texas. You know Texas?"

"Ah, yes. Cowboys."

She sipped her bitter coffee. My, it really was *serré* in Paris. The dying leaves of autumn and the harsh coffee and her cousin's insincere smile combined to make her shoulders sag. When would she go home? She longed for that beach. How much longer would this estate business take?

"I understand you have not been back to Paris for many years. Is that right?"

She nodded. "Bad memories. I left in 1968."

"Ah. You were involved in the protests?" She nodded. "But that was long ago. Paris and France are still here. Still beautiful."

She shrugged. "I was an only child. My parents died, one after the other. My father visited me in America once, a few years earlier. My mother didn't bother. We did not get along."

She had thought so much over the years, and especially in Paris, about that last conversation at home with her mother and father, the yelling, the incriminations, how they said they despised what she had become, a modern girl who does awful, lurid things for irrational reasons. And how she had told them she thought they were ignorant and backward and would never understand. And they really never had.

If only she could take it all back—would she? Probably not. Her small expat life wasn't that bad, was it? No, it was just fine.

Lucien said, "But what of Mathilde? You say you loved her. And yet you didn't come back for her either."

"At least I have an ocean as an excuse." She lowered her eyebrows.

"Touché." He spun his coffee cup distractedly.

"What do you want from me, Lucien? Why are we here?" She was tired of playing games. One thing she liked about Americans was their ability to cut through the *merde*—the bullshit.

His eyebrows raised in surprise, as if caught being impolite. The biggest sin in France. "To be friends, Cousin. That is all. I do not need the money from Mathilde's estate, I assure you. I make a very nice salary as a physician. Whatever happens with the estate is fine with me. It will be a cushion for my boys. But that's the end of it."

It was almost convincing. "And your wife, Severine? She thinks this way too?"

He shrugged and looked askance. "She works in finance. She thinks a bit differently. The money people, you know how they are."

"Did she tell you to meet with me, become friends?"

"She encouraged me, of course." He smiled his smarmy smile. "But I wanted to, Axelle. May I call you Axelle now?"

"If you wish. I won't be in Paris long."

"Here is the thing, Axelle. I would very much like for all this to be resolved and everyone to be happy. My wife always says I am the peacemaker. So can we make some kind of peace? An arrangement about the estate? Something that will make you feel good? I do not like to fight about these things. They are just things, even the art."

She squinted, suspicious. "Of course. Give me the Roy."

"Ah." He picked up his phone. "I have just heard from the lawyer. She sends me a list of the estimated values of the art. She tells me the appraiser thinks that the 'Roy,' as you call it, will sell for three to five million euros at auction."

"So don't sell it. Give it to me."

He sighed. "Look at the list, Axelle. She will have sent it to you. You pick the most expensive thing in the apartment. It is unreasonable. And the Pompidou would love to have that piece to share with all art lovers."

"It is the only thing I want." She crossed her arms across her chest. "What is it that you want?"

He pushed back from the table, his color rising now. "What about the Matisse? It is lovely. You said yourself that it is valuable."

"I have no connection with that painting. Do you want it?"

He shook his head. "No. What about this? I give you the Matisse, then you agree to split the proceeds of all the other items at auction?"

"You aren't hearing me, Lucien. I only want the Roy. Mathilde and I had many conversations about it. It means something to me. It is valuable to my heart." She placed a hand on her chest dramatically.

He sighed angrily. "You are too rigid, Axelle. We all must make compromises."

"Must we?" she snapped. "What is your compromise?"

"Don't you think I would love to have some artwork in my home? I am quite fond of the Rothko actually. But I know it must sell. I am resigned to never owning it." He leaned in. "And what of the apartment itself? My wife would give her eyeteeth to live at that address. So airy, so large, she goes on and on. But she cannot have it. I tell her that every day. 'No, Severine, forget it.' And yet I must listen to her complain incessantly."

Axelle smiled. "Poor Lucien. With all you will make on the art you can probably buy the apartment outright. Severine will be so happy."

He huffed and rolled his eyes as if his wife would never be happy. This too cheered Axelle. She liked the image of Severine pecking on him constantly. "How much is the Rothko worth, according to the appraiser?"

He tapped his phone. "She says, two to four million."

"And the Matisse?"

"He must be out of favor. Only five hundred thousand."

"It is a dreary little thing for a Matisse."

Axelle thought about the Mark Rothko piece, a large canvas, about three by four feet, with squares of ochre and rust against a gray background. It was gloomy too, as Rothkos went, with none of the vivid reds that he was famous for. But Lucien liked it, that was what seemed important.

"All right. I will compromise. I will take the Rothko and split the proceeds of everything else with you. On the condition that you and I help the Pompidou come to a fair price for the Roy, not an auction price. Somewhere in the middle so we are donating a portion. Also including attribution from Mathilde so her legacy will live on."

He blinked and opened his mouth to speak. She raised a finger. "And you will sign a document that says that anything else found that belonged to Mathilde goes to me alone."

"What else is there?"

"I have no idea. Hidden bank accounts perhaps?" She gave him a mysterious look. She'd made up this part of her bargain on the spot but was liking the effect it had on him. "I know of nothing, Cousin. But it helps my peace of mind if I know there will be no more lawyers involved. Do you like lawyers? I am not fond of them."

"They are picking the bones of the estate as we speak."

"*Exactement.*"

Lucien looked at her with new respect, contemplating her proposal. He wanted a compromise and she had provided one. If she couldn't have the Roy, at least she would stick it to her cousin and take his beloved Rothko. It might be worth a lot more than the appraiser reckoned. One never knew about these things.

"What will I get outright?" he asked. "As long as you're getting the Rothko."

"What do you want? The dreary Matisse? The crystal? The moth-eaten books?"

He gave her a steely stare. "The apartment. I want the apartment, Axelle. It is worth a similar amount, I'm told."

Her eyes widened. "What? It is worth twice the Rothko. At least four million, possibly six. Have you looked at Paris real estate lately?"

He folded his arms now. "It's in bad shape. It will take all of my share of the estate to repair and modernize it. But Severine wants the apartment. And I must make my wife happy."

"You are such a dutiful husband, are you?" She glared at him with his set jaw and hard, dark eyes and saw that it had come to the final offer. Check and mate. They each got something they wanted, more or less. It would pain her to think of that skinny, petty woman entertaining her superficial socialite friends in Mathilde's home. But Axelle would never have to see Severine again, or Lucien for that matter. It was time to go home.

"Ah, Cousin. If that will make your wife happy, who am I to stand in her way? At least it will stay in the family. I see you refinishing floors in my mind, on your knees, sanding. I see you putting in a new toilet. You will keep a guest room for your cousin?" He gave her a sly, satisfied look. He had won, and he knew it.

Fortunately for him she didn't care.

CHAPTER FOURTEEN

The lawyers for Docteur Fourcier met in the Bozonnet Patroni office the next morning. Axelle and Francie arrived together, sharing a cab again. Élodie Maitre was gracious and grateful, especially to Francie, who she assumed had talked her French friend into making a devil's bargain with her cousin. Francie hadn't been particularly optimistic about the plan when Axelle called her yesterday afternoon, but now she could see that it was set. Axelle just wanted it done so she could go home.

The three women sat in Élodie's sumptuous office, a feminine version of the formal law office with purple velvet armchairs, a colorful modern rug, and a streamlined glass desk that looked spotless. How in the world did she keep that so clean? Francie wondered. The fresh flowers in the plain white vase on the window ledge were just too perfect.

The lawyer uncapped a fountain pen. She looked up expectantly at both of them, a smile transforming her rigid expression. "Shall we begin?"

"You prefer French?" Francie asked. "Axelle can translate for me."

"*C'est bon,*" Élodie trilled. She wore a pink Chanel-style suit today, very formfitting. Black ruffles graced her wrists as she began to write down what Axelle was telling her. They talked about the Mark Rothko painting, the Lichtenstein, and the apartment. The key items.

The lawyer nodded along, then Axelle began discussing something else, Francie wasn't sure what. Élodie frowned. Francie looked at Axelle.

"I'm telling her about the agreement. That anything else that is discovered in the estate from now forward will become my property, without any legal recourse by Lucien or involvement with the law firm."

"He agreed to that?" Francie asked.

"He did." Axelle explained something to Élodie then to Francie. "There is nothing that I know of. Mathilde had the art and the apartment, those were her precious things. She had no more than a thousand euros in cash at the end. Has Monsieur Corne found anything more in the estate?"

The lawyer said no. It was unusual to cut off any future benefits without recourse, but if the heirs agreed, they agreed. Giving Lucien the apartment was a huge gift, a generous one. He would probably have to pay massive taxes on it, so there was that. Axelle got the more portable item.

"Are you sure about this particular painting, the Rothko? Didn't you want the other one, the Lichtenstein?" Francie asked, a little confused by this sudden turn of events. What had happened to Axelle that she'd suddenly changed her mind?

"Lucien wanted the Rothko," she explained. "So I thwarted that desire. And I am quite sure the estimate by the appraiser is low. Even if he is correct it is fine. There will be plenty of money to go around. I must go home, it is time. It makes me very happy to think of all the people who will admire the Roy at the Pompidou and see that Mathilde donated it. But I will tell her exactly the bargain on the Roy. Thank you for reminding me."

Francie daydreamed a little while Axelle spoke in French. It was Friday already, and Merle and Pascal were due back this afternoon. She couldn't wait to see her sister, to tell her about the Belle Époque apartment and the fabulous pieces of art. While she gazed at the chartreuse and yellow flowers on the windowsill, her phone buzzed. She reached into her purse and looked at the screen.

The text was from Dylan. He was coming back. Her heart lifted. There was still time to have the romantic sojourn they had hoped for, a repeat of the search for pink flowers from the spring or something similar. He would arrive early Sunday morning, he said. And he was bringing Phoebe.

Oh.

Francie startled, staring again at the flowers. Phoebe was traveling to Paris with her father? Francie hadn't spoken to Dylan since he'd been back in the US. They'd only exchanged short text messages. What was going on? Did he get custody of his daughter? Had something happened to his ex? Who was going to take care of Phoebe while Dylan worked?

She shut off her phone without replying. She didn't want to say the wrong thing. What did he expect of her? Her disappointment in the way this Paris trip had turned out was making her sour. She didn't want to be sour, she wanted to be sweet and optimistic.

Axelle was standing, and Élodie followed suit. The two women shook hands. It was all remarkably civilized after their last encounter.

"I will get a document drafted for you today, Madame."

"Good. We must move on." She asked another question in French. "*Bon. Merci,* Madame. *Bonne journée.*"

As Axelle and Francie walked out into the lobby, the older woman said, "It should be final by Monday, she says. At least the part between Lucien and me. The donation of the Roy will take a while."

Axelle asked Francie to accompany her to lunch, and since that was her actual duty here in Paris, she found a good brasserie nearby, hailed a cab, and got them in before the noon rush. She smiled at Axelle and gazed at the menu, still thinking about Dylan.

"What is it?" Axelle demanded after their wine arrived. "You think it's a bad deal, what I did with Lucien? Is that it?"

"I'm sorry. I got distracted by a text from Dylan." Francie took a welcome sip of rosé. "I think you did very well on your bargain with Lucien. Everybody got something, nobody feels screwed. Right?"

Axelle's lined face sagged. "He was cagey."

"But you feel okay about him getting the apartment?"

"Oh, yes." Axelle chuckled. "His wife will make him suffer for that place. So many repairs. Only one bathroom! It will be a money pit, as they say in the US."

"I think it turned out as well as it could. Everyone is more or less happy."

"So what did Dylan say? Is it true he is your boyfriend?"

"He was my boyfriend years ago in law school. It didn't last. Then we ran into each other again last spring, here in Paris."

"Ah, kismet."

"Yes. It was nice. Magical, even. So we decided to come back. He works over here pretty often. We were going to have a romantic work/play couple of weeks over here. We were going to go down to the Dordogne and visit my sister. Who by the way arrives in"—she checked her watch—"three hours. And now I don't know if we'll have any play time."

"Why not? The estate work is nearly done."

"His nine-year-old daughter is returning with him."

Axelle nodded sagely. "I see. A dampening on romance."

"Exactly."

"Do you like this girl?"

"Sure. I mean, she's nine and I'm dating her father. I don't really know her very well. Dylan and I have only been seeing each other about six months. She lives with her mother most of the time. I'm a little confused about why she's coming here. I hope everything's all right on the home front." She glanced at Axelle. "I worry."

"Life is a worry, *chérie*. You have experience with children?"

"Not really. I have nieces and nephews. But none of my own."

"Same as me. I find talking to them as you would adults is very effective though."

Francie perked up. "How so?"

"It shows you respect them and their feelings. They feel on an equal footing with you. Don't treat them like babies. Sometimes they can get bossy and you can remind them that you don't boss them around. That sort of thing." Axelle waved a hand as if that was the end of it.

As they finished their meal Francie got another text. This was from Élodie. She crumpled up her napkin and said to Axelle, "The documents are ready. Let's go back."

BACK IN THE LAW OFFICE, Élodie Maitre sat with her hands folded on a manila file folder. She looked pensive now, not so giddy about the solution as she had been in the morning. Francie squirmed in her seat. What was wrong now?

"Madame," she began solemnly. Axelle translated for Francie. "There has been an offer for the Rothko. From an important museum here in Paris."

"The Pompidou?" Axelle asked.

"*Non,*" Élodie said. "Le Musée d'Art Moderne. Their collections are similar. You may have heard they are doing major renovations and wish to expand into more American artists than in the past. I have spoken to Monsieur Corne and he believes you should sell, or donate, the Rothko to them."

"Oh, he does, does he?" Axelle muttered in English. "Why is that?"

"For the good of the country, our culture."

Axelle frowned at Francie. "What the hell? Can't I just take the painting home?"

"Is there an export issue, Madame?" Francie asked.

Élodie blinked and stood up. She returned a few minutes later with Cédric Corne, resplendent in gray worsted and a pink shirt, his silver hair perfect. The two French lawyers looked like a matched set.

"Mesdames, *bonjour.* Madame Maitre has asked me to explain the tax laws." He proceeded into a complicated delineation of the issues involved with taking cultural items out of the country, a practice frowned on by the French state. Because the Rothko had been in the possession of a French citizen for so many years, it was considered a French cultural icon, something that should be enjoyed by the masses. A severe penalty was levied on items taken out of the country.

"What sort of duties would have to be paid?" Francie asked.

"That depends on the valuation, Madame. In this case it could be quite high: thousands, perhaps even millions of euros. This is why we discouraged you, Madame Fourcier, from claiming the other piece you desired, the Lichtenstein crying woman. It would have been subject to the same heavy duties designed to prevent it from leaving France."

Axelle sprang up from her seat and stalked to the window. She stared outside, her hands clasped tightly behind her. The lawyers exchanged worried glances, as if Axelle might be violent. Francie turned to her. "It will be all right, Axelle. The people of France will enjoy the Rothko as much as you would. Right?"

She didn't answer, rubbing her eyes with one hand. An awkward pause, then she sighed and returned to her seat.

"Why must the French state thwart me at every turn? Tell me that, Corne."

He blinked, taken aback at her tone, or the use of his name without the honorific. He stuttered softly: "Madame, if you please. I have explained. It is not personal, just the way of the state."

"To use their power against citizens. To confiscate personal items from everyday people."

"You will be compensated, Madame. I assure you we will negotiate a fair price."

"Will I have to pay taxes on that?" she demanded.

Corne pulled his lips in. His answer, it seemed, was yes. "There are *droits de succession*—inheritance taxes. Yes, Madame. I am sorry if that was not explained to you. Because of the high value of the estate, the apartment, the paintings, we expect you will have to pay the maximum amount for nieces and nephews, fifty-five percent."

In the end, the will to fight seeped out of Axelle Fourcier. Francie could see the color drain from her face, her hands go limp in her lap. She closed her eyes wearily. She had been so happy with her bargain this morning, or at least happy to have it done, to have thwarted her cousin by taking the Rothko home. And now, the hated French government was exercising its power over her again. Whatever had happened in 1968 had made her hate France, and here was just another example of why.

She signed the papers, agreeing to sell the Rothko to the museum and granting the apartment to Lucien Daucourt, who she cursed as a thieving bastard out on the sidewalk. Francie could see why she was angry. She was truly helpless against the French bureaucracy: lawyers, government, taxes, and inheritance laws. It was an untenable position for a proud, independent woman who had made her way in the world by herself, alone, without help.

"Hey," Francie said at the corner as they waited for the light. "Let's find a bar."

"What?" Axelle glared at her.

"Let's celebrate. Get a flute of champagne. A Kir Royale. It's over."

CHAPTER FIFTEEN

*M*erle and Pascal climbed the three flights of stairs with their luggage as Francie unlocked the door to Dylan's apartment. She helped with one bag, thumping it down in the hallway near the second bedroom. She had persuaded her sister to stay with her for a few nights at least. She had the apartment, there was no real argument.

"Oh my, Francie, you minx." Merle spun around in the salon, taking in the view and the eighteenth-century details of the small flat. "You didn't tell me it was so lovely."

Pascal took a deep breath after the climb with two huge suitcases. "Not all your sisters are enamored of houses like you are, blackbird."

"I have wine, you two. Take off your coats."

Francie opened a bottle of Provence rosé, her sister's favorite, and poured them glasses, delivering them to the salon. Pascal took his and made his excuses. He needed to shower and report in to the Police Nationale that he had returned.

"He has to go to work immediately?" Francie asked as they settled into the velvet chairs.

"I think he's on duty for the weekend," Merle said. "But we had a great week at home. Jack and Bernie think the world of him."

"He cooked for them, didn't he?" Francie had been a bit jealous of their relationship in the past, but she was over that. She was just happy for Merle now. "Dylan's coming back on Sunday morning."

"Oh. Will we be in the way?"

Merle looked tired. Transatlantic flights will do that to you. There was a gray cast to her complexion and dark circles under her eyes. But she had to be told what was up.

"His daughter is coming back with him." Francie still hadn't replied to his morning text. She had to do that soon or he'd think she was mad or something. "I don't know what's happening with her, or them. But I imagine we'll need the bedroom."

"Of course. We'll be out by Sunday. How old is she?"

"Nine."

"That's a great age. I remember you at nine." Merle was seven years older, so she had lots of stories about Francie's childhood. Some were very embarrassing.

"Was I cute?"

"Adorable and knew it. Red hair and freckles, vivacious smile. Bouncy ponytail. You took dance lessons and collected butterflies." Merle smiled maternally at her, making Francie stick out her tongue. Merle laughed. "Yes, and you were a handful."

Francie sighed. "I don't know if Phoebe and I will get along. I don't think she likes me."

"It's probably just the situation. I love that name, by the way. I bet she's as adorable as you were."

"Is nine really a good age? Because she barely speaks to me. And before I left the US I intercepted a call from her to Dylan where she cried and cried."

Merle frowned. "What about?"

Francie shrugged. "Something about her mother. She said she hated her sometimes."

"Nine-year-olds can be such teenagers sometimes."

"Ugh. I hate teenagers."

"You do not." Merle clinked her wineglass against Francie's. "Here's to Paris. May it never let us down."

Francie sipped her rosé and wondered if this time Paris had let her down. Its magic hadn't helped Axelle. She'd left the older woman at a table in a small bistro, eating *frites* and drinking Sancerre. Axelle had bitched for a good hour about the lawyers and France and Lucien and how much she hated them all. Finally the wine calmed her. Was she still in that bistro, ranting away? Maybe Francie should call her, make sure she got home all right.

But she wasn't driving. She wasn't a child. And Francie was technically no longer her minder. The deal was done. Let her get sloshed. She was an adult. She'd earned it.

Merle was watching Francie's face intently. "Tell me what's been happening."

"It's a long story," Francie warned her.

Merle stood up. "Then we need more wine."

THE SISTERS WENT out to dinner late that night, taking a cab to the wine bar they'd discovered that spring. They ate charcuterie and cheese and bowls of onion soup. Francie had missed Merle. They hadn't spent much time together since the spring. Even back in the US, Merle was busy seeing all her relatives, going to her son Tristan's college, making sure their parents were healthy and happy. She was a good sister, a good daughter and mother. She sometimes made Francie feel petty and selfish in comparison. This summer Francie had devoted all her free time to Dylan, and look how that had turned out. Still there was hope, she told Merle, that this time things might work out for them.

She wasn't sure if she believed it. There were so many obstacles. And now the big one—Phoebe—was coming to town.

THEY SPENT SATURDAY SLEEPING LATE, going shopping and out to lunch. Pascal disappeared back into his job in the wine investigative unit of the national police. Merle said he had to leave midday to go out into the vineyards somewhere. He could never say where.

"How are you two then?" Francie asked at lunch, wiggling her eyebrows. "Everything *super*?"

Merle grinned. "Yes, everything's good. Very good." She looked around the small, touristy brasserie with its tacky decorations and dusty plastic fruit baskets. "I'm so happy to be back in France."

"My client, Axelle Fourcier, is just the opposite. She hates France with a passion and can't wait to go home."

"You mentioned that. What do you think happened to her that makes her hate France so much? It must have been something drastic."

"All I've gotten her to explain is that she got arrested in 1968, during the student riots."

"That was fifty years ago."

"There's more. There must be. But I don't know what."

AXELLE BLINKED OPEN HER EYES, letting them adjust to the light coming through the window of her hotel room. What time was it? She rolled over to look at the clock and realized she was fully dressed, lying on top of the covers. She fell back on the pillows and felt the pain in her head. What had happened? Oh, yes. She'd drunk a lot of wine. This was a hangover. She'd one or two in her life.

Staring at the ceiling, bits of the night before flashed in her throbbing head. There was a man. Yes, it was Xavier. Her old boyfriend who appeared out of nowhere and bought her more wine. He was as handsome as ever, as charming. How had he found her, she asked him. He had heard she was back in Paris, he explained. He had read about her aunt's passing. He gave her much sympathy for her loss. He wanted to know everything about the apartment, the paintings, the inheritance.

She poured out all her grievances to him. He was so attentive, so kind. He was an old friend from her student days. They had marched together, rallied together, burned a few desks in the street together. He told her how much he admired her courage back then. And her beauty. He was a flatterer, for sure, but she was in no mood to tell him to stop. She needed a friend, and Xavier had appeared, like a guardian angel.

Had she kissed him? Oh, she thought she had.

She closed her eyes and groaned. She didn't really like men, as she told almost everyone who wondered. But there were certain ones who broke through her resistance. At least she hadn't slept with him. Had she? She felt for her undergarments and found them all in place. He was a gentleman after all. Just a chaste kiss between old friends.

How had she gotten back to the hotel? She seemed to remember him putting her in a taxi, telling the driver the name of her hotel. She must have told him where she was staying. It was all a blur by then. So much wine. She was ashamed.

She took a long shower, until the hot water ran out. As she dressed her stomach reminded her she had missed dinner, and now breakfast as well. She needed sustenance. She picked up her phone to check the time. It was nearly one o'clock in the afternoon. Also there was a text message.

It was in French. "*Comment ça va, ma belle?* How are you, my dear? It was so lovely to find you in that resto. And to catch up on your life. Call me and let's have dinner. X."

So he had her phone number. She must have given it to him last night. Struggling into her coat, she sighed and walked down the stairs to the sidewalk, giving the girl behind the desk a nod. Had anyone seen her in her cups last night? How embarrassing. But she put her shoulders back and held her head high.

After an omelet and several coffees made her feel human again, Axelle sat on a park bench in the Tuileries and watched the boys push sailboats in the fountain. *Such innocence,* she thought. If only she could go back and relive her youth in Paris, find some joy, some happiness. Then she wouldn't have this nut of hatred that she carried with her everywhere. But now, at her age, it seemed unlikely to go away.

She wanted to talk to Blandine suddenly, tell her about the chance meeting with Xavier. Blabla would understand. They had all been friends. She pulled out her phone and found Blandine's number. It rang, then a voice told her to leave a message.

"Blabla? It's Axelle. The most incredible thing happened last night. I ran into Xavier. Can you believe it? We drank and reminisced. I wish you had been there. Call me, dear one. I have much to tell you about Aunt Mathilde's inheritance. Can we have dinner tonight?"

Her friend didn't call back. Axelle waited in the park for an hour then walked back to her hotel, took two aspirins, and went back to bed.

CHAPTER SIXTEEN

Francie made the decision late Saturday night to go out to Charles de Gaulle Airport in the morning to meet Dylan and Phoebe. By eight A.M. on Sunday she clutching onto the door handle of an Uber driven by a Moroccan as he barreled along at top speed. At the terminal she asked him to wait and went to find father and daughter inside. She found them, eventually, collecting their luggage, and gave them both hugs. Phoebe looked sleepy and out of sorts. Her brown hair had come loose and wafted around her small, sad face. Dylan's dark hair was matted on one side of his head and his eyes were rimmed in red. A charming couple.

Francie slipped her arm through his and smiled at him. "How's it going, Dad?"

He jerked his head toward her then smiled faintly. "A little rough. But—we'll talk about it later."

Phoebe wore dirty, worn-out white sneakers and stained blue track pants with a pink puff jacket that hung off one shoulder. Her backpack looked heavy, sagging against her. She dragged her rolling bag and clomped along behind them, scowling.

"Could you see anything from the plane, Phoebe?" Francie asked, trying to be pleasant.

"It was dark. Duh." Phoebe rolled her eyes.

Francie squeezed Dylan's arm and ran ahead to find the Uber, a sedan that was clean enough though not too new. Phoebe scrunched up her face and said it smelled. Dylan sighed. The three of them squeezed into the back seat.

"Hang on," Francie whispered. "He drives fast."

By one, the Hardy family of two had taken short naps and showers and joined the Bennett sisters for lunch. The brasserie was at the end of their block, a family place with high ceilings and big plate glass windows on the sidewalk. They got the last table. Everyone was out for Sunday dinner, even the dogs.

Phoebe stared at a chihuahua sitting on a woman's lap at the next table. The white-haired lady fed him tidbits off her plate. "Yuck. That is not sanitary," she complained loudly.

Dylan patted her hand. "Good vocabulary. And science! But this is a different country. You'll have to get used to seeing different things. Things you don't understand until you ask, or observe a little bit."

His daughter slouched back and sulked. "How long am I going to be here? Like, forever?"

Dylan caught Francie's eye. They still hadn't discussed why Phoebe was here, and what the time frame was. Francie raised her eyebrows in question.

"Just a week or so, sweetie. Then we'll go home and figure out a new school."

"You don't like your school?" Merle asked. Phoebe shook her head. "My son Tristan had trouble at his school. He got in a fight, got a black eye, and had to leave for a while. Sometimes it's good to take a break."

"I haven't done anything," Phoebe said belligerently.

"No. You didn't," Dylan agreed. He turned to Merle. "She was just having some social things with other girls."

"Bitches," Phoebe whispered angrily.

"Phoebe. That's enough," Dylan said sternly.

"That happens. I had some problems in school with friends too," Francie said. Not too many, but if necessary she would make something up.

"They aren't my friends. I hate them! And stop looking at me!" Phoebe bent her head so they couldn't see her face. Merle looked sad. Francie stuck out her lower lip. Poor girl. She had been tossed between parents and something nasty was going on with fourth-grade bitches.

They changed the topic of conversation to the work at the apartment and the deal that Axelle had struck with her cousin. Dylan was startled that she'd agreed to give Lucien that beautiful, historic property but agreed it was her call.

"He told her his wife was lusting after it and he had to make her happy."

Dylan rolled his eyes. "And she fell for that? Well, she got that nice pop art piece."

"Apparently the state doesn't like you to take artworks out of the country. Export taxes and all that, and the high value the state places on cultural items. So she's selling the Rothko to a museum."

He nodded. "We should have thought of that. She never would have been able to take the Lichtenstein home."

"Even though it's American?" Merle asked.

"Not without a huge amount of red tape. It could have taken years and lots of money."

"So that's how France has amassed such great art collections," Merle said.

"There is one more thing she made Lucien agree to," Francie said. "She said anything else that is found in Mathilde's name will belong to her exclusively. He will have no rights over it. I asked her why she wanted that in the agreement and she said because she doesn't like lawyers. She wants us out of it from now on. We are apparently eating into the estate with our fees."

Dylan shrugged. "No question about that. But she can't just fire us now."

"What else is there?" Merle asked.

"Probably nothing," Francie said. "But who knows? Maybe there's another Lichtenstein tucked away."

Dylan snorted. "Right."

Back at the apartment Merle packed her bags and took them, with Pascal's suitcase, down the stairs to catch a cab for the train station.

Francie felt she was leaving too soon. "Then come visit me," Merle encouraged. "All of you, please come. I have room."

Francie hugged her. "We'll see. I'll try."

"Don't look so down," Merle said, chucking her under the chin. "Just because a whiny little girl is along doesn't mean you can't still have some fun with your boyfriend."

Francie wasn't so sure. She felt beaten in a way. Whipped by a nine-year-old, it was pathetic. She hadn't had one moment alone with Dylan. She helped load the suitcases and waved her sister off, smiling broadly just in case that thing about smiling making you feel better was a real thing.

Upstairs in the apartment Phoebe was taking another nap. Francie changed the sheets on the second bed and ran the washer. When she finished she found Dylan sitting in a velvet chair, staring out the window, a solemn, bemused look on his face. She busied herself making tea. Handing him a steaming cup, she carried hers to the other chair and sat down. She had a bad feeling about this. It was go-time. He was going to tell her to go home.

She cut to the chase. "I can get a flight tomorrow."

He glanced at her over his teacup. "Why? What? No, no. I know this is awkward as hell." He set down his cup and reached for her hand. "Please. Don't go."

She smiled tightly. "Tell me what's going on."

He sighed. "Of course. You deserve to know. I just—I don't like to diss my ex even if she's acting badly." He rubbed his face with both hands. "Something's not right. She's drinking more than she used to. Not that she's endangered Phoebe. At least I don't think so. She just refuses to deal with Phoebe's stuff. She plays tennis instead. She got laid off from her job. Or fired, maybe. I told her to figure it out. We had a big blowup. I told her I was going to go back to family court and get custody if she didn't get it together."

"I'm sorry. That sounds difficult."

"Ya think?" He laughed sarcastically. It wasn't a good look. She knew he must be tired and angry and confused about what to do. But she'd never seen this side of him, the cynical, bitter side. She frowned into her tea.

"She's my only child," he continued in a warmer tone. "Francie, I have to think of her well-being above anything else. You understand, don't you?"

She softened and caught his tortured look. "Of course. I'm sure I'd do the same in your shoes."

"She's hurting and I don't really know why. It makes me hurt, here in my chest. She says it's these girls at school who pick on her, call her names. But could that be all of it?"

"If she's feeling vulnerable, sure. Your life is your friends at school at that age."

"I never even had a sister. I have no idea about girls."

She reached out and laid her hand on his shoulder. "If I can help, I'm here. Just ask me, Dylan. I don't want to butt in, but I *do* have sisters. Lots of them."

He sighed. "I don't know if she'll talk to you. She barely tells me anything."

"Well, we'll take it slow. Maybe Paris will work its magic."

He smiled at her finally. "Good old Paris."

THAT EVENING Francie showed Dylan the letters. From Axelle to Mathilde, she told him, going back to her childhood. Francie explained that Axelle had thrust them on her, said she couldn't deal with the past.

"You think she was damaged by something?" Dylan asked, holding the envelope in his lap.

"Maybe. Why does she hate France so much? I mean, does anyone hate their homeland like that, for so long? It's France—Paris for god's sake! She's got a serious grudge. Nobody hates Paris like that, do they? Did I tell you she got arrested in the student riots?" He nodded. "Do you think the cops did something horrible to her?"

He shrugged, unconvinced. "Have you looked at them?"

"The letters? Yes, a few. But I can't read them. They're in French."

He looked at her seriously. "You want me to translate them. Is that what you're asking?"

"I don't know. Is that prying?"

He drew one brittle folded letter out of the packet. "Yes. But now—"

"I've made you curious too?"

He smiled at her conspiratorially. "What if we make sure Phoebe is tucked in and go to bed ourselves? The letters can wait."

"Are you saying Paris has worked its magic on you? One more time?"

He pulled her out of the chair and into his arms. "At least, *chérie.* At least."

WHEN FRANCIE WOKE up the next morning, feeling well-loved again, the bed beside her was empty. She had wondered how Dylan was going to work it with Phoebe right next door. Apparently he had slept in his daughter's room, or on the sofa. Anything to lessen the blow that he no longer shared a bed with her mother.

Francie tied on her robe and padded into the kitchen. Dylan wasn't in the salon. She struggled with the espresso maker and managed to eke out a small cup. As she sipped it, gazing out at the morning light on the roofs of the elegant buildings opposite, she heard a door creak open. Dylan slipped out of Phoebe's room in blue dad jammies, his hair at weird angles. He was tiptoeing into the salon when he saw her and smiled.

"Good morning," he whispered. He gave her a quick kiss and gazed at her coffee. "Make me one?"

He had slept on the floor in Phoebe's room. His daughter had woken up in the middle of the night and called for him. She was disoriented and thought it was morning. He calmed her down by reading aloud from the book she'd brought, a harrowing young adult novel that clearly was too advanced for her. He had to skip the scary parts for his own sake. Today, he declared, he needed to find her better reading material.

"What was Rebecca thinking, letting her read about kidnappings and abuse?" He shook his head. Francie handed him the demitasse of espresso. "How long have you been up?"

"Since I realized you weren't in my bed," she whispered.

He sighed. "I read some of those letters last night. I think you're right about Axelle. She was clearly disturbed—no, not in that way—just worried about something even as a preteen."

"Like what?"

"I can't really tell. She complains about her parents a lot. She actually reminds me of Phoebe. Teenage angst on steroids."

Francie tucked her feet under her in the chair. "So maybe just normal stuff."

"Maybe. I'll read some more later." He leaned toward her. "What are we doing today?"

"I finished the cataloging. Or at least as much as I care to do."

From a bedroom the sound of a cell phone ringing was faint. "Is that yours?" Dylan asked. He stumbled back down the hall to their bedroom and emerged with his phone. He was tapping it when he got back to the salon. "From the office. Voice mail."

> *Bonjour*, Dylan. You are back in Paris, I assume? I am prompted to tell you that there was some untoward activity at Madame Mathilde's apartment over the weekend. If you could meet me there as soon as possible, I would appreciate your help. This is Cédric.

Francie sat up straight. "Untoward activity?"

"I think that means a break-in." He turned back to the hallway then spun back. "Can you stay with Phoebe?"

At that moment his daughter's door opened and she appeared before them, fully dressed in jeans and a purple sweatshirt with cats on it. Dylan stared at her.

"You're up, honey!"

She looked at her wristwatch and then showed it to them. "It's nine, isn't it? I'm not allowed to be in my jammies after nine. And I'm starving."

Fifteen minutes later they were standing in line at a patisserie for croissants and more coffee. Phoebe was surprisingly helpful, and Francie saw the sweet side of her for at least a minute. It gave her hope. Maybe the girl just needed more sleep.

The streets were quiet, and the taxi made good time to the ninth. Up the stairs to the apartment, they passed three young women in chic outfits on their way out. Francie sighed to herself. She had shopped a little with Merle on Saturday. But basically none, as Merle wasn't very interested. This was not the way it was supposed to work in Paris. She had intended to stroll slowly through the boulevards, finding out-of-the-way shops and unique and beautiful things. Oh, well.

"Come on, Phoebe," Dylan urged as his daughter slumped against the wall on the last landing. "We're almost there."

They reached the door of the apartment on the fourth floor. It had large gouges around the knob, like those made with an axe or the claw of a hammer. Dylan pushed the door open gently, looking inside. He stepped in, waving them to follow. Francie let Phoebe go in first as she had a frown the size of France on her face.

Three policemen in dark blue uniforms stood in the salon, surrounding Cédric Corne. Monsieur Corne was in what must have been weekend duds: khakis and a blue sweater. He was running his hand through his hair.

"Dylan. *Merci d'être venu si vite.*" He looked relieved until he saw Phoebe hanging on her father's arm.

"This is my daughter, Phoebe. Say hello to Monsieur Corne. He's my boss, Phoebe."

"Hello," she squeaked.

"*Bonjour, petite,*" he said, frowning but nodding to her. "There have been burglars. The door, you see, broken down. The lock gone."

Francie stepped toward the hallway and saw it was empty. The artwork that had been lined up along the walls was gone, vanished. This was horrible. Her heart sunk.

"They have taken some things, broken some things," Corne continued. "But it is all because of Élodie we are saved. She had the auctioneers come in on Friday and remove the paintings to their showroom for safekeeping."

Francie took a breath. "That was very good thinking on her part."

"*Oui.* It has saved us," Corne repeated, clearly freaked out by the close call. "Madame Bennett, can you go see what might be missing in the *cuisine?* You have your notes? I fear the burglars took the silver there."

"Of course." She moved in that direction. "Do you want to come with me, Phoebe?"

She didn't, glaring hatefully at Francie. So that was back in play. Dylan waved Francie on with an eye roll. The kitchen was clean now, and smelled a lot better. Still a little musty but okay. The intricate piles of crystal and china still sat undisturbed on counters and the small table by the window.

In the dining room things were different. Some china was broken in pieces on the floor, but it seemed selective, as if the burglar didn't like that pattern. The line of champagne flutes had been tipped like dominos and many were broken. She sighed, thinking of all the glasses that had been thrown drunkenly into fireplaces. But this was no celebration.

She got out her notebook and paged through, checking on items on the long dining table. Most were still here, some were broken, a few were missing. As Corne had surmised, two silver candelabras were gone, several large platters and bowls in sterling silver, a set of gold ashtrays, four cigarette holders in pearl and ivory, a pair of ornate fire irons, and two large sterling silver ladles.

She made a list of the missing items on a separate page then double-checked she hadn't missed anything. She could find photos of the missing things for Monsieur Corne if he wanted.

It was almost an hour before she went back into the salon. One policeman remained with Monsieur Corne. They both sat silently in the ancient upholstered chairs. Corne was working his phone. He looked up. "Ah, Madame. How did we do?"

"They took some things, the most valuable stuff, as you predicted." She tore the sheet from her notebook. "I have photos of everything. It should be easy to get valuations for insurance."

He grimaced. There wouldn't be insurance apparently. No wonder he had been so relieved about the artwork. He stood up and put on a brave face. "*Merci beaucoup.*" He waved her list. "Dylan says he takes the girl home? I think. Maybe you should call. I must wait here for the workers to fix the door. But you may go—*merci encore*, Madame."

"Did you look in the library or the bedrooms?"

He blinked. "Is there anything of value there?"

"Shall I take a look?"

She opened the doors from the hallway to the first two bedrooms. The bedding looked rumpled, as if someone was searching them, or maybe had slept over. In one the mattress was askew. This looked like the typical ransacking that burglars were apt to do as they looked for money stuffed in mattresses. She stepped into the library and paused, her foot kicking a book.

Books were strewn over the floor. Every book had been removed from the shelves and tossed randomly. The first editions, piled on the desk, had been toppled but not taken. What was the burglar looking for then? Not valuable books. She stepped gingerly into the room. Was something hidden in the books? Not that she or Axelle had found. Except for the box of letters, of course. And who would want those? Not even the person who wrote them was interested.

Leaving the mess, Francie took a look at the last two bedrooms. In one the dresser drawers had been yanked out and thrown into a pile. In the other the armoire stood wide open, the hat boxes on the floor. Were hats stolen? What the hell was this guy—it had to be a man, didn't it?—looking for?

She returned to the salon to find a man in a blue worker's jumpsuit setting down a large toolbox by the front door. Corne and the policeman were talking to him in French. She put up a hand to wave, intending to go, when Corne stepped aside to speak to her.

"And what do you find, Madame?"

"The first editions are still there. Just some tossing in the bedrooms. All the books are thrown off the library shelves."

"All right. We will get this door secure. Thank you."

Francie hesitated by the broken door. "Have you told Docteur Fourcier? Or her cousin?"

Corne rubbed his forehead. "Not yet. *Mon Dieu.*"

"I can call her if you'd like. I don't have Lucien's number though."

"*Oui, oui. Merci.* You call her. I call Monsieur Daucourt."

. . .

AXELLE WAS AT A CAFÉ, enjoying a pastry and espresso, when Francie called. She filled her in briefly about the break-in—no art lost—then made her way to the café. The older woman looked as she always did, a bit fierce with a scowl and messy hair. She was back in her old man's sweater, which didn't look any better, still with egg and dandruff clinging to it.

Francie ordered at the bar and sat down opposite her. "Well, that was interesting."

Axelle smirked. "You didn't lose anything. Why should you be upset?"

"I'm not." Francie straightened, trying to remember not to engage with her client's bad mood. "I hope you're not."

"What happened?"

"Someone broke in sometime over the weekend. Pried open the door, broke the lock. With nobody else on that floor it was probably easy to avoid being seen. Then inside they took some silver pieces. I made a list for Monsieur Corne."

Axelle sipped her espresso calmly. "Silver? Anything else?"

"The books were tossed around. Thank goodness the artworks had been taken to the auction house. I couldn't tell that anything was taken in the library though. Or the bedrooms."

Axelle flicked crumbs from her fingers. "I feel bad for Mathilde's memory. But it appears I don't really care anymore about her things." Instead of frowning she smiled, as if remembering something fondly.

Francie's coffee arrived with a croissant. She hadn't seen Axelle since Friday, she realized. And she wasn't interested in the break-in, at all. So, new topic. "Did you do anything interesting over the weekend?"

She blinked, a funny look on her face, guilty but enjoying whatever it was. Then it passed and her world-weary attitude returned. "Not really. You?"

"Dylan came back. My sister and her boyfriend arrived, then left."

"And the girl? Did she come too?"

"Yes." She set down her cup. "She's a cute kid. Have you seen your old friend again? What was her name?"

"Blandine. I tried to call her but only get her machine. She hasn't returned my calls."

"Do you know where she lives? Maybe you could go check on her."

She reached into her purse on the floor, drawing out an address book. "I do have her address. She gave it to me the other day when we had dinner."

"Maybe she's sick. Bring her flowers or something. Unless you have something else going on today."

"I'm hoping to get those documents back from the lawyers. Have you heard when that will happen? I'd like to get a flight home as soon as possible."

"I'd better get over to the firm and find out then." Francie put some money in the little tray and stood up. "I'll call you as soon as I have them in hand."

As she walked away through the café, she heard a cell phone ring and Axelle's voice say in an odd, pleasant trill: *"Oui. C'est moi."*

Francie turned back to see Axelle grinning like a cat. Maybe Blandine had returned the call at last.

CHAPTER SEVENTEEN

*A*xelle agreed to meet him at L'Orangerie, an art museum small enough to find someone in, but big enough to provide distractions. She used the hour until their meeting to walk through the Tuileries at her leisure, stopping at the fountain again and admiring the statuary as she strolled. The day was pleasant, warming with autumn sun shining off the creamy gravel.

What am I doing? The thought flitted through her mind and was gone. She'd thought about Xavier all weekend, trying to bring up old memories of high school, those heady strikes, the promise of youth and change they all clung to. Now they were all old and little had changed. If anything France was more fascist than ever. This was why she hated Paris, all these hopes and plans that went nowhere. Their youth was gone and it would never be back, and they had nothing to show for all their passion.

Xavier had replied several times in texts, charming her with his flattering words. What would it hurt to see him again? She wasn't going to get tipsy like last time, not in the middle of a Monday in a museum. She would talk to him, reminisce, then she would go home tomorrow or the next day when the estate business wrapped up.

She passed through security and bought her ticket for the museum. There were a surprising number of visitors at Old Louis's long, rectangular greenhouse. It had been converted several times over the centuries and was now airy and light, with skylights and glass everywhere. She had never been in the place. When she'd left Paris it was not a museum at all, just some boring state function building.

She decided against the audio gizmo and wandered with the crowds into the rooms with the huge Monet water lily panels. They were enormous, but that didn't stop the young and old from trying to take photographs of them. In several corners, young women were getting their pictures taken by young men. It was the same everywhere.

Axelle had never been that enamored with art. In her youth, yes. When talking to Mathilde, sure. But for a long time it had felt elitist and bourgeois. Why did people make such a fuss about it? But the colors on the panels, especially if one put a nose right up to them, shone like a rainbow. The magic of Monet's blues was calming, entrancing. She waited until a seat on a bench opened up and settled herself.

He appeared in the corner of her eye, a tranquil figure in gray slacks, a navy blazer, and a big blue scarf wrapped around his neck. He was still so easy to look at, just as he'd been when she was fifteen. How was it men retained that sparkle and women seemed to just fade away like dust as they aged? Maybe French women worked harder at maintaining their magic. She certainly had done nothing to retain her youth. It had all leached away, neglected and ignored, years before. But Xavier—he remembered it. Maybe that's why she was here.

He spun on dirty canvas sneakers, surveying the room. He stopped spinning when he spied her on the bench. A smile broke open on his face. He skipped over and reached out both hands. "*Ma belle* Axelle!" he exclaimed. She took his hands and he pulled her to her feet. "Have you been here long, waiting for me?"

Up close Xavier didn't look young, not in the face. His hair was thinning and white. His nose was veined and lumpy; his eyelids drooped over his eyes like a sleepy dog's. His neck, cleverly camouflaged by the scarf, was quite saggy. She remembered that now from the other night. They had compared necks and determined drunkenly that they both had terrible waddles. The memory of their laughter came back to her and she smiled.

"How are you today?" She pulled away her hands and put them in the pockets of her raincoat. She didn't like men touching her in public places, even touchy Frenchmen.

"Good, good." He rattled on about some film he'd seen the day before, a Swedish one that baffled him. Why was he telling her this? But she enjoyed the companionship of a handsome man. Did he want to take her to a film? She would go if he asked.

They walked slowly through the Monets, down the stairs, and into another gallery with smaller paintings of a similar period. He talked incessantly, gesticulating about the art, about America, how much he'd like to see it, about the changes in Paris since she'd been gone, and on and on. His French washed over her like a balm. Never had she been with a man who needed no prompting to talk. Well, some professors liked to pontificate, but their small talk was deadly. Not Xavier. He seemed to revel in it, laughing at his own jokes, cajoling her, making her smile. It was freeing in a way. She could listen, or let her mind wander, as their feet wandered through the rooms.

Then it was time for lunch. They walked across the Seine and found a typical Parisian bistro, big and busy with tourists and locals. It seemed natural that they would go to lunch. Xavier told her he'd once worked in this neighborhood and came here all the time. That he had retired from a boring state job deep in the French bureaucracy. When she asked in what field, he waved his hand. It was too boring to explain. Shuffling papers, that sort of thing. Her father had done much the same. Received forms, stamped them, filed them: what a life. Xavier hadn't minded it, he said. It was valuable work. Someone had to do it. But now he was done with it.

"What will you do in your retirement?" she asked as they ate their soup outside on the sidewalk in the sunshine. It was just warm enough to sit outside and she wanted to savor it. There was really nothing like this in Oklahoma.

"I plan to travel," he said happily. "Greece, Italy, South America if I can. I want to see the world."

She decided not to tell him she was a homebody now. That the peace and tranquility of her own safe environment warmed her, made her feel calm. "Where first?" she asked, and he was off, describing cruises and volcanoes and archaeological sites until her eyes watered.

After lunch he walked her back to her hotel, showing surprise at how small it was. The rooms, she assured him, were quite grand. He didn't need to know how tiny they were. He gave her a little bow and said goodbye. She watched him walk jauntily down the sidewalk, leering at the bottoms of all the passing girls.

Quel typique. Frenchmen.

Upstairs in her room she sat on the bed. She was so over Paris. That thought made her laugh, as she had never been "into" Paris, not for fifty years. Her colleagues always wanted travel tips: what to see, where to eat, what were the chic areas. They were baffled when she simply shrugged and said she had no idea. Now at least she could give them the benefit of a week in Paris.

But there was something undone—Blandine. Axelle looked at her phone again. Still no reply. She called her friend again, and again it went to voice mail. She should say goodbye before going home. They would likely never see each other again. These morbid thoughts clung to her as she put her coat back on and walked out into the street to find a florist. Some bright autumn flowers for their friendship. It was the least she could do.

The cab got to the corner near Blandine's town house and stopped. "You walk from here?" the driver said in heavily accented French. Axelle peered down the street and saw white barricades. Her heart skipped a beat.

"Of course." She paid the man and slipped across the seat.

Blandine's street was one of the nicest in this area, with mature trees turning yellow and red, pots of evergreens on doorsteps, colorful doors in every shade. *Her husband, whoever he was, must have been successful to afford this neighborhood,* she thought bitterly as she passed one lovely *maison de ville* after another. Clearly Blandine had sold herself out to the bourgeoisie. What had he done? Blandine hadn't spoken too much about him, and Axelle hadn't wanted to pry. She got the idea he was in business. A damn good business apparently.

A policeman stood at the first barricade, stopping pedestrians and vehicles, turning back onlookers. She asked him if she could visit a friend at Number 154, and he shook his head. She pleaded, but he was firm. She couldn't see what was happening, as the officials had erected a tent of sorts in front of one of the houses down the block. The young, arrogant policeman wouldn't tell her a thing, and she got a bit angry. Damn police state.

Spinning around, Axelle marched back to the corner. She would find another way to Blandine's. Perhaps it was past the barricades. Yes, she would walk the block and come at it the other way. She passed a cluster of men in front of a bar, staring down the street and smoking cigarettes as if enjoying the show. She kept moving.

The block was quite long in both directions. Axelle cursed her old feet as she trudged past apartments, falafel joints, cheap jewelry shops, a small church, more bars. After more than thirty minutes she had turned into Blandine's street from the north and reached the barricades on the other side. She peered at the numbers of the houses and saw 122 and, across the way, 131. Still she could not get close to her friend's house. She pulled out her phone and called Blandine again. No answer, again.

She stood, wondering what to do, worrying a little. There had been a break-in at Mathilde's apartment. Perhaps the same had happened to one of Blandine's neighbors.

Or to Blandine herself. Axelle felt the skin crawl up the back of her neck. She set down the bunch of flowers, orange and yellow chrysanthemums, on a trash receptacle and turned away from the scene. She walked back toward the corner, hoping she could find a taxi in this *arrondissement* without wearing out her feet. Ahead a woman stood on the sidewalk in a sweater and apron, arms crossed against her chest. She eyed Axelle and stepped forward, spilling out a train of angry French.

Axelle startled to a stop. "Madame, *plus tard, s'il vous plaît.*" Slower please.

The woman swallowed hard, clearly distressed. Her blond curls bounced as she waved her hands in a manic fashion, as if she couldn't contain herself. In French, she said, "A terrible tragedy. That poor woman, she lived alone. It is not enough that we have the bombings, the shootings, but now, here, this on our quiet street."

"What? What has happened?" Axelle said softly, but already, she knew.

"That sweet woman. Madame Baudet. It is the filthy terrorists, the Arabs, I know it. They do not even try to belong. They are all criminals."

Okay, sure. Axelle took the hysterical woman by the shoulders, shaking her. "What happened to Madame Baudet?"

"They have killed her, Madame! Dead in her own home. That poor woman. So kind."

FRANCIE GOT the call from Axelle as she was walking home from the law firm. She'd had to wait a long time to get the finished documents. She hung out with Phoebe, if you can call being soundly ignored by a nine-year-old "hanging out." The girl was back to not speaking to her. Dylan had brought her to the office and fallen into anxious relief when Francie showed up before lunch, palming off his daughter on her.

She didn't really mind. She could take the silent treatment. One day they might be friends, but that day wasn't today.

"Hello, Axelle," she said, tapping Phoebe on the shoulder to wait. They were near a big open square, one of those old ones that are basically a big field of pretty sand with some black Gothic stuff thrown in. She whispered to the girl: "Just a second, okay?"

A stream of French came through the phone. What was happening? Another woman was yelling. A shuffle and crunch, then: "Francie? I need a taxi. Can you get a cab and come get me? I'm in the nineteenth somewhere."

"Are you all right?"

"No, I am not. But get a damn cab and come get me. I can't find one anywhere. I'll send you my location on my phone."

"Okay." Francie frowned as the ping came through and she could see where Axelle was. "I've got it. Sit tight."

She grabbed Phoebe and began walking briskly toward the busiest street surrounding the square. "Ow!" Phoebe cried, pulling her arm away. "You're hurting me. I'm telling Dad."

Francie stopped. "I'm sorry. Are you all right?" Phoebe rubbed her arm dramatically then shrugged. "I just got an emergency call. My friend is in trouble and she needs us to find a taxi and go get her. Can you help me with that?"

"How?" Phoebe curled her lip.

"By being fast. And helpful. Okay? Let's go."

They found a cab quickly and jumped in as it idled at the curb. Francie gave him the address but fumbled the numbers. *Leave them out, of course.* She closed her eyes to remember her pronunciation: "Rue Côte de Villette. *Vous la connaissez?*"

The driver turned back to her and she showed him the map on her phone. *"Oui,* Madame.*"*

Traffic was heavy and slow. Francie called Dylan and he answered right away, no doubt because Phoebe was with her.

"So, listen," she said. "We're on our way to get Axelle. She called in a panic. Phoebe's here with me." She turned to the girl. "Do you want to talk to him?"

Phoebe nodded. "Hi, Dad. Yeah, I'm okay. We're just on some wild goose chase." She handed the phone back.

"I was on my way to deliver her the papers anyway."

"Call me when you figure out what the panic is about." He chuckled. "That doesn't really sound like Axelle, does it?"

"The traffic is terrible. I'll call you when I get there."

When she hung up, the girl asked, "Is she a kid like me?" Francie said no, a grown-up. "What's her problem?"

"She didn't say." At least the girl was talking to her again.

They found Axelle eventually, after some wandering, sitting on a bistro chair outside a bar on a corner. She sat still, hands on her knees, until she saw Francie wave from the taxi. Then she stood up and smoothed her trench coat. Francie jumped out as the taxi stopped.

"Are you all right?" Francie ran up to her. She looked a little distraught but unharmed. "What happened?"

"I couldn't find a taxi. Then—" She looked back down the side street. Francie saw crowds halfway down, standing in the street. "No, it was before. Before I looked for a taxi I looked for Blandine's house. Down there." Axelle gripped Francie's arm. "She's dead. Blandine is dead."

CHAPTER EIGHTEEN

Francie huddled over the teakettle, willing it to boil. A pile of coats and shoes sat inside the door to the apartment where Phoebe and Axelle had each dumped their things unceremoniously. Francie managed to keep the conversation away from violent death on the ride home in the taxi, and to send Phoebe into her room with her iPad to play games, but she wasn't sure how long she could keep up this routine without hot liquids.

Finally she poured hot water into the cups waiting with tea bags. And one more with hot cocoa mix for Phoebe. The day wasn't even that cold and the sun was still bright in the sky, but warming beverages were nevertheless required.

Axelle sat shivering at the dining table, gazing mutely out the window. Francie set down her cup. "Warm your hands on it for a minute."

In the kitchen she blew on the cocoa then delivered it to the girl's room. Phoebe lay on the bed on her stomach, watching a video on the tablet. She barely looked up when Francie set her cocoa on the bedside table. Back in the salon Francie sighed as she sunk into the velvet chair.

"Tell me what happened. Did you see anything?"

The older woman shook her head and took a sip of tea. "No. Just police everywhere. A big white tent set up. I guess that was her house. I couldn't get close enough to make sure."

"So it might not be her?"

"A neighbor told me. She seemed quite sure. She said Madame Baudet had been killed. By Arabs, she assumed, because she's one of those people."

"How can we find out for sure?"

Axelle shrugged. "On the news?"

We're not waiting for the news reports, Francie thought. "I'll call my —my brother-in-law. He can find out."

Francie punched in Merle's mobile number and waited while it connected. "Hey! Are you coming south?" Merle asked cheerily.

"Hey, yourself. I have a favor. Can you have Pascal call me?"

"Of course. What's up?"

"Someone we know might have had an—unfortunate event. You know what I mean? We need to confirm."

"Or deny," Axelle added.

"Right," Merle said. "I'll send him a text right now. Sometimes it takes him a while to get back, if he's out in the field."

Francie thanked her and rang off. "Now we wait. Her boyfriend is a *policier*. He goes undercover in vineyards, looking for wine scammers."

"That's a job?" Axelle rolled her eyes. "Only in France."

It took a half hour—not long, but Francie was at the end of her patience by then, pacing the rug. "Thank god, Pascal."

"And the same to you, Francie," he replied with a laugh.

"Sorry. Listen, we need some info. The police are investigating something that happened today on Rue Côte de Villette here in Paris. It may involve a friend of our client, Axelle Fourcier. Can you find out if it's her friend? The name is Madame Blandine Baudet."

Pascal said he would make some calls. Francie fell back into the chair. "He's on it. Now we wait some more."

Axelle stood up. "Would it be possible for me to lie down?" Francie showed her to their bedroom, pleased with herself for having made the bed that morning. Her mother, Bernie, always said making your bed was like wearing nice underpants: you never knew when someone would see them in an emergency.

The return call was ominously swift. Pascal said, "Your fears are correct. The victim is unfortunately Madame Baudet."

"And she is—"

"*Morte.* Deceased. A head wound. Victim of a bungled burglary, it appears. She gave him a good fight though, *le pauvre chou.*"

"They think she surprised the burglar?"

"He must have picked the lock. Or talked his way inside. No sign of forced entry. All the chaos is in the house."

"Thanks, Pascal."

"*De rien.* I am sorry for her friend. "

Francie stared at her phone. What a strange turn of events. She punched in Dylan's number to give him the news. He was equally shocked and unsure what, if anything, it meant to their work with Axelle. The two break-ins at places related to Axelle was at least curious.

"Do you think Axelle's in danger?" Francie asked.

He paused. "Maybe she should stay with us tonight."

THE DANGER CAME from a different angle, as they discovered the next morning. The night before Dylan had brought home ingredients for dinner and made them lemon chicken with a white wine sauce and asparagus and pappardelle noodles. He concentrated on his daughter and spoke little to either Axelle or Francie until Phoebe went to bed. By then they were all so exhausted, and had so few answers, that they soon turned in themselves.

The knock on the door at eight thirty the next morning surprised them all. Phoebe had been moved to the sofa and was reluctantly folding blankets. Axelle sat in yesterday's clothes at the dining table, drinking a second cup of espresso. Dylan was in his suit, holding his briefcase, talking to Phoebe about the day. They all stopped what they were doing at the sound at the door.

"I'll get it," Francie said. She looked through the peephole and saw the uniforms. She opened the door slowly and stepped back. "Dylan? Can you come here?"

Two tall, well-built policemen in navy blue, with radios and gadgets and guns on their belts, stepped inside. Dylan came from the hallway, eyes wide.

"*Oui?* What can I do for you, messieurs?" he asked in French.

They replied in a serious tone, looking around the room at each of them.

Dylan whispered, "They're looking for Axelle. I told them at the office she was staying with us."

"*Je m'appelle* Docteur Axelle Fourcier," she announced as she stood up, putting her shoulders back and glaring at the men in uniform. "What is it you want with me?"

They wanted to question her, it soon became apparent. Not here, but at police headquarters, like she was a criminal or something. Francie frowned, her stomach beginning to clench. What was going on? Was she suspected of something related to Blandine? She looked at Dylan, willing him to translate for her.

Axelle was getting her coat from the closet. She picked up her purse. "It's always something with these jackbooted thugs, isn't it?" she said in English, smiling in a false, hateful way to the policemen.

Francie tugged Dylan's sleeve. "What is it?"

He whispered: "It's the break-in at Mathilde's. Some of the silver has been found at her hotel."

"They searched her room?"

"Sometime yesterday. And that's not all." He glanced at Axelle and narrowed his eyes. "They found a crowbar with paint on it that matches the paint on the door."

Francie stared at Axelle, dumbfounded. Yes, she'd been upset about not getting the "Roy," but never had it occurred to Francie that she would try to break into the apartment to get it back. Was it possible? Was that why she said she no longer cared about Mathilde's things?

Dylan said, "I can come with you now, *Docteur*, but we will find someone else to represent you."

"Do I have to go with them?" Her composure cracked, and fear showed on her face. For a moment Francie saw the teenage girl, arrested for protesting against the government. What memories were flooding through her mind?

Dylan looked at the policemen. "I'm afraid you do."

THAT EVENING Phoebe and Francie met Dylan at a brasserie near his law office. Initially he'd thought he might have to go back to work, but when he arrived he was in a good mood. He kissed them both lightly on the cheeks and ordered a glass of wine.

Phoebe had her book open at the table and was reading, barely looking up at her father's arrival. Francie had helped her pick out two new books, checking them over to make sure they were age appropriate. The selection of English children's books was not huge, but there was an adequate selection to make good choices, Francie thought. She was quite pleased with herself on that front.

She sipped her wine. "What happened with Axelle? You never called."

"She's still being held, I'm afraid." Dylan glanced at his daughter. He leaned closer to Francie and lowered his voice. "Now it's the Blandine situation."

His wine arrived. They let him order for all of them as Francie tapped her fingers impatiently, wanting to know about Axelle's fate. Finally the waitress left. "Did they charge her with"—she glanced at Phoebe—"something?"

"No. But there have been some worrying details exposed."

"Such as?"

"A letter Blandine was writing, or had written, I'm not sure. Something about being afraid of Axelle."

"That's ridiculous."

He shrugged. "Also she was struck with a silver candlestick that was not her own."

"Oh, no. From Mathilde's?" He nodded. "Did they recover it?" Another nod.

"This is like a game of Clue," Phoebe piped up, bright-eyed. "Colonel Mustard in the library with the candlestick. I love that game."

Dylan pulled in his lips, embarrassed that his daughter had over-heard such details. Francie sighed. It wasn't like they could keep it from her. She'd been there when Axelle got taken into custody. "Where is she?"

"In France they can hold you for several days without charging you. They're investigating."

They ate their meal quickly, in a very un-French manner. This was no Michelin-starred restaurant, and the *frites* were a bit soggy and the lettuce was limp. Best to get it over with quickly.

They walked across Paris, back to the apartment, even though it was nearly two miles. Dylan said he needed the fresh air, such as it was in the city, and Phoebe could use the exercise after reading all day. Francie had somehow managed to wear the right shoes for once, and she threaded her arm through Dylan's as they watched Phoebe skip ahead to the corner.

"She seems happier," he said. "Thank you for taking her to the bookshop."

"The right book makes the world seem a lot better."

"And lets you forget your troubles for a while."

She squeezed his arm. "I love walking around Paris with you, Dylan Hardy. I'm glad you came back. I wasn't sure you would."

"Well, you certainly orchestrated a grand return party, complete with big cops."

"If it had been me, I would have used puny little Frenchmen. They were pretty intimidating. Will she be all right—Axelle? I sort of warmed to her while you were gone. Her bark is worse than her bite. She seems so alone."

"We found her a good criminal lawyer. Not the one from the spring. I'll never recommend him again." He smiled at her. "Good thing you did the gumshoe work."

"It all worked out, didn't it?" Francie was quite pleased with herself again. Twice in one day. She'd have to stop being so proud. But being with Dylan was like that. He saw the best in her. "To think it all started with a bunch of letters."

He stopped on the sidewalk. "I forgot to tell you. I read some of Axelle's letters while I waited at the police headquarters. I had them in my briefcase." He started walking again as he rummaged in his brief-case. "I must have left them at the office." He touched his forehead, remembering. "Right. I put them in the safe before lunch. Such a day."

"In the safe? Why?"

Dylan turned toward the corner where Phoebe was yelling, "Dad!" and waving her arms. He called for her to wait and picked up his pace. Francie skipped to keep up.

Phoebe was waiting for the light, dancing on one foot then the other excitedly. "Look," she said when they arrived, breathless. "There!"

She was pointing at the end of the bridge, the Pont des Arts, the one that had once been weighed down with thousands of padlocks, the "locks of love." A few remained around light posts, but most had been removed and sleek plexiglass panels put in place to deter lovers from leaving their marks. At the midway point of the bridge, under a lamp-post, an old-fashioned organ grinder worked his contraption, turning the wheel with the handle, as a small monkey in a red pillbox hat and vest danced on the man's head.

"It's a monkey!" Phoebe hollered as the light changed and she raced across the street toward the music. The tinkling of the organ was light in the night air. A small crowd had gathered by the time they got close, tapping their feet, clapping along.

The organ grinder was a round fellow in a waistcoat and straw boater, his handlebar mustache jumping as he turned the crank and grinned at his audience. Francie leaned around an old man standing in front of her to get a better look. Something about that monkey. Then she saw the organ grinder pull strings attached to his hand, making the monkey's legs move. It was a puppet.

Phoebe pushed her way to the front, standing right in front of the organ. She grinned up at the man, who returned her smile. An upturned black hat sat on top of the organ with the word "*merci*" etched in white chalk. She ran back to her father. "Can I put some money in the hat? For the monkey?"

Dylan put a few coins into her outstretched hand. He glanced at Francie and made a small grimace. He must have realized the monkey was only a stuffed animal too.

Phoebe was entranced, whether she realized the monkey wasn't real or not. They tried to leave once, calling to her, but she refused, planted in front, watching raptly. Finally the organ grinder's paper roll ran out and the tune came to a halt. Several people approached and put coins in the hat. Phoebe asked the man loudly, "Can I pet your monkey?" He replied in French and shrugged, looking for her father for help.

"Come on, honey," Dylan called. "Time to go."

"But I want to pet the monkey," she protested as he took her hand, leading her away. "He is so cute."

"That was fun, wasn't it?" Francie said. "I love all the street music in Paris. The other day I saw a four-piece brass band with a tuba."

"We'll see some more musicians, Pheebs," Dylan said.

"But I want to see monkeys," she replied. She stomped her feet to the corner. "I love monkeys."

The dark streets stretched ahead, lit with spots of gold from street-lamps and café windows. Finally they made it to the apartment building and trudged up the stairs. Dylan took Phoebe to the bath-room to brush her teeth then off to bed, reading her a few pages from her book. When he emerged from her room and took off his tie in the salon, Francie asked him about the monkey business.

"She thinks it's real, doesn't she?"

He nodded. "Almost too excited by monkeys to sleep. But I think she's tired from the walking."

"It wore me out too."

"A sip of wine?" he asked, eyeing the remnants of a white Bordeaux in the bottle. He poured them both a small glass and sat down, kicking off his shoes. "Now, where were we?"

"We were walking along—oh, Axelle's letters."

"I put them in the safe, right. Because"—he leaned toward her, eyes dancing—"there are clues in them."

"About Axelle? What was she like?"

"The same as now, whiny and self-important. But that's not the interesting thing."

Francie sipped her wine. "Well?"

"She wrote those letters to her aunt, but not to that address in

L'Opéra. Most were sent to an address in the Lot-et-Garonne. They were still in the envelopes."

"Wait. Mathilde lived there? When?"

"The letters range over seven years, all in the summer. I'll have to do a little sleuthing tomorrow. I can have one of the clerks work on it, get the state records of the place. I think it's a country house."

"Does it have a name?"

"Villa Pardoux. I looked it up on a map. It's on some sort of rural route, somewhere in the north central of the province."

"The province is Lot-et-Garonne?" He nodded. "Is it close to the Dordogne?"

"I think it's right next to it."

"Does Mathilde still own it? Or did she, I mean."

He wiggled his eyebrows. "Or did she ever? We don't know yet, do we. It's a mystery."

THE INTRIGUE of the country house was overshadowed the next day by the announcement by the Police Nationale that Axelle Fourcier was being charged in connection with the violent death of Blandine Baudet. The break-in at Mathilde's was also mentioned. She was charged with burglary as well.

They got the news at midday. Francie and Phoebe met Dylan for lunch. She'd taken the girl to an art museum, for both of their educations. Phoebe lasted about an hour then began complaining. She stared at her sandwich suspiciously as Francie and her father talked about Axelle.

"This is horrible, Dylan. How could they think she'd hurt her old friend?"

He shrugged. "The incriminating stuff from Mathilde's was enough, I guess. They don't really need a motive."

"But anyone could have stolen it and planted it in her room, and used it to smash poor Blandine."

"Her lawyer needs to establish some alibis, but—you didn't see her over the weekend, did you?"

"I left her in a bistro Friday afternoon. Then I didn't see her until I met her in a café on Monday and told her about the break-in."

"How did she take it?"

"Calmly. She said she didn't care anymore."

"Did she say what she did over the weekend?"

"Not really. She seemed a little secretive about it. You don't think she's violent, do you? Or crazy? Sometimes I'm a great judge of character, and sometimes I get it really wrong."

He shook his head. "She doesn't seem violent to me. But sometimes scary?"

"I know."

"I don't understand why she would have returned to the scene of the—on Monday."

"Right. Makes no sense."

Dylan saw Phoebe was watching and listening, her eyes darting from one face to the other as they spoke, her face solemn. Dylan patted her head fondly, but she jerked away from him. "What are you talking about? The old lady?"

Dylan grimaced. "Yes, she's in some trouble."

"With those cops?"

He nodded, glancing at Francie. She said, "Her friend was killed. They think she did it." Dylan startled at her bluntness, and she shrugged as if to say, *How else do you explain it?* "But we think she's innocent. You know what innocent means, right?"

"She didn't do it."

"So we're going to figure out what really happened. If we can."

"Then she'll be free?"

Francie looked to Dylan. "Does she have to stay in jail?" He nodded. "Yes, Phoebe, she'll be free when we figure it out."

If we figure it out.

Phoebe took a big bite of her croque monsieur and chewed, cheese dribbling down her chin. She seemed satisfied with that explanation. Francie was not a big believer in keeping children in the dark. Axelle's words: *Talk to them as adults. Show them respect.*

• • •

AT BOZONNET PATRONI, Francie and Phoebe waited in Dylan's office while he spoke to some of the partners. One had grabbed him as soon as he walked in. *At least he still has work,* Francie thought. What was happening at home? Did anyone miss her? She'd hardly given work a thought since arriving in Paris. Not a single email. The assistant managing partner she'd hired was going to get flowers, at the least.

She found Phoebe some paper to draw on and retrieved the markers they'd bought at the museum from her purse. "I can draw as good as that Van Gogh guy," the girl declared.

"I bet you can." Francie sat in a chair, deliberating over telling Merle the news about Axelle. She'd promised to keep her up to date. She composed a quick text, told her sister not to worry, that there was a great attorney on the case. And that she would try to get to the Dordogne soon.

Finally Dylan walked in with the envelope of letters. Phoebe looked up from his chair, holding her drawing aloft. "Look, Dad. Van Gogh." He admired the smears of blue and gold and asked her to move to another chair. He handed the envelope to Francie as he sat down.

"That country house? It's in Mathilde's name. Has been since the 1940s when her brother died. It went first to his wife, but she couldn't keep it up, so she sold it to Mathilde for sixty thousand francs. About a hundred and fifty bucks in fifties dollars."

"And she's had it all this time?"

"Apparently no one has paid taxes on it since 1995. That's when Bozonnet took over her finances. The folks here claim not to have known about it."

"Did she have dementia or something?"

"At the end, maybe. But Corne says she was charming and funny and totally with it for many years. That he enjoyed his visits with her. He's baffled that this house of hers never came up in conversation."

"Has anyone spoken to the caretaker? What was her name?"

"She called her Ceci. Quite devoted apparently. No idea what's happened to her."

Francie frowned. "Does the house go to Axelle? Did she know about it?"

"She wrote letters to Mathilde there. And she put in that paragraph about 'if anything else is found it's mine.' That looks suspect now."

"Is it going to be voided?"

"I imagine Lucien will be interested."

"He's signed the agreement though. They both have, right?"

Dylan nodded. "Notarized and delivered to the court."

"He's getting that huge apartment that has to be worth a lot more." Francie sighed. "We could ask her what she knows, if they'd let us visit. And I'd like to make sure she's okay."

"I'll ask. Listen, how would you feel about a trip to the Dordogne?"

Francie perked up. "When can we go?"

"I can't. Not right now. But maybe you could pop over and inspect this country house. See if it's worth wrangling over."

"And visit my sister, of course." Francie eyed Phoebe's artwork, another splashy blue composition of indeterminate subject matter. "What about—" She jerked her head toward the girl.

Phoebe's head rose. "Me?" She was quite a talented eavesdropper. She looked anxiously at her father, then malevolently at Francie. "I'm staying with you, Dad."

"Wouldn't you like to see some different parts of France?" he asked.

"No. Like—farms? Cows?"

"It's a big country, Phoebe," Francie said. "It's not just Paris."

"As big as the United States?"

"No, but it's pretty interesting. And you could ride on a train."

The girl hunched her shoulders and pleaded with her father with her eyes. She obviously didn't want to go. Not without Dylan. Part of Francie wanted her to stay here too. What would she do with the girl in Malcouziac? Francie had warmed toward her, but Phoebe needed her father. She was obviously more fragile than she appeared. Last night's happy moments with the organ grinder's fake monkey were a distant dream.

Dylan raised his eyebrows at Francie then addressed his daughter. "If it's all right with Miss Bennett, I think you should get out of the city. See some horses and geese and vineyards. It would be fun, sweetie."

"Miss Bennett? You mean *her*?" Phoebe crossed her arms, fuming. "You're just trying to get rid of me. You're just like Mom. You don't care anything about me. You just want me to disappear so you can have fun. You both suck! I hate you!"

FRANCIE THOUGHT it best to make herself scarce. This was a problem between Dylan and his daughter, and though she might take on a role as nanny, her input wasn't needed as they worked out a plan. Her parenting skills were exactly zero. She followed Dylan out the door of his office as he went in search of Phoebe.

She asked the polished, middle-aged woman behind the front desk if Monsieur Corne was available for a moment. Francie knew all these people by now, and they seemed to know her. Their politeness was so intense she wasn't sure if they recognized her. But the receptionist did and made a call.

"He will see you, Madame. He has but a few moments," she warned.

Corne's corner office was massive, as befit the head of the law firm. Ornate brocade drapes hung on large windows overlooking the street, where the golden leaves of autumn glowed in the afternoon sun. His desk was tidy and broad, a slab of maple burnished to a gleam. He sat with a fountain pen in his hand, reading glasses halfway down his nose, and smiled in his formal French way as she entered.

He stood. "Madame. Please sit."

When they were seated she smiled, hoping this wasn't beyond her role here. What was her role with the estate besides minding Axelle?

"Mr. Hardy tells me there is a country house just discovered." He nodded. "And you never knew about it?"

He twitched, ever so slightly. "How such an oversight happened, I cannot say."

"I was wondering if it might be possible to talk to the caretaker. The woman who looked after Mathilde. Did she work there long?"

"Five years, I believe. What is it you wish to talk to her about?"

Francie bit her lip. "I thought she might know something about the house."

"I am not confident we still have her contact information. But I can try."

"Will this discovery be a problem with Lucien Daucourt? The papers have been signed."

"I will speak to him. Madame Fourcier was so kind as to offer him the apartment, so he should not have a problem with a country house. I believe his own father left him a small château near Toulouse."

"How nice. The apartment is probably worth much more anyway." His eyebrows seemed to agree. "But what about Doctor Fourcier? Can I visit her?"

"We no longer represent Madame. Her *avocat* is now Marcel Garnier. He is a well-regarded criminal attorney."

"So I should contact him? She has no friends here in Paris. I'm worried about her."

"She had *one* friend," he said archly.

Francie winced. He thought she was guilty, it appeared. He was washing his hands of this woman who may have murdered her only friend, as weird as that sounded.

"Do they have a motive?" He frowned, not comprehending. "A reason why she would harm her old friend. I'm struggling to make sense of this."

Corne folded his hands on the desk. "I am not privy to discussions with the police." He looked at her from under those dark eyebrows. "May I give you some advice?"

She nodded warily.

"Leave Monsieur Garnier to do what he does best. The estate business is settled. That is why we engaged you to help us. Being a helper to Madame Fourcier was most generous and I hope not terribly exhausting. All the items you detailed for us have been packed and taken to the auction house. The silver, the dishes, the books. And to another auction, the artworks. It is done, Madame. Your little lists were very helpful. But now it is finished. Perhaps it is time for you to go home."

They locked eyes. His held a glint of amused contempt. Francie felt her blood start to boil up her neck, into her ears. His patronizing tone was, of course, not a new thing, but as unwelcome as ever. He was a pompous ass, one of a type the world over, French or not.

For a moment she composed a silent narration in her head for the mythical readers of her now-defunct blog, *Lawyrr Grrls*.

> A battle of wills, one that has raged since the beginning of time. Man vs. Woman, Wise Old Man vs. Uppity Young Woman. His steely blue eyes glittered and cut, opinions shooting out of them like daggers: weak, clueless, emotional, but mostly INCONSEQUENTIAL. A gnat on the daily calendar, a speck of dust. In return her glare held up a shield: Your opinion, sir, is just your own. You do not know me, affect me, denigrate me, or manipulate me. You can try, but you will never succeed.

She rose slowly from her chair, holding his stare until she turned and walked out of the room.

CHAPTER NINETEEN

*I*n Dylan's office Phoebe sat at his desk again, drawing something red and orange. A Van Gogh sunset perhaps. She didn't look up when Francie stuck her head in, so she spun around and went to find Dylan.

Her blood was still hot from the special moment with Corne. She walked with angry purpose to the break room then back to the receptionist, who told her Dylan was in conference with another lawyer. She walked to the lawyer's office and found the door shut. Leaning against the wall next to the door, she checked her watch. How long would they "confer"?

Five minutes passed, very slowly. Then, at eight minutes—but who's watching the clock—the door opened suddenly and Dylan stepped out, files in his hands.

"Hey," Francie said, making him stop abruptly in the hallway.

"Oh, sorry. Where did you go?"

"To talk to your asshole boss," she whispered. "I am ready to go. To the Dordogne and wherever. Give me the details."

Dylan searched her face, looking for something. Answers to questions he didn't know how to ask perhaps. "Come on," he said, taking her arm and dragging her back to his office. He stopped at the door, seeing Phoebe at his desk.

"Pheebs, sweetie. Could you give Miss Bennett and me a minute to talk?"

She frowned, gathering up her art supplies. "Where should I go?"

"Into the waiting area. Just for a few minutes."

Dylan sat down in his chair, waving Francie into the other. They waited as Phoebe stomped out, and the receptionist said something to her down the hall. Dylan sighed.

Francie crossed her arms. "I'm going to the Dordogne, to Lot-et-Garonne, whether you come or not. I'm going to figure out if there's anything in that country house. Axelle got screwed by Lucien and that boss of yours. And now by the whole damn government. I owe it to her."

"I want you to go, remember? But there's Phoebe. She's agreed to go with you, but it won't be a cakewalk, I know that. She's rude and angry and—"

"A preteen. I get it."

"I can't keep up with her mood swings. I'm worried about her. I can't send her back to Rebecca on her own. Maybe next week I can take her back. I have to do my job. I can't afford to take time off again and keep in the good graces of Monsieur Corne."

"That jerk. Being a man must help."

"I warned you. A fully functioning patriarchy."

She eyed his kind face, thinking about what a delicate dance he had here as an American in France. "What are you offering then? Fifty cents an hour is what I used to get babysitting."

"Come on. I'll put you on the payroll for the estate."

"Are you saying Corne took me off?"

He looked pained. "I'll get you back on, plus a per diem. As much as I can, I promise. Can Phoebe go with you—that's my question."

Taking Phoebe would certainly ingratiate her to her boyfriend. But it would make matters difficult. Francie had sincere doubts about whether she was parenting material. 'Motherly' was the last thing she'd expect anyone to say about her. Her experience was so light, extending only to scattered moments with nieces and nephews. She was a well-known social butterfly, with scant maternal instincts. The girl was a handful, with emotional issues that ran hot and cold. Maybe some time in the country would calm her down, smooth things down, make her forget her parents for a while. It would be sort of a science experiment. No, that was wrong. She was a living child who deserved happiness. So, she could go. Francie would try to be a good substitute parent if such a thing were possible.

But what about Merle and Pascal? "I'll have to ask Merle."

He looked relieved. "Of course."

Francie got out her phone and sent a brief text to her sister, asking if it was all right if she brought Phoebe instead of Dylan to Malcouziac. Merle wrote back almost instantly: "I would love to see her again. Don't worry about a thing. We will pick you up at the station."

"She says it's okay. She's good with kids."

Dylan slumped onto his hands. "What a royal fuck-up." He looked up. "Thank you, Francie. I know it's a lot to ask. I really owe you."

"What else are you going to do, hire a nanny?"

"I already asked. Those are permanent jobs in France. And not for nine-year-olds. They're all in school. Like she should be."

"Maybe we can stash her away in a French school in Malcouziac."

His eyes widened. "She doesn't speak French."

"Kidding, Dylan." She smiled. "We'll take good care of her."

He pulled an envelope from his desk and turned it over on his blotter. A small ring of keys fell out with a jingle. "Guess what was discovered in an armoire in the final cleaning of the apartment?" He held out a dirty flag of linen attached to the ring. "It says 'V Pardoux.' Here's hoping."

~

THEY BOARDED the train the next morning at the Gare Montparnasse, a madhouse of travelers with horrible, confusing signage amidst construction zones. Dylan ran to the platform with Phoebe's suitcase in hand, hugged her, and put her on the car. Francie gave him a hurried kiss and jumped on. The rush was unavoidable and everywhere travelers looked disoriented and harried. Francie and Phoebe found their seats, spent a few hours gazing at pastures and cows and eating rich French railroad food, then changed trains in Bordeaux.

Phoebe held tight to the stuffed monkey Dylan had bought her the night before, stroking its brown fur and fiddling with the brass buttons on its tiny vest. She answered Francie with a grunt or a nod but never more than a couple of words. Was she angry or sad or just bitter at her parents—or at Francie? It was impossible to know. She looked like she hadn't taken a bath or washed her hair for days. Her clothes were dirty, her fingernails filthy. These could at least be remedied at her sister's house. Francie hoped Merle had the magic touch with the girl. She'd been known to work wonders with hard cases.

Last night Francie made Dylan promise to get the word to Axelle about the country house. No one had spoken to her for days except, one hoped, her lawyer. Dylan said he would call the lawyer, the famous Marcel Garnier. The villa grew in Francie's mind, reaching château status with turrets and moats. She smiled to herself. It was probably a little farmhouse.

It was midafternoon when they reached Bergerac. The last leg of the trip had been slow but scenic, traveling through picturesque wine towns like Saint-Émilion, along rivers, and through forests bright with fall color. Phoebe didn't appreciate the sights, having fallen asleep against the window. Francie nudged her awake when they were pulling into the station. They gathered their belongings and waited in the aisle.

Francie spotted Merle in the crowd on the platform, her brown hair blowing in the breeze. Relief flooded through her. Her older sister would make this right. If anyone could.

"Come on, honey." Francie put her hands on Phoebe's shoulders as she walked the girl forward. She wriggled out of Francie's grasp, gripping her suitcase and the monkey to her chest. At the door she flung her bag down the stairs and jumped off. Francie followed, more sedately.

"Hey, girls," Merle cried, giving each of them hugs. "How was the train ride?" she asked Phoebe. She didn't answer, watching a boy who was kicking a soccer ball into the air.

"No problems," Francie said.

"That's an improvement," Merle said. "I had a two-hour delay when I came down."

They walked through the station to the car park. Merle put the suitcases in her trunk. As they buckled their seat belts, Francie asked, "Is Pascal here?"

"He arrives tonight," Merle said. "I can't wait. We'll have a full house. We'll have so much fun." She glanced in the rearview mirror at Phoebe then at Francie. "Won't we?"

"We sure will," Francie said with false gusto.

Phoebe made Merle stop near Monpazier while she threw up her lunch by the side of the road. Francie cringed and passed her a tissue. Dylan hadn't mentioned motion sickness. They arrived at last in Malcouziac, Merle's village. Phoebe and Francie got the twin beds in the loft at the top of the stairs, hardly ideal. Francie prattled on to the girl, trying to make her feel at home. Phoebe was silent.

Merle's house, an eighteenth-century stone *maison de ville* at the end of a street overlooking vineyards and orchards, was cozy that evening with a fire in the big fireplace and a delicious stew to warm them. The *boeuf bourguignon* was rich with carrots and potatoes and bacon. Pascal, who arrived just as they sat down to eat, praised it; they all did, except Phoebe.

"Your tummy is not so good?" Pascal asked her. "The ladies tell me you felt bad in the car."

She looked at him in wide-eyed wonder, as if she'd never seen such a man. "I got carsick."

"Perhaps you should not eat then," he suggested.

"I don't like this. It smells funny."

He laughed, a booming happy sound that made the sisters smile. "It is the garlic. I keep telling Merle she uses too much of the garlic."

"That's not true. You tell me to use more," Merle said.

"It tastes just right to me," Francie said.

"Thank you, Goldilocks," Merle joked.

"And to me as well." Pascal leaned over and kissed Merle on the mouth. Phoebe made a face. He saw it and asked, "You don't like the kissing?"

She shook her head. "It's gross. That's how people get germs."

He laughed again. "I can see, *mon chou*, that we will get along just fine."

That evening it was Pascal who talked the girl into taking a shower and washing her hair. She didn't respond to Merle's suggestion, or Francie's nagging. But one word from Pascal and she ran upstairs to get her pajamas. Then back down to the shower in the bathroom off the kitchen.

"Wait, *petite*. It is cold in there. I will run you some hot water. Make it all cozy."

Merle smiled at him after he closed the door on Phoebe in the bathroom. "Aren't you the charmer."

"She is a poor, dirty urchin. Who would not feel sorry for her? Her papa sends her to the country like a castaway, with only two old sisters to care for her? What a cruel papa."

Francie frowned. Was he trying to crush her? "I hope you're kidding, Pascal."

Merle swatted him. "We're doing our old lady best, *chéri*. What do you suggest?"

"Leave it to me. I will get her cleaned up and happy again."

Francie looked at Merle. "It's a deal."

PASCAL WAS good to his word. The next morning he helped brush Phoebe's hair then encouraged her to let Merle braid it for her. Off they went to the boulangerie to buy croissants and other good things. Francie stood at the window, mystified, watching him catch her hand and swing her along.

"Is he a wizard or something?"

"Shhh. We don't want to break the spell," Merle said. "Are you going to that country house today?"

"I think tomorrow. I have to rent a car and make sure Phoebe is okay."

"Oh, good. Because today the weather is nice. We can have a

picnic on the river. Would you like that? I know a great spot with a little bit of sand beach."

It wasn't market day in Malcouziac; the only place to buy food was the convenience store, Le Petit Casino, and the bakery. Merle and Francie shopped for whatever delicacies they could salvage to put in the picnic basket: cheeses, a fresh baguette, olives, salami, mandarin oranges, a chocolate bar, and for Phoebe, they bought Nutella just in case. It was Merle's experience that no child didn't like Nutella on bread.

And so it turned out. They drove the short distance to the River Lot and climbed down the bank to the tiny strip of sand, where they spread a blanket. The sun obliged. Phoebe wolfed down two large slices of bread with the chocolaty nut butter and joined Pascal skipping stones into the slow-moving water.

Francie lay back on the blanket and shut her eyes. "This is heavenly. I needed this."

"Paris can be hectic."

"Did we bring wine? I thought there was wine."

"I thought you'd never ask." Merle unscrewed the top on a bottle of white from the supermarket. She poured them both a paper cup of it. She sipped and made a sound. "Not the best, I'm afraid."

Francie drank hers. "Tangy but not bad."

"*Buvable.*"

They watched Pascal and Phoebe laugh and throw rocks. "He should have had children," Merle said. "He's so good with them."

"You're no slouch yourself," Francie said. "Me, on the other hand . . ."

"You're fine." Merle patted her shoulder. "It was very generous of you to bring her here. To get her out of Dylan's hair."

"I don't know if I'm cut out to be a parent, except maybe as an evil stepmother."

Merle sat taller. "Are you and Dylan thinking about marriage?"

"We haven't talked about it. No. I feel so awkward around Phoebe, like she's fragile and I might break her."

"It'll come to you. I can tell you care about her. What is going on with the mother?"

"I'm not sure. She drinks a little?"

"Well, I drink a little. So do you. It must be more than that."

"He hasn't told me. I don't know anything about his ex, really. Except her name, Rebecca. And she has red hair and that's why he married her." Francie grinned playfully, throwing back her hair.

"That's a dumb reason," Merle said. Francie pushed her playfully. "Maybe she'll open up to Pascal."

"If anybody, it would be him. Where can I rent a car around here? Maybe you can drop me off on the way home."

Pascal worked his phone and reserved Francie a rental at the Cahors train station. It was out of the way but the best place nearby to get a vehicle, he said. He went inside with her and talked his way into a good deal for a shiny black Citroën, very small but up to the job.

"Do you want me to drive it back to Malcouziac for you?" He jingled the keys in the parking lot as they looked for the numbers painted on the asphalt. "I don't mind."

"Phoebe might," Francie said. "I think she likes you best."

"But of course. She is a sensible girl." Pascal laughed. "She seems to be having a rough pop."

"Patch? Maybe you can get her to talk about it."

"Ah, here it is. Number Sixty-Seven. Such a pretty little Citroën. I will drive. You keep Merle company."

He revved the engine loudly as she walked back to Merle's car, making her laugh. Pascal just wanted to drive a new car, that was obvious. He pulled up behind Merle's beat-up Renault and revved the engine again for maximum effect. Phoebe turned back and waved at him, smiling.

WHEN THEY GOT home in the late afternoon, the Citroën was already parked at the end of Rue de Poitiers, next to the broken rock of the old bastide wall. Pascal had passed them somewhere near Figeac, going about ninety miles an hour.

Merle's village—she thought of it now as hers—was walled, a bastide town, built in medieval times and fortified during the time of the Hundred Years' War around 1300. This part of France had been owned by the English crown in the thirteenth century. The fighting was fierce along this line as the French tried to retake the territory and the English kept taking it back. In the last five or six hundred years the wall had held up marvelously, a sweep of golden rock, dry stacked in the old way. In a few places the top ten feet had crumbled, leaving debris on the countryside below and here on the street. Pascal had been talking about cleaning up the huge stones for several years, but they sat where they fell, a barrier to extra parking for Merle and her opposite neighbor, Madame Suchet.

Madame was out on her front stoop, sweeping. Her steel-gray hair was a little longer but still in a chic bob. Her pearls and heels and immaculate dress never changed. She came out to sweep whenever she was curious about what was happening in the neighborhood, or when she wanted you to come over and chat. Merle handed Francie the picnic basket and she and Phoebe went inside. A cool breeze had picked up, and below in the vineyards the harvest was almost done. Merle pulled her jacket tight as she walked over to her neighbor.

"*Bonjour,* Madame!" Merle liked to talk to Madame Suchet because it made her use her French. Madame, whose first name, Paulette, was never mentioned, returned the greeting then asked if she had company.

"*Ma sœur,* Francie. Do you remember her?"

"Ah, *les cheveux. Très belle.*" Everyone remembered Francie's auburn hair.

"And also her friend's daughter. Phoebe. She's nine."

"*Bon, bon.*" She said she would bring over a dessert for the girl. Merle thanked her. There was no denying the politeness of the French, and friendliness once you passed some kind of test. Merle had passed her tests by fire here the first year, but it still took a while for people to become truly friendly. She still knew only a few of her neighbors.

"We'll plan a dinner while they're here. They would love to see you."

Her face lit up and she thanked Merle. Then, as she turned back to her broom, she held up a finger. In French, she said, "Would it be all right if I bring something? A dessert? Also, perhaps, my sister Ninon?"

Madame S's sister lived on the same block, about five houses down. Merle had met her the summer before when Ninon's son was suspected of vandalism. The two women were as different as night and day—one tall and cranky, the other plumper and sweeter. Not unlike Merle and some of her sisters.

"Of course, I'd love to see her again." Merle had passed Ninon in the market a few times, unrecognized or ignored. She was not very pleasant. But Madame Suchet was more than pleasant, a friendly, lonely neighbor. Plus her desserts were divine. "*Á bientôt.*"

CHAPTER TWENTY

Lot-et-Garonne

*T*he morning light dimmed as Francie Bennett maneuvered her rental car through the narrow lanes of the backwoods of the Dordogne and into Lot-et-Garonne to the south. The trees grew thick, arching over the road. Where once the skies were fierce and blue, the sun warm on the side of her face, now the oppressive greens and browns of the woods blotted all that out. Was it some kind of omen? She doubted it. But nothing about this estate had turned out ordinary.

She wound her way on the ever-smaller roads, following the directions from her phone. Otherwise she'd have been lost for days, driving in circles down shaded lanes, far from civilization. She'd once marveled that cosmopolitan France, land of manners and fashion and cuisine and sophistication, could still have such neglected backwaters. Where were the house-flippers and Brits on the prowl? These places seemed untouched by modernization, neglected and gone to rot.

The mission, to find this old house, had sounded delicious, even mysterious, evoking a girlish curiosity that Francie was glad to discover she hadn't outgrown. To outlive curiosity, to be jaded about the unknown and undiscovered, would be tragic. So here she was, deep in rural Aquitaine, far from vineyards and goats and, well, people. To open an old woman's manse that no one had cared about for nearly forty years.

There was no village, no town square, post office, or store. Not much of anything but overgrown lots, cows, and sparse stands of trees. The destination was approached carefully, with intention, winding around hummocks and along streams. It was on no maps, just a blip on an unnamed road. A hamlet, something she somehow associated with small ham sandwiches—ridiculous, yes—that's what it was. A collection of a few houses of varying sizes, on acreages with falling-down barns and grass up to your knees.

She slowed to a crawl, phone in hand, looking at directions. This must be the place. She turned off the car and stepped into the weeds. Putting aside visions of rats and pigeons, she stood outside the stone house, dangling the keys. Of course she was curious. She'd read about apartments in Paris that had been boarded up during the war and never touched for sixty years, museums of a long-gone time. Would this old house be fabulous, or simply disgusting? Merle's cottage had been more filthy than delightful at first.

The house was much larger than her sister's. Not a château like she fantasized but a good sized villa. The old lady apparently came from a family of aristocrats, what was left of them in secular, socialist, post-Revolution, postwar France. A lapsed duke, a long-ago count: they remained, their wealth often tied up in land and houses no one wanted, or their fortunes gone forever along with their heads.

Two stories of weathered gray stone, the mansion had a roof that sported fancy gables with odd-shaped windows, indicating a third floor under the slates. Windows were shuttered, a soft, peeling rose color, or smothered by vines. The yard was flat cream-colored gravel overrun with weeds. Dry, prickly thistles scratched those who dared to enter. A half-dead tree stood guard, its leaves yellow and black.

Villa Pardoux was not quite a mansion, not anymore.

The first padlock, on the door shutters, was awkward and rusty. But with a few trials it popped open. The shutters creaked and one hinge fell apart. Now, key in the door lock, she wiggled it for two minutes before she felt it give. The house didn't want to give up its secrets, that was obvious. Then it turned, a loud, metallic click, just as her cell phone rang.

It was Dylan. "Did you find it?"

"I think so." He read off the address again, which didn't help. "There are no street signs. No numbers, no signs of any kind."

"Well, if the key works, there's your answer."

"I'm unlocking the door right now. The padlock on the shutters opened."

"What's it like?"

"On the outside, about what you'd expect: dirty and weedy. Pretty big, but in the middle of serious French nowhere. Not another house or person in sight. All the shutters seem intact though, and the roof looks good from the front at least. Nothing growing through the slates."

"Okay, call me once you look around inside. How was Phoebe this morning?"

"She seems fine, Dylan. Give her a few days to adjust." Francie was afraid to mention how the girl had attached herself to Pascal. It might hurt Dylan's feelings.

"Call me later? I'm hoping to come down next weekend. I'll be waiting for your call."

She slipped her phone back in her pocket and pushed open the double doors. The stale stench of dust, mold, and animal droppings swept past her as if glad to be free. But there was something else, flowery, powdery. Her eyes blinked against the darkness.

She paused, pulled out a small flashlight, and stepped inside.

The house was pitch-dark. Her flashlight hardly made a dent. The only light came from the open door behind her. She felt the wall for a light switch. It was an old-style push button that did nothing. Waiting until her eyes adjusted, she felt along the front wall, stumbling over something that cracked against her shins. A crusty lace curtain fell apart in her hands. She dropped it, sneezing, and felt for the window latch. It was one of those with a long bar that locked it in place at the top and bottom. The knob refused to budge. She whacked it with her flashlight a couple times and tried again. With a grunt she turned it, but it only moved a little. She gave up and went to the next window.

This one was more accommodating, turning after a few tries. She pulled the two sides open then shined the flashlight at the shutters. More latches, but really, the house wouldn't have lasted all these years without them. They were rusty and needed a few whacks. Then they were free. She pushed the shutters out, letting the midday light flood the room.

This must have been the grand salon, with groupings of sagging upholstered chairs and one long, lumpy orange velvet sofa. A faded Oriental rug was bunched up in front of a blackened fireplace. Above it a de-silvered mirror with an ornate gold frame hung at an angle. A chandelier was covered in cobwebs.

Moving through the furniture, Francie walked to the back of the room where large glass-paned French doors took up much of the wall. A key sat in one of the doors' locks, obligingly left behind. She unlocked the door, yanked it open, but failed to budge the other half of the pair. The shutters behind them were locked. She rummaged through the keys, hoping one of them worked on this padlock. None did. She moved to a window nearby on the same wall and managed to free it and open the shutters. The damp air outside did little to dispel the odors of the old house.

At least she could see now, the light revealing the holes in the upholstery, nests of rodents, piles of debris, and plaster from the ceiling in chunks on the floor. A royal mess, much worse than Mathilde's apartment, even though they both smelled pretty bad. This house hadn't seen a human for decades and it showed.

The dining room was bare, stripped of furniture. No table or chairs, just an empty built-in china cabinet that stretched across one wall. The glass was broken in a couple places. Her footsteps echoed on the wood floor. She pushed open a door to find the kitchen. How old was this house? It had a proper kitchen like the Paris apartment, but fixtures from the 1920s: an enamel stove, an icebox, a sink with a well pump, a large table in the center.

Back at the front of the house Francie climbed a staircase. The bannister was wobbly, and she tread carefully on the wooden steps. At the landing she opened the window. The back of the house was over-grown with vines, making the shutters hard to open. Breaking through them, she managed to get a view of the land back there, a jungle of dead things, a fountain tipped on its side, broken glass, and a dry pond.

Up on the second floor little remained. A bed frame without a mattress. A child's stuffed bear, gnawed by something. Had Mathilde lived on one floor like she lived in one room in Paris? A sliver of light in a bedroom wall tipped Francie to a door hidden in the dusty blue paneling. She pried it open and found a stair to the third level, shining her flashlight up the narrow steps. Exposed rafters, spiderwebs, and the smell of dead mice—*Save that adventure for another day.*

She quickly passed through the second-floor rooms again, looking for closets (none), armoires and dressers (zero), trunks (nada), and any other hiding places for valuables. Back downstairs she found a room she'd missed behind the kitchen, some sort of butler's pantry full of cabinets. She opened the lower ones, peered through the glass of the upper ones, and swept her flashlight to the ceiling and floor. The house had been cleaned out.

She took photos of the rooms for Dylan then fastened the shutters and windows again and exited the front door. She tested the padlock for security and pocketed the keys. From the road she took a few more photos. Standing for a moment in the yard, she listened to birds in the forest and trucks somewhere at a distance. Well, this could bring a few more euros for Axelle when she sold it.

Or would she want to keep it to remember Mathilde? Francie started up the Citroën and backed out onto the rural road. There seemed to be little here to remember. It was a sad, abandoned place, hardly the summer villa of legend where garden parties and dancing under the moonlight enchanted visitors dressed in gowns and tuxedos. Some millionaire could fix it up, but Axelle probably didn't have the interest.

As Francie approached Malcouziac from the west, the sun broke through scattered clouds and her mood lightened. Whatever she could do for Axelle, she would do. The woman was in prison and likely to remain so for months until her trial. She was considered an American now, after renouncing her French citizenship years ago. She was a flight risk, charged with murder. Which brought up the question: Who actually did kill Blandine Baudet—and why? What was it they had argued and fought over? And why was Axelle framed for it?

Something connected the two women. Was it the protests in 1968? High school? Sure—but what?

As she pulled up to Merle's house she called Dylan. She had to speak to Axelle. As soon as possible.

"How was the house?"

Merle sat outside in the sunshine at the green metal table. The garden had been vandalized last year, but you wouldn't know it now. Merle had spent most of her summer here planting, trimming, painting, and repairing. The wisteria had been whacked back but had regrown a lot. The espaliered pear trees against the house looked healthy. There was a new fruit tree against the east wall, an apple tree. Everything looked perfect.

"Was it a moment in time, like the apartment?"

Francie sat down, her back to the sun. "This place is pretty bare. A few chairs and rugs, that's about it."

"Shoot. I was going to take photos and make a million bucks." She smiled. She had started taking photographs of France, pretty decent ones for an amateur. Francie showed her the photos on her phone.

"If you like spiderwebs you'll be in business. The bedrooms were cleared out except for one old bed frame. I didn't go up in the attic. It smelled."

Merle's eyes sparkled. "What do you think is up there?"

"Not much. The house has been stripped. No dishes, nothing."

"But some furniture, you said."

"Moth- and rodent-eaten."

"Maybe I could reupholster some pieces. Are you going to sell them?"

"I thought we'd get an appraiser down here, like we did in Paris. But there isn't much stuff. You can probably have them, Merle." Her sister gave a yip of delight. "Don't get excited, honey. Where is Phoebe, by the way? Don't tell me you've lost her already."

"Pascal took her out to the vineyards with him. To watch the harvest."

"Good. Hey, Dylan says he might come down next weekend. I don't know where we'll put him though."

"I have one of those air beds. I can set you two up in the living room."

Francie frowned. "I'll make a reservation at the hotel as soon as I hear he's coming for sure."

Merle looked around the garden. "Or you could camp back here. Phoebe wants to do it. She says she's never slept outside."

"I am not nine, Merle, or a Girl Scout." Francie stood up. "Come on. I'll take you to lunch."

The café was their usual place, just off the cobblestone town square with its large, now-dry fountain. Tourist season was nearly done. Getting a table was no longer a challenge. They decided to sit outside, taking advantage of one of the last warm days. It was almost October now and the rains might start at any time, signaling the end of summer.

Merle shivered a little as Francie picked a table on the edge of the sitting area, roped off from the square. "What is it? Are you cold?" Francie asked.

"No, this is fine." Merle sat down. "Just some memories of last year. The man with the scar, remember him?"

"Never had the pleasure, but your description is seared into my mind."

Merle gave a forced smile. "Forget I said anything. I just want to enjoy your time here. I promised Madame Suchet a dinner party. Should we plan it for when Dylan is here?"

"That would be nice. I hope he can come on Friday night."

"If he has to work Friday that will be stretching it. Unless he flies. He could fly to Bergerac directly, like we flew to Brittany."

"I'll tell him." She looked at the menu. "Now. Food. The warm goat cheese salad as usual?"

LATE THAT AFTERNOON, just before five o'clock, Francie got a call from Dylan saying to expect a call from Axelle Fourcier. Her lawyer had arranged it, somehow. She hung up quickly and went into the garden and paced. It took fifteen minutes, but finally her cell phone rang.

"Axelle?" The line was scratchy with background noise.

"It's me. Prisoner of the state." She sounded feisty. That was good.

"How long do we have?"

"Five minutes. Hurry up."

"Okay, I went to Mathilde's country house, Villa Pardoux. It's all fine there. I'll tell you that later. Here's what I'm thinking now. Someone is framing you, using that candelabra and planting it in your room." Francie hadn't really discussed Axelle's guilt or innocence with her. It was lawyerly to just go with "presumed innocent" when dealing with clients. You don't want lies, or confessions.

"But who?"

"Did you have any dealings with Blandine over the years?"

"No. But she kept up with my family, she said. She went to my parents' funerals, and to Mathilde's." She made a choking sob, then cleared her throat.

"Could she have met someone at Mathilde's funeral? Do you know anyone else who was there?"

"Lucien and his wife attended the service. I was told it was a small gathering."

"Could they have met Blandine?"

"It's possible. But—are you saying you think Lucien could murder someone? Over an inheritance?"

"He *is* a doctor," Francie admitted. "It's a stretch." Although doctors have been known to kill people. "Maybe he met someone there, and can describe to us who else attended."

"What about his wife, Severine? She's got a vicious streak."

"Can I call them and poke around? Is that okay with you?"

"Do what you want. I'm just sitting here turning to dust."

"How's your lawyer—" The line went dead.

Francie swore under her breath and punched in Dylan's number. "Did it work?" he asked.

"Yes, she called. Thank you. Listen, I'm curious as to who attended

Mathilde's funeral service. Can you pull up the obituary and find out what funeral home did the service?"

"Sure, I guess. When was it again?"

"In May, I think. Do French funeral homes have a place to sign in —a guest book?"

"No idea. But you want it if they have it?"

"Yes. Hey, are you coming next weekend? Merle suggested you fly. It takes quite a while on the train, with transfers and all."

"Maybe early Saturday."

"Let me know. We're planning a big celebration." She laughed. "Well, a dinner party with the elderly neighbors. And can you bring Axelle's old letters? Maybe Pascal can help translate some of those parts you said were too faded."

She told him about Phoebe going out into the vineyards to watch the locals harvest grapes. He seemed pleased, then he had to go. He promised to do what he could about the funeral home.

Merle stuck her head out the back door. "Done? It's Wine O'Clock."

CHAPTER TWENTY-ONE

The next morning Phoebe was given a choice: go explore a creaky old house that was a forty-five-minute drive away, or stay home with Pascal. He had some chores lined up, replacing some guttering, painting the interior of the laundry fashioned from an old stone latrine, and planting a bush. She chose Pascal, of course, and the two sisters took off before she could change her mind.

Merle wanted to see if any of the furniture was salvageable. She brought along cleaning supplies. A bucket with cleaner, dust rags, a feather duster, and mousetraps sat in the back seat of the Citroën, along with Merle's toolbox. Francie volunteered to drive. The law firm had paid for the rental, she may as well use it. If possible they would find a nice place for lunch.

"Phoebe seems better. Calmer," Merle said.

"She even ate your food last night."

"Amazing." Merle laughed. "I did use less garlic. I was afraid she wouldn't like spinach."

"Your quiche was fabulous. As usual." The spinach and goat cheese quiche was becoming one of Merle's favorite French meals. No one was complaining, not even nine-year-olds.

They chatted as they drove, rounding bend after bend, playing chase with farmers' trucks and handyman vans. Finally Francie pulled into the gravel drive, giving Merle her first look at the house.

"It's huge," she cried, jumping out. "Look at that stone. It's lovely, Francie." She focused on the neglected yard. "I see what you mean though. Pretty sad."

Francie grabbed the bucket from the back seat. "I wonder if we can get someone in to clean up out here. Do some weeding at least."

Merle shrugged. "Hard to find that sort of person out in the middle of nowhere. And we are really far from everywhere here."

"How close is the nearest village?"

She checked the map on her phone. "That last one we passed was fifteen miles back. And that was pretty small." She took the bucket from Francie. "Well, open it up. Let's explore."

It took an hour, a small hammer, and a lot of elbow grease to open all the windows and shutters. When they did, light flooded the rooms. The padlock on the door shutters on the back wall of the salon had to be cut with bolt cutters. It took the strength of both sisters to get that job done. When the lock fell away the doors swung open on their own, as if free at last.

"Let's just leave everything open for a few hours," Merle said. "Air it out while we clean."

The chairs in the salon were deemed possibly repairable. The orange sofa with a broken leg and cracked arm was not. The rug was full of holes. They dragged it outside and left it in a heap.

"We forgot a broom," Francie said, looking at the mess where the rug had been.

"We can't do everything," Merle said. "All we're doing now is assessing the damage and hitting the worst of it. Later some pros can come in. The estate will pay for it. Now," she said, hands on her hips, looking around the big salon. "There was no art this time? No china, no silver?"

"I didn't look in the attic yet."

"Let's go."

Merle marveled at the door hidden in the faded blue paneling of the upstairs bedroom. "There's no doorknob. How did you find it?"

"Just luck. A little light shone through the crack." Francie pried the panel open with her fingernails and handed Merle the flashlight. "You go first."

"Age before beauty?"

"And I'm afraid of spiders."

They tiptoed up the steep, narrow flight of wooden stairs, touching the walls for balance. At the top step, Merle stopped and moved the flashlight around the room. "No shutters." Two gables on the south side, the front, had small, mullioned windows, filthy with grime. "Let's open the windows."

"Careful," Francie said. "The flooring might be rotten."

Opening the windows was a struggle. The wood was swollen and warped. They only got one open and gave up on the second. At least there was more light, and fresh air.

"Trunks. Oh, goodie," Merle said. Three old steamer trunks lined up against the north wall, the dark side of the attic.

"And look. Over here." Francie pointed to the big area to the east. "Furniture for you."

A broken rocking chair, a dresser, a rolled-up rug, some cushions, a lamp, a folded mattress. Merle made a show of examining it. "Not much of interest, honestly," she said. "Let's check the trunks."

They opened the first trunk and found old clothes. A lacy dress. A man's suit. A homburg, a veil. Antique shoes, well worn. "Wedding stuff," Merle said, picking up the lace dress then dropping it back in the trunk. "Open the next one."

That one had old photographs in it, and a bulky antique camera. "Could these be Axelle's family?" Merle asked.

"Maybe. Let's take a few for her." Francie scooped up a stack of photographs, all very small and faded. Merle picked up the camera and decided to take it too. Then they opened the third trunk. It was empty.

"Well, that was anticlimactic," Merle said as they stepped carefully back downstairs.

In the salon Francie spread the photos on the small tea table next to the broken sofa. She shined the flashlight on them. Portrait shots mostly, of men and women in their finery from some bygone time. Women in cloche hats. Children in white dresses. Who were they? They might have some sentimental value.

Merle prowled around the first floor, knocking on paneling for another hidden door. She returned disappointed.

"Nothing?"

"Nope." She turned in the salon. "What about a wine cave? All these old houses had one."

"Where would the door be?"

"Maybe outside. Come on."

They had worn old pants and running shoes, in case of cobwebs and dirt, and now they didn't worry too much about stickers and thorns as they crashed through the jungle that had grown up around the house. Francie complained a bit, as usual, but kept up with Merle. "Why didn't we bring a machete?"

Finally they stood by the overturned fountain and stared at the back of the house. Vines covered most of the stone, creeping over shutters and up onto the roof. At ground level a patio of blue stone had heaved and buckled below the big French doors.

"This must have been very grand," Merle said.

"Hard to picture it now."

"Use your imagination, Francie. Champagne in a silver bucket. Little candles on the patio on a velvety night. The lilting sound of a violin or an accordion or a Victrola. House parties on long summer evenings."

Francie squinted and tried to imagine it. Her first thought of gowns and tuxedos faded into the dry weeds. She was just more literal than Merle. It looked like a mess. "Okay. But where is the wine cave?"

They stepped along the perimeter walls, all the way around the house. There was no door to a basement, or any wine cave that they could see. They did find one tiny window on the west side of the house, with bars across it. That made Merle think there had to be a basement. And where there was a basement, there would be a wine cave.

"What do you think you'll find, Merle? There can't be another stash of expensive old wine in your life."

"That would be too much, wouldn't it? Don't give up though. Let's look for a door inside."

Francie volunteered to use the feather duster on the cobwebs while

Merle continued her quest for a wine cave by stomping her feet all over the first floor, listening for echoes. That released dust from draperies into the air, making both of them sneeze. She disappeared into the kitchen, stomping away. Francie cleaned the glass windows in the front door. Fifteen minutes passed without any noise from Merle; then, a shout came from the kitchen.

"Francie!"

"Did you find it?"

Francie skipped through the old scullery into the butler's pantry. Merle stood, hands on hips, a triumphant smile on her face, next to an open trapdoor.

"Oh, my god. How in the world did you find it?"

"Just luck, like you said. I figured it had to be in this area, where the servants could run downstairs for a bottle."

Francie went back for the flashlight. Merle shined the beam down the stairs. "Ready?" Francie shrugged, grimacing. "Come on, scaredy-cat."

Francie was like Merle had been before she'd inherited her house, a lover of the clean and tidy, a hater of any sort of filth. But now Merle had seen plenty of moldy, smelly places in her time in the Dordogne. Her cottage had been abandoned for years and had a squatter living in the garden and rotten sacks of grain in the kitchen. A dormouse, *le petit loir* in France, lived in her attic along with a family of pigeons. Her basement had swarmed with mice and damp, rotten things. But she had learned, she told Francie now, to look beyond the mess. That was where the best things hid.

Francie reached the bottom of the stairs. The floor was dirt. The smell of mold and mildew was rank. The air was cool and ripe. Francie pulled the neck of her T-shirt over her nose and said, "Eeeuw."

Merle laughed, shining the light on her sister. "You are so sensitive."

"You can say it. Such a girl."

"You're such a girl."

"I didn't mean you had to actually say it. What's down here anyway?"

Their eyes adjusted to the dark. The beam of the flashlight found heaps of wood, firewood, bits of broken furniture. Old wine boxes, crates. Empty wine bottles. Another rug.

"This must be where old rugs come to die."

Merle said, "Look for a door. Come on." She tugged Francie's sleeve to keep her close. They found iron hinges then the door itself, across the big open space, inset into a wood partition across the west end of the house. A large iron ring hung below a keyhole. "Do you have another key?"

"Not for this type of lock. Just modern types."

"We'll have to break it down then," Merle said, turning toward the stairs. "Wait here."

"Hell no," Francie said, grabbing her sister's back pants pocket and following her up the stairs. They brought the whole toolbox back down the stairs and set it in front of the locked door.

"Okay, what to use," Merle muttered, looking into the toolbox. "Hold the flashlight." Francie watched as Merle picked up and rejected various tools. "Bolt cutter again?"

"What are you going to cut, the hinges?"

Merle straightened. "Ooh, good idea. Point the light on them." The iron hinges on the door were rusty but not overly large. Merle thought she could break them with the claw end of the hammer. She wedged it between the door and the wall, inside the hinge, and pulled hard. She kept at it for ten minutes, then finally a vertical crack appeared in the middle of the door.

"Look," Francie said. "The wood is splintering."

Merle moved her hammer to the space above the crack and yanked hard. The wood split more, halfway down the door. She broke off a six-inch-wide section and pulled it away. "Give me the flashlight."

"What's in there? Wine again?"

"I don't see any bottles."

Merle handed Francie the flashlight and went back to work on the door. Half an hour later there was a gap big enough for them to squeeze through. Merle cupped her hands to help Francie step up and over into the cave. Merle was a little taller than her sister, enough that she could put a foot on the opening and hoist herself up. Francie helped her jump down.

"Hey. A key." Francie pointed the flashlight at a big black key hanging by the door's inside handle. Merle grabbed it and reached through the gap to unlock the door, letting it swing wide into the basement. Then they turned back to the cave itself.

Long stretches of empty wine racks lined both walls. Francie traced the length of them with the beam of the flashlight. "No wine, Merle. Bummer."

"This house seems to have been completely cleaned out. I guess she knew she'd never be back."

At the end of the room a large rustic cupboard sat against the wall. "What's in there?" Francie asked. "Open it."

"Get ready for mice," Merle warned.

Francie stepped back. Merle turned the skeleton key in the cupboard door. It opened easily, revealing something large wrapped in cloth. "Bring the light."

Francie pointed the flashlight at the lumpy thing. The object was about three feet long and wrapped in pale, off-white oilcloth. "Let's take it upstairs," Merle said.

They carried the thing up the stairs, each taking an end. It was heavy and awkward. They set it gently on the dining room floor.

"This is weird," Francie said. It looked strange, like half of a body or something. She shivered. "Right?"

The oilcloth had a picnic pattern on it, like an old tablecloth, complete with wineglasses, cheese, and grapes. It was a little sticky but not filthy, unlike everything else in the house.

"It must have been in that cupboard for years," Merle said, squatting next to it.

"Do you think it's a dead body?" Francie asked. "Like desiccated or something? Remember when Tristan found those bones?" She stepped away from it. "I think I—" She turned toward the salon.

"Suddenly you get an imagination," Merle said. She felt the object through the cloth. "It's hard. It doesn't feel like a dead body. Or bones." She looked at her sister. "Be brave, Francie. Brace yourself for the worst."

"Are you intentionally trying to scare me?" Francie cried. "It could be something really gross, like a dead animal."

"It could be anything. But it's probably just one thing, and if we unwrap it we'll find out what it is."

"All right." Francie took another step back. "You do it."

Merle stood up. "I'm getting the gloves." She returned wearing yellow cleaning gloves. Kneeling by the oilcloth, she searched for the edge and peeled it away. She had to roll the object several times to get all the oilcloth off it. When it was free they stood and stared down at it.

"What is it?" Francie asked, baffled.

One side of the object, the side facing up, was rough and white, apparently plaster of Paris with finger and palm impressions that had hardened into it while it was wet. Merle tipped it carefully to its other side. "It's a woman. A woman's torso."

Francie kneeled down beside it. The breasts were exact and perfect, as well as the nipples, the collarbone, the belly, the groin with indistinct mound of pubic hair; then it stopped below the crotch, cutting off the tightly pressed legs. It was in reverse, as if molded from a real person. There was no face, just the neck, shoulders, and half arms like Venus de Milo.

"Wow. It's beautiful. And so blue."

The interior was painted an iridescent blue, glowing in the dim light from the dining room windows. Some color had rubbed off on the fuzzy side of the oilcloth, but it hadn't harmed the effect.

"Something else Mathilde collected, I guess." Merle said. "Were there sculptures in the apartment?"

"I don't remember any. Just paintings by pop artists, plus that one Matisse."

Merle shined the flashlight up and down over the piece. On the back, down by the bottom, something was inscribed in the white plaster. She could feel it with her fingers and see it, sort of, but it was rough and unreadable.

"Is it signed?"

"I think so. But it will take an expert to read it."

They stood up, staring at the strange object. "Is it a sculpture, or just a random cast of a woman? Maybe that was a thing in France," Francie said.

"Whatever it is, it's old. Maybe we should put it back in the cupboard. It's been safe there all these years."

Francie frowned. "Now that we've opened up the house, there might be some curiosity, even way out here. We don't have a padlock to replace the one we cut off. And the door to the wine cave is wrecked and wide open, thanks to us."

"You're right," Merle said. "Help me wrap it back up."

CHAPTER TWENTY-TWO

Dordogne

*T*he week flew by, with cleaning trips to the old villa, entertaining Phoebe and her moods, shopping end-of-season markets, painting projects, and general countryside laziness. Merle found a used bicycle in the village that fit Phoebe and bought it for her. The girl took to exploring the village on her own. A local girl around the corner had come over briefly to meet Phoebe, and the language barrier proved difficult. But it had been a fairly good week all in all.

Dylan flew into Bergerac at seven thirty in the morning on Saturday. Francie drove the rental car into the city to pick him up. She begged Merle to come along and navigate. On her own she had no confidence that she'd make it on time. Merle was happy to go, leaving Phoebe sleeping late and Pascal in charge.

After searching for coffee, Dylan and the Bennett sisters drove back to Malcouziac. The sun rose over the fields of shorn wheat, down through the undulating rows of grapevines, and peeked over woods that clung to the tops of hills. The day was crystal clear after a light rain the day before. Dylan asked about Phoebe. He was disappointed she hadn't come to the airport to meet him.

"She wanted to," Francie said. "But then she remembered about how she gets carsick."

"Did I mention that?" Dylan said. Francie gave him a glance. "Sorry."

"Sometimes I get carsick on these winding roads," Merle said. "But not now. I'm good."

"How's she doing?" he asked.

Francie tipped her head to Merle. "She has good days and bad days, to be honest," Merle said. "I'm not sure what's bothering her, but something seems to be. She had a little tantrum yesterday when we told her you two would stay in the hotel," Merle said.

"I thought she'd like that," Dylan said softly. "I loved staying in hotels when I was her age."

"Listen, you should know," Merle said. "She's gotten pretty attached to Pascal. He calls her his little shadow. They have private jokes of some kind."

Francie glanced back at him. "She seems calmer, Dylan. But still not particularly cheerful."

"I'm going to get her to see somebody when we get home."

"In the meantime," Merle said, "we'll have fun. She's been doing stuff with Pascal and he distracts her."

"Like a father." He sounded sad.

"I think she's just better with men. Because she trusts *you*, Dylan."

There was an awkward silence for the last ten miles. Then finally the village came into view, giving them a topic of conversation. Merle knew all the history, Eleanor of Aquitaine, the Hundred Years' War, the French Revolution, and more. She answered questions before they were asked and gave him the short version of how she came to live here, glossing over some of the less-than-pleasant aspects.

"It's so French. Even more than Paris," Dylan gushed. "I love the walls, the way they slant up. And the arched doorways. I didn't know you could live inside these little walled villages."

"There are challenges," Francie said as she pulled up to the broken wall. "Like parking."

Phoebe crashed out the front door as Dylan got out of the back seat and they hugged. He swung her around and held her tight. "How's my girl?"

"Good, Dad."

He set her back on her feet. "You look good. I like your hair in a braid like that."

Pascal stepped outside. "She's been so excited that you are arriving."

"I hear you've been entertaining her. Thanks, man." Dylan shook Pascal's hand.

"My pleasure. But I'm glad you're here so I can get some rest."

They gave Dylan a tour of the house, ending in the garden. Phoebe insisted on sitting on Dylan's lap, although she was clearly too big. Her legs dangled to the ground. But he didn't complain, hugging her close. They all went out to lunch, sitting inside now as the weather was definitely turning. Merle pointed out the hotel where a room was reserved for them. "I've stayed there myself. Some rooms have been renovated. We asked for one of those for you."

Hotel Quimet, a squat yellow building with half-timbering on the upper level, wasn't the fanciest of provincial hostelries, but it had served Malcouziac well. Merle and her son Tristan had stayed there several years earlier while the legal issues about the house were worked out. It was damp and dreary but mostly a decent country inn. Limp orange geraniums hung from the window boxes on the second floor.

After lunch Francie dropped Phoebe and Dylan and their gear at the hotel. Then she drove to the parking lot outside the walls to park her car. Walking back through the village on a sunny afternoon was hardly a trial. There were old men talking on the square, the baker standing in his whites in his doorway, smoking a cigarette, covered with flour. She passed the hotel and paused. Should she go in and see how they were doing? It had only been fifteen minutes; she should give them some space. She kept walking, back to Rue de Poitiers.

Francie hadn't told Dylan yet about the sculpture thing, whatever you called it. "Plaster cast" made it sound like something you wear on your broken ankle. And yet it was something like that, a cast of a body, a woman's figure, slender and delicate. That's about all you could tell about her. How long had it sat at Mathilde's? Who was it? It couldn't be a cast of the old woman, could it? Would a woman of that era get naked for an artist—back in the twenties or thirties when she was young? Oh, who was she kidding? This was France, and Mathilde was an avant-garde character.

She'd mused about it all week but focused on getting Phoebe back to a happy state. The plaster cast was sitting, still wrapped in the table-cloth, in the upstairs loft bedroom. Francie had tucked it next to her bed, against the wall. It wasn't ideal. She worried. Was it worth some-thing? She couldn't read the inscription on it. None of them could. Pascal had squinted and shook his head.

Now, wandering back through the avenues and alleys of Malcouziac, she thought of Merle's own wine cave. Of course, why hadn't she thought of that earlier? Why not stash it in there? It had a lock. No one actually used that dank, moldy place anymore.

Unlocking the front door, she walked through the house to find her sister. The garden was deserted. Turning back, she opened her mouth to call out for her then heard the bedsprings squeaking upstairs in Merle's room. She paused, smiling. Her sister had come so far since Harry's sudden death. Her whole world had been turned upside down, but she'd put it back together in spectacular fashion.

Francie tiptoed up the stairs and lifted the cast from the floor, setting it on the bed. They had found an old blue blanket at Villa Pardoux and wrapped it around the oilcloth, securing it with duct tape. It now looked like the body of a large dog ready for burial. Francie sighed: another memory, another summer in France, a kidnapped dog, and a close brush with fate.

Onward, she told herself, even as she recalled her silly anxiety about going into the villa's basement. Was she still carrying the fear, the utter helplessness of that summer's adventure? Here in France it kept popping up in her mind. She carried the bundle downstairs and set it on the dining table. Now where was that trapdoor to the base-ment? She found it, but it had a large dish cupboard sitting on it. She would have to wait for Merle and Pascal to help.

She was sitting in the sunshine in the garden, looking at photos on her phone, when Dylan called. A walk through the village was on the agenda. She grabbed a sweater and took off toward Hotel Quimet.

~

ON SATURDAY AFTERNOON Axelle sat in the visitors' room, at a small table. This facility, a *maison d'arrêt*, or remand facility for those awaiting trial, was part of a larger prison and spare and cold. She hated it, but that was a common sentiment. At least it was close to her lawyer's offices, so he had been consulting with her often. He had told her he had to pull a few strings to get Xavier in to see her. She had pleaded with Garnier. She had so few friends, and her cousin Lucien hadn't even bothered to contact her after her arrest, obviously washing his hands of her. Garnier took pity on her, worked his connections. He was well known in the justice community. That was helpful.

Now, in the big cement-walled room with its peeling paint and smattering of other female prisoners, she felt nervous as a schoolgirl. She smoothed her gray sweatshirt and cotton pants, clothes the lawyer had provided for her. What if Xavier couldn't come? What if he changed his mind? What if he looked down on her now, in her "reduced circumstances"?

He had said just the opposite on the telephone. His voice soothed her frayed nerves. Waiting for the French bureaucracy to grind its gears was excruciating. Garnier warned her it could be months before she got a trial. It was to her benefit, he suggested, that she wait, because new evidence could come to light to exonerate her.

Easy for him to say. He didn't have to sit in a dirty French prison.

Head in hands, Axelle cursed silently. She should never have come back. She knew it then and she had been right. She'd known it all her life. Why had she let greed overtake her judgment? Did she even care about Tante Mathilde's art or apartment or even this country house she'd forgotten about? No. Of course the funds would be nice. But money was never her object; she had a nice retirement fund. How much money did a single retiree need? She had let avarice lead her astray. She had only the vaguest memories of the country place. Mr. Hardy had told her it was in Lot-et-Garonne. She may have gone there once with her parents as a small child. Her memory was as vague as a faded postcard: trees, soup, sky, chocolates. All so distant.

A small commotion at the door. A guard was patting down Xavier, making him empty his pockets and take off his jacket. His shoes too, the guard said. Xavier was making comments, joking that he forgot his boarding pass. "What gate is the flight to Barcelona?" he cackled. The guard was not amused.

He had come.

Axelle straightened and tried to smile. Her heart suddenly seemed so full. He looked jolly, a word no one used in the US. Despite all the humiliations of visiting someone in prison, he had come, willingly, in good humor to see her. His silver hair flopped over one eyebrow as he stepped over to her table. He held out his arms then pulled them back. "No touching, my friend. They give me my orders." He sat down and smiled at her. "How are you? They treat you well?"

She grunted. "It was good of you to come."

"What else would I do for an old friend?" He blew her a kiss, making her smile. "*Merci beaucoup* for using my brother's name. Do you mind?"

"Of course not. But why?"

He looked chagrined. "Years ago, remember the trouble?"

"They still hold that against you?" She was appalled. But then, the French government. What did she expect? Of course they would make him suffer.

"Ah, well, they hold it against us all. You were lucky to get away, make a new life in America." He sighed. "We lost, all those years ago. It is hard for us to admit. But the republic won't let us forget."

"I remember it all," she said, eyes twinkling. "The marching—oh, how we marched. The thrill of it, out in the open. We were the resistance, the *new* resistance. We were so young, so proud."

"Until the tear gas, the batons, the beatings." He leaned a little closer and lowered his voice. "My head was broken, Axelle. I had a concussion. My brain was broken. I could not work or go to school. For *years*."

"I'm so sorry, my friend. I had no idea." She felt so bad for him, then angry. "Those dirty *keufs*. In the US they call them pigs."

He smiled. "I like that. Whatever they are called they just want to crack your head, right? What is this all about then?" He waved dismissively at the room.

"Blandine Baudet. You remember her?"

He squinted, thinking. "Was she in our class?"

She nodded. "She and I were arrested together under the Arc de Triomphe. During the sit-in."

"Ah," he said vaguely.

"You remember that?"

"Of course. I do not remember all the girls though. Just you."

"You flatterer. Still so French."

"What else is there to be? It is the apex of the male."

She laughed then sobered, thinking of Blandine. "She was called Blabla for short. She was hit on the head, much like you, I suppose. A few days ago. She did not live."

"*Mon Dieu.*"

"They think I am the person who did it. She was my friend. It is inconceivable."

His forehead crinkled in concern. "Do they have evidence?"

"They think I stole some things from my aunt's apartment. Tante Mathilde, the one who died recently. The estate was a mess—the apartment crumbling and smelly, the house in the Aquitaine, full of mice and memories. My aunt collected art, do you remember? They say I used a candlestick to hit poor Blabla. I don't understand it. My friend, my dear old friend. I would never hurt her." She wanted to cry when she pictured Blandine, lying dead on her floor. What were her last thoughts? Had she cried out for her daughters? Her dead husband?

He gazed into her eyes. "Poor thing. I wish I could give you a hug. Should I offer my services to your attorney? Perhaps there is something I can do. I will give him my word about you?"

She wiped her eyes. "No, no. It is not necessary. He is a good lawyer."

He tipped his head, examining her. "Why did you never marry, *petite?*"

Petite? There was nothing small about her. Yet it was *charmant.* She felt another wave of emotion pass over her. She needed to be admired, to be loved, suddenly. To be *seen.* To have her life acknowledged. To *matter.* She assumed she had put all that vanity behind her. Perhaps not.

He was smiling at her, head cocked at an angle. She straightened and looked him in the eye. "I never met the right man."

He wiggled his eyebrows and licked his lips in comic rapture. "Perhaps France draws you back for a reason."

It felt so good to laugh. *Zut,* Xavier. So, so good.

CHAPTER TWENTY-THREE
DORDOGNE

*T*he dinner party was set for midday on Sunday, the usual time on the day of rest to have a long, leisurely meal. Merle and Pascal had worked up a menu on Saturday and done all the marketing, even driving to a neighboring town that had a market that day. They returned with a leg of lamb, many potatoes, vegetables, cheeses, and bread.

After their walk around the village Francie and Dylan drank wine in the garden as Phoebe played on a new tablet that Dylan had brought her. He had loaded some books onto it, but his daughter was content with playing games. He was just happy if she was happy, at this point.

When Merle and Pascal returned with all the food, Francie asked them to help move the cabinet and open the trapdoor to the basement. Merle was a little anxious about putting something potentially valuable in her wine cave again, but Pascal said it was the safest place. Besides, no one knew if it was valuable or not. It could be just some child's project, he said, although that would be a bit weird.

Merle unlocked the old wooden door for Francie. The cast with its wrappings was set on the wine rack, the door relocked. The low-ceilinged basement was empty now, all the moldy debris removed. The sisters stepped back up the wood stairs and dropped the trapdoor back into place. Pascal and Dylan pushed the cabinet back over it.

Dinner on Saturday night was nutritious but quick, as they had lots of cooking to do the next day. Soup, baguette, green salad, and they called it good. Francie asked Pascal about the student riots of 1968. Axelle had been a participant, she explained. Pascal wasn't old enough to remember them but explained it was a seminal moment in French history. It caused President de Gaulle to flee the country and eventually lose power. Strikes all over the country, and riots too, took France to her knees.

"Did you bring Axelle's letters?" Francie asked Dylan. "Maybe Pascal can read them."

Dylan retrieved the packet from his briefcase then snuggled up with Phoebe on the horsehair settee. "There are a few that are messy. I couldn't make them out." He rifled through them, picking out two. "They seem to be the last two written."

Pascal put on reading glasses and peered at the thin onionskin sheets of paper. "Messy, yes." He squinted. "Nineteen sixty-eight on this one. Fifteen June." He scanned down it then read it aloud for them, slowly translating:

 'MY DEAR AUNTIE,

What exciting times these are. I led the students from my high school down Boulevard Arago to meet the Sorbonne crowd at Boulevard Saint-Michel on the seventh. We were twenty thousand strong, *côté à côté*, shoulder to shoulder down the boulevards. I thought my heart would burst from my chest, I was so proud to be a small part of such an event. Barricades were set up everywhere. My friends and I helped burn three cars but don't tell *les flics* [the cops]. Or my parents.

The next day we were arrested while we occupied the circle around the Arc de Triomphe. Such bravery, such glory—I've never been more proud of my friends! Blandine and I cried a little, huddling in the cold cell, but were released the next day. They told us the high schools were open but when we went back the police were everywhere and no teachers. We returned to organizing against the Fouchet reforms, for the socialists, for free university and higher wages. On the tenth the entire Latin Quarter was occupied by students with microphones, barricades, anger, and fury. We yelled and chanted until we were hoarse.

Yes, so exciting in the moment. I worry, aunt, that now it is all for nothing. Have you seen any revolts in the South? I hear there is rioting in Bordeaux and factory strikes all over. But will we really succeed? De Gaulle comes back. He will hate us more now. My spirits are low.

The only thing that keeps me happy is my boyfriend. I think I can call him that. He is right beside me in the marches. But he does not believe in universities. He says they are for the bourgeoisie, for those who do not believe in the power to all people. Can't we have both education and power? Prosperity and equality? My parents dislike my boyfriend. They call him a communist. They forbid me from seeing him.

Always and forever: *Soyez réalistes, demandez l'impossible.* Be realistic; ask the impossible. Axelle.'

PASCAL FOLDED THE LETTER. "That's all in that one. That last is a rally cry from May of sixty-eight. *Demandez l'impossible.*"

"They were so idealistic." Merle glanced at Francie. "And she had a boyfriend."

"I thought she was a lesbian honestly," Francie said.

"Maybe that's why she left France, because her parents hated her boyfriend."

Francie shrugged. "What's the other one say?"

They all sat forward as Pascal opened and read through the next letter. "Okay," he said, wiggling his eyebrows. "This one was written three years before, in 1965."

> 'My dear aunt,
> What is wrong with my mother and father? Do they hate me? Can you please explain? Do they hate all young people?'

"CAN'T READ IT—THEN—"

> '—art classes last month. I was so excited to be in the company of artists again. They are so creative, so bold, I sometimes feel like—*un balourd.*'

"A dullard, an idiot," Pascal explained. He read on.

> 'But they inspire me and reach my soul. And now Papa and Mama forbid me from even going to art galleries or museums. Why do they hate art so much? What did it ever do to them?
> Nothing can make up for what they did. They have ruined everything for me. I wish I could run away, go to Africa or India and be free. But of course I will not. I am too much the dutiful daughter. Haha. I do respect my parents but not their antiquated opinions. They seem to relish my despair. I am so miserable.
> Inconsolably yours,
> Axelle'

A moment of silence passed. Then Francie said, "What did they do? Banish her from art classes?"

"She was what—fifteen or sixteen?" Merle asked.

"Her parents sound very strict. Of the old school, many rules," Pascal said. "I had an uncle like that. They went through the hard times then the war. Many people never really recovered, in here." He touched his chest. "They were afraid of it happening again."

"Like Madame Suchet?"

"At least Madame and her sister were young during the war. For the older generation it made some of them very rigid, authoritarian. Seek out the rules and stick with them out of fear," Pascal said.

"Axelle was a rebel. A child of the sixties," Merle said.

"She did run away, to Canada then the US. She got away from them," Francie reminded them, remembering the photograph of Axelle as a small child with her parents. How they all scowled in their drab, stiff clothes. "They sound horrible."

"Every fifteen-year-old thinks their parents are horrible," Dylan remarked.

"That's true." Merle sighed. "Now she's back in a French jail, just like back in her salad days."

They came to no conclusions about Axelle Fourcier that night. Her past was her own and it was unlikely they would ever understand what happened or why it had scarred her so badly. They could ask, Francie supposed, but it seemed unlikely that answers would be forthcoming. Could she acknowledge whatever happened? Her pain was too great and apparently, even after all these years, too fresh.

THE PREPARATIONS for the Sunday dinner took all morning. Pascal rose early to get the leg of lamb started. By the time they were drinking espresso, the delicious smells of the roast perfumed the house. Merle sliced potatoes and Pascal instructed Francie on a bean dish that was the classic side for the lamb, he said. He called the lamb dish *gigot à la cuillère*. Something about a leg and a spoon. Francie tried not to make a mess of her cooking: white beans, lots of garlic, whole cloves, onions—it began to smell heavenly. She got hungry and took surreptitious bites of it.

Albert, the retired priest who lived across the alley, arrived with his bottle of *eau de vie*, apologizing for not bringing more. Pascal told him he was thrilled, and they each had a quick shot of the distilled plum brandy. Pascal's father had been an old friend of Albert's. Francie and

Merle put up their hands in mock horror. The stuff was as strong as white lightning. Pascal opened a bottle of wine for them and poured it reverently.

The sisters who lived across Rue de Poitiers, Paulette and Ninon, arrived about one in the afternoon. They each brought a dessert. Madame Suchet—Paulette—had made a magnificent thing, layers of almond and hazelnut meringue on cake and biscuit, that she called a dacquoise cake. She also carried in a small pan with chocolate sauce and placed it on the back of the stove.

Merle's tiny kitchen was jammed with cooks. Luckily the tall, grim sister, Ninon, had brought an apple tart—very simple, she explained, except she added dried lavender blossoms. It was complete, she said dismissively, setting it on a table in the main room. She frowned at the chaos in the cramped kitchen and stepped outside into the garden.

"The son didn't come?" Francie whispered to Merle.

"I didn't ask." Ninon's son had been hospitalized for depression last year and was considered delicate.

A last frenzy of cooking, pouring, and setting the table peaked. Francie went to find Phoebe. The girl had been out of sight, and Francie wanted to make sure she wasn't off moping somewhere. Dylan lounged on the sofa with a glass of wine. "Just chilling," he said with a smile. "It smells amazing." Phoebe was in the garden, he said.

Outside, next to the acacia tree, bright yellow in its autumn finery, Phoebe and Ninon sat next to each other on the low wall. Francie stopped, startled by the smile on the cranky old woman's face, reflected in Phoebe's face as well. They had their hands together, wrapped in purple yarn. Phoebe seemed to be teaching her some kind of finger knitting. She had the tablet in her lap and kept looking at it. "Wait, no. It's this way," she said, laughing at her mistake. Ninon looked enchanted.

Francie backed away and went inside. She took Dylan by the hand and they stood in the doorway to the garden, watching them. "It's so sweet," Francie said.

"Look at their faces," Dylan whispered.

Pascal yelled *"C'est l'heure! Diner!"* inside the house. Phoebe glanced over at them, smiled, and dropped her hands. Ninon was left with a tangled mess, but she didn't complain. She pushed the yarn off her fingers and marched toward the door. She gave Dylan a catlike smile like now he owed her something.

"Ready to eat, Phoebe?" he called. "Bring the tablet inside."

"It smells good," Francie said to her. "But I think Pascal used too much garlic."

Phoebe looked up at her. "But I love garlic now. I am getting French-ified. That's what Pascal said."

There were in truth *twenty* cloves of garlic in the lamb. A lot. But after half a day of cooking—it was also called *gigot de sept heures* or "leg of seven hours"—the lamb was so tender it could be eaten with a spoon, *à la cuillère*, thus its other name. The garlic had long since cooked down, fallen apart, and become sweet, the way onions do when you cook them a long time.

"*À confit*," Pascal explained. "That is what we call it."

"Like duck confit," Merle said. "Cooked slowly for a long time."

"I can still taste the garlic," Phoebe said. "Good thing I like it now."

Pascal grinned. "Way to go, Frenchie."

The talk ranged from English to French to translations to Franglais. Albert helped translate for the two older sisters, and they seemed happy just to eat *en famille*. They praised Pascal's lamb, so tender and delectable. Ninon gave him a complimentary pinch on the shoulder. Francie got kudos for her white beans. Merle's potatoes sliced and fried in duck fat with shallots went over very well. The *haricots verts* were devoured. They laughed and talked and groaned and drank wine, slowing down to French speed to savor every bite.

The meal took three hours. Three delicious hours. By the time the desserts were served Francie was pleasantly full, as were they all. Phoebe had a look of stunned wonder on her little face and leaned against her father.

Francie took a small portion of both desserts and washed them down with the last of the red wine. She looked around the table at the happy faces, full of camaraderie and community and food and love, as the French do so well. She could get used to this.

• • •

DYLAN'S FLIGHT back to Paris left at ten that evening. Everyone agreed that Phoebe shouldn't drive with Francie and her father to the airport because of her carsickness. Even Phoebe agreed. All very civil. Then, as they were saying goodbye in front of Merle's house, Phoebe collapsed into tears. She clung to her father, wailing, desperate to keep him from leaving. He held her, tried to talk to her, soothe her, but she refused to listen. Hands over her ears, shaking her head to block out what she didn't want to hear, she looked more like a four-year-old than a preteen. Merle and Francie exchanged concerned looks. Dylan took her blows against his chest stoically, as if this wasn't the first time he'd been the subject of her rage.

Finally Pascal stepped in, taking Phoebe's shoulders and peeling her off her father. He held her arms at her sides, turning her toward him. He gave her a hug then looked at her little face.

"*Mon chou*, what is it? Why are you so angry? Your papa must go to work. You know that. Hasn't he gone to work your whole life? He will be back. He doesn't have holiday time right now. You understand? This is what papa must do."

Tears streamed down her face. She calmed a little, listening to Pascal, but now she was just so, so sad. It broke Francie's heart. This poor girl. Divorce was awful for children, she knew that. But to see that pain so clear and present felt tragic.

Pascal kept up the conversation, one-sided that it was. "He will come back for you very soon. Or better yet, we will take you to Paris. Would you like that? Go up in the Eiffel Tower, ride the carousel? Have you done that yet? Oh, you must do all these things, Frenchie. Have the time of your life. You will go home soon and see your mama—"

Here she tore away and threw herself against her father again, clinging to his legs, sobbing. Dylan took her hands and crouched down to where she now sat on the cobblestones, quietly crying into her chest. "Oh, baby, don't be sad. It's only one more week, I promise. Then we'll go home together. Okay, honey?"

She took a deep, rattling breath and looked up into his face. "Okay, Dad," she whispered. "Together?"

"Yes, of course, together. I love you, sweetie." He helped her to her feet, wiped her cheeks with a thumb, and gave her a kiss on the fore-head. He glanced at Francie, nodding to the car. *There is no best time to leave,* he seemed to say, *so let's do it fast.*

Pascal walked around to the driver's side where Dylan had slipped behind the wheel. Francie got in on the other side, buckling her belt quickly. They needed to make a getaway before more tears slowed them down. Dylan was on the last flight to Paris, and he had to make it back tonight. But now Pascal was leaning down. Dylan rolled down the window.

"Listen, Dylan, I'm not sure what to say. I don't have any kids, so I am just spitting here, is that what you call it?"

"Spitballing," Francie said. She made a *hurry* motion with her hand.

"Right. So Phoebe has something she's not telling us. Not me, not Francie or Merle. And apparently not you either. Am I right?" Dylan shrugged. "I hoped to get her to talk to me about whatever this secret is."

"Did she call it a secret?"

"Yeah."

He got agitated, reddened, took off his seat belt. "Did you ask her —did someone touch her or something?"

"First thing that came to my mind too. She said no. No one is touching her or hurting her. Do not be alarmed."

Dylan sighed and rubbed his face. "I don't know what to do."

"I will keep talking to her. But I thought you should know."

"About a secret that she won't talk about."

"Sorry. I wasn't sure if I should mention it. Then—this." He glanced over the roof of the car. Phoebe and Merle stood in front of the door to the house, solemn, holding hands, waiting to wave good-bye. "That was too much."

"Way too much." Dylan looked at his watch. "I have to go. Do whatever you can, Pascal. And thanks."

Pascal clapped him on the shoulder. "*De rien.* Good travels."

They all waved as the black Citroën roared away down the street. At the end of the block Dylan stuck his whole arm out the window and waved madly.

Francie leaned back into her seat and sighed. She was still stuffed from dinner. "I'm glad you came down," she said quietly. "We all are."

Dylan gave her a half smile as he steered around a roundabout. "What a mess," he muttered. "Still."

"Do you think it's school? Some mean girls?" That seemed likely. "Girls get pretty whacked out if their friends turn on them."

"You know what? I hope it's mean girls. Because that would mean a new school will solve at least that problem."

"A new school can be pretty traumatic too, you know. It won't solve everything."

Dylan swore loudly and hit the steering wheel with his palm. "I should be home with her. Not going back to work."

"She'll be okay," Francie said, patting his shoulder. "She's got three adults looking out for her."

Suddenly the law firm with its petty grievances, long hours, and office intrigues looked downright civilized. Comforting even, an oasis of rational duties and logical agendas. Maybe that was the purpose of a vacation after all: to dash your silly expectations and make you happy to go back to work.

INSIDE THE HOUSE Merle got Phoebe to put on her pajamas. Merle took out her braid, messy now, and brushed her hair. Phoebe had thick, dark brown hair like her father's, but no one had taught her how to care for it apparently. Well, this wasn't the time for a lesson.

"Pascal is making you something. Run down and see."

Downstairs Pascal poured hot cocoa from a saucepan into a cup. Phoebe waited patiently, taking it carefully back to the dining table and sitting down.

"Are you hungry?" Merle asked her.

"No."

None of them were after that incredible meal. Even Madame Suchet and her sister had broken out of their formality and gotten a little giddy about the lamb and all the fixings. Albert had waxed poetic. Now Pascal put his arm around Merle and kissed the side of her head. She leaned into him, glad for his warmth and caring. She had been so lucky to meet him when he came to fix her roof. It hadn't always seemed like luck—in fact it wasn't—but to her, finding him was the best gift France could give.

"I must go tomorrow. Back into the vineyards."

Phoebe looked up at him, her face blank. She said nothing. Maybe she'd used up all her fury earlier. She picked up her cup and took a cautious sip.

"So soon?" Merle asked. And more to the point: *What would they do with Phoebe?*

"Don't worry. It will be fine." He walked over to the girl and kissed the top of her head. "You will be okay with Merle and Francie, won't you? Tears all finished?"

He stepped back and nodded to Merle. She wrapped her arms around him again and hoped he was right.

CHAPTER TWENTY-FOUR

The next afternoon, while Phoebe and Merle were finger knitting, Francie drove over to Lot-et-Garonne to meet a real estate appraiser that Bozonnet Patroni had contacted. The appraiser had offices in Périgueux and Bordeaux but also some staff who lived not too distant from Villa Pardoux. Francie liked the sound of Villa Pardoux; the name had a rich, old-world ring to it. Now that her imagination had been piqued she could see it fixed up, modernized with bathrooms and a working kitchen, the plaster patched and the mirrors re-silvered. The yard overhauled and manicured. A lot of work, obviously.

It was too bad, she thought as she pulled into the driveway to wait, that Axelle couldn't keep it. But in these circumstances—charged with homicide and fighting for her life against a government, a system, she'd rejected so many years before—it was impossible. She needed to sell it and be free of France. Thinking about that beach house back in the US was probably keeping her sane in jail. Luckily she'd already closed on the sale before she left. All she had to do was finish packing and move in. And beat this murder rap, of course.

Francie tried to reach Lucien Daucourt that morning, to ask if he remembered anyone from the funeral service. He was busy in surgery, his staff explained, but would return her call. She waited the rest of the morning. He never called back.

She wondered now why Dylan hadn't been interested in driving over to see the villa. But his time was so short in the Dordogne, barely a day and a half. He wanted to spend it with Phoebe; that must be the reason. Sitting in her rental car, gazing at the facade, she admitted there was not that much to see. The photos she took had been enough.

Fifteen minutes late and looking harried, the appraiser drove up in a rattletrap, or rather, a vintage car. It looked like Merle's neighbor's old car, the one that no longer ran. This one, labelled "2CV," the same as Albert's, was a rusty blue with a torn brown convertible top and lopsided headlights. It was cute, she had to admit, even though she'd been told the top speed was about 35 miles per hour.

The appraiser was also cute, in a rumpled, elderly French way. He rolled out of the car, his belly stretching his shirt buttons under a waxed field jacket. He wore a tweedy hat and dirty khakis. "*Bonjour,* Monsieur," she said, smiling. She put out a hand as he approached her. He shook it quickly.

"*B'jour, ma'moiselle.*" He glanced at his clipboard. "You are Miss Bennett, *oui*? I am Théo Lejeune. You wish English, okay?"

"Yes, thank you so much. My French is sadly lacking." She led the way to the front door, unlocking first the padlock on the shutters then the door lock. "The house is mostly empty. But being unoccupied for so long may not be a problem?"

He hemmed and hawed, shrugging. He switched on a large flashlight and pointed it this way and that. "We will see."

"Do you want me to open the shutters? There's no electricity."

"This will be enough."

He pointed the light at the loose ceiling pieces, hanging by a thread. Francie and Merle had cleaned up the worst pieces that had fallen. "Some damage, eh."

"Does that mean water damage—a leak?" They stared solemnly at the crumbling lath and plaster above.

"Sometimes. Other times it is just old. Ancient, eh?"

"How old would you say this house is?" Francie asked.

"I have not an idea. I must look in the property decrees."

"One hundred, two hundred years?"

"I must, how do you say? Dig." He glanced at her suspiciously. "It matters, the historic value?"

"Not to me. Just curious," she said. "This way to the dining room."

She pushed open the door and stopped, causing Monsieur Lejeune to bump into her and apologize. "Oh, no," she whispered.

In the dining room the French doors swayed in the gentle breeze, open to the elements. The shutters were wide open too. Dead leaves, grasses, and animal waste littered the herringbone wood floor. "How did that happen? I know I locked that door, and the shutters. There was no padlock on these, but see—" She pointed to the latch on one door. "A really decent latch." She pulled the old shutters closed and latched them. With a metallic creak they slowly fell backward onto the patio pavers with a loud crash.

Francie and Lejeune stood in the open double doors and stared at the broken shutters. "What happened?" she repeated. The appraiser stepped outside to examine the hinges. He poked at some twisted metal.

"They have been tampered with, *ma'moiselle*. You have had a burglar."

"There's nothing to steal."

He stepped back inside and shut the French doors, turning the dead bolt. "Perhaps. But the burglars do not know. Or maybe they come in for a party. Local youths, the worst. They have no morals."

Francie glanced around the empty room. The dish cabinets were still barren. No signs of a party unless it was squirrels.

They walked into the kitchen and looked around under the beam of the flashlight. Nothing seemed disturbed here. Then they went through to the butler's pantry. The trapdoor was open.

Francie teetered on the edge of the hole. "Jesus," she muttered, grabbing the appraiser's meaty arm.

"So, a party in the cave. Hmmm." Lejeune pointed his light down the wooden stairs. "You have been down there?"

"There's no wine. Nothing really, just mice and dirt." She followed him down the stairs, stepping carefully now. Her heart was still fluttering from the near tumble into the basement.

He shined his light on the broken door. "Ah, they have broken into the wine cave. *Tant pis.*"

"My sister and I did that. We didn't have a key, and we thought there might be something valuable in there. Like wine, you know."

She could feel his eyes on her in the dark, questioning her judgment. "You broke the door?"

"My sister is very strong."

Lejeune reached into the gap and unlocked the door from the other side. Francie waited outside as he stepped in and looked around. He walked down to the cabinet, unlocked it, looked inside, and relocked it. "So, it has a wine cave with a broken door. Still it is a necessity for a country house."

Back upstairs they closed the trapdoor then climbed to the second floor, did a cursory walk-through, then Francie showed him the hidden attic door. They walked up the steep stairs, looked around from the top step, and returned to the main floor. Lejeune wanted to look around the property, so Francie let him go on his own. She'd already battled the thistles. When he returned he stopped midway to her car to make some notes on his clipboard.

"Will there be any repair work before the house is marketed?"

"What do you suggest?"

He frowned. "Turning on the electricity, of course. The water, or well, whatever it is, get it tested. Checking the slates." He peered up at the roof. "Then repairing the shutters, painting them would help but is not necessary. Cleaning."

"I will tell the lawyers about your recommendations." They shook hands. "I think those broken door shutters are the first thing. Keep the burglars and the squirrels out."

"Squirrels?" He frowned then broke into a smile. "*Les écureuils.* Ha." Then he was gone.

FRANCIE BROUGHT Phoebe with her the next day when she returned to Villa Pardoux. The girl had been quiet and sad the previous evening, missing her father, and Merle had work of her own to do today. She was now helping their oldest sister, Annie, do some environmental consulting work in Europe. Merle's part of it was mostly connections, finding the right people to help the cause, but it kept her busy. She had an idea for another book but was happy do just talk to the French about climate change for a while.

Phoebe stared out the window as they drove. She answered Francie's softball comments with a grunt or nothing. *At least she isn't crying,* Francie thought. Why had Pascal had to leave? He was the best girl-sitter.

Well, Phoebe wasn't his daughter, or his responsibility. She couldn't blame him for having to work. So now it was only the two of them, the girl and the girlfriend. Francie grimaced. She had no idea what to say to Phoebe.

Her cell phone rang as she was pulling into the villa's weedy drive. It was Lucien Daucourt. "Thank you for returning my call, *Docteur.*"

His voice was cool. "What can I do for you?"

She explained she was trying to run down a guest book list from the funeral home but wondered if he recalled who had attended. He seemed surprised, then stuck. He did not remember. He didn't ask about his cousin but rang off, saying he had patients to see.

Phoebe made it to the villa without having to stop to upchuck. As Francie parked the car, the girl unbuckled her seat belt and glanced at Francie. "Get out and explore. It's a cool old place. But watch out for stickers."

"Stickers?"

"Thorns. Weeds. Sticks and stones."

Phoebe opened her car door, stepping out onto the gravel in her canvas tennis shoes and jeans. She wore her hooded sweatshirt, the pink one that was her favorite, and put the hood up against the breeze, or random adults.

The handyman from the nearest town had promised to meet Francie here at ten o'clock. It was now ten fifteen. She unlocked the front shutters and doors but waited outside for him, watching Phoebe take tentative steps into the side yard. As a child Francie would have loved an adventure like this. It was like being Nancy Drew. But this girl? Who knew.

A few minutes passed. Phoebe appeared at the front door. "Hey," she yelled. "The back door is open."

Muttering curses, Francie stepped into the house and followed Phoebe, who skipped to the dining room. Once again the French doors were wide open. More leaves and yard debris littered the floor.

"Dammit." Francie looked at Phoebe. "Sorry. I didn't say that."

"My mom says it all the time."

Huh. "So this is why we came over. To fix this door. Someone is breaking into the house." She shut the French doors and latched them —again.

"Are they sleeping in here?" Phoebe asked.

"There's really nowhere to sleep."

"What about that couch?"

They walked back to the living room. Francie opened a window and the shutters behind it, letting in a flood of morning sun. The long velvet sofa with the broken leg had a dent in its orange cushion now. She didn't remember that. It could be a person's outline, she guessed.

"Look." Phoebe pointed at one end of the sofa. Something was rolled up—used, perhaps, as a pillow.

"Don't touch it," Francie said, leaning in close. It looked like a sweater, navy blue knit.

"Can you get DNA off it?" Phoebe whispered next to her. "Like on TV?"

Francie smiled, putting a hand around Phoebe's shoulders. Her new partner in crime. "Maybe. Do you see any hairs?"

Noise outside made Francie turn back to the front door. A utility van had roared up and skidded in the gravel. "Keep detecting, Phoebe. I'll be back."

The handyman was about forty and a chain-smoker. A cigarette hung from his yellowed fingers. He grinned at her, sizing her up. "Madame Bennett?"

"*Oui. Parlez-vous anglais?*"

No, he did not speak English. Francie took a deep breath and used hand signals to get him to follow her into the house. In the dining room she opened the French doors, pointed at the dislodged shutters lying flat on the flagstones, and said, "*Voilà!*"

They stepped outside, jumping to the sides of the shutters to avoid breaking them further. Francie pointed at the hinges and made a broken sign. Then shrugged. The French must understand shrugging; they did it constantly.

The handyman, whose name was not offered, scratched his chin, smoked the tiny bit of cigarette that remained, and crushed it on the bottom of his shoe. He tucked it into his pocket and bent over the broken hinges. He wiggled the twisted metal and shook his head sadly.

"*C'est dommage*, Madame." That's too bad. Then he let loose a string of French that blew right over her.

She blinked, tipping her head. "Can—you—fix—it." This was ridiculous. "Hold that thought. *Un moment.*" She jumped back inside, went out the front, and got her purse from the car. The little French dictionary had already saved her bacon a few times on this trip. Back inside she leafed through and found the word for "to fix." Weirdly it was "*fix-er.*"

"*Vous fixez? Reparez?*" she asked, trying to remember her accent.

He hung his head. "*Non*, Madame. *Les charnières sont cassées. Je n'ai pas de charnière.*"

The hinges were broken and there were no more. Francie sighed and referred to her dictionary. "*Vous sécurisez la porte?*" She stepped out and indicated something to put over the door to secure it. After several tries at pantomime, he seemed to understand.

He brightened and nodded. "*Bien sûr*, Madame." He said something and pounded his chest like he was the man for the job.

When he didn't move she added: "*Aujourd'hui?*" Today? By any fricking chance?

He brightened again and scurried off around the house. She hoped he had brought the right supplies with him. She had mentioned the broken hinges on the phone, and he hadn't bothered to bring any. Back in the living room Phoebe was still staring closely at the rolled-up sweater.

"I have a clue!" she cried. Francie joined her in front of the sofa. "See, right there. A white hair. It must be an old person."

Sure enough, there was a short silvery hair on the sweater. "Good work, detective." She patted Phoebe's back. "We'll get this door fixed so whoever the sweater person is, they can't get in again."

"But—?" The girl frowned. "What if it's a homeless person and this is the only place they have to sleep? It would be cruel! It's getting cold and soon it'll be winter, right?"

"True. Winter will be here soon." What a compassionate child. "Good thinking. What should we do though? We can't have homeless people sleeping in here."

"What if we leave them a note?"

"What should we say?"

Phoebe screwed up her face, thinking hard. "I'll work on it. Don't worry."

The girl ran outside and got into the car, rummaging in her backpack. The person, assuming they *were* homeless, probably didn't speak English. Whatever Phoebe said to them would be of no consequence, but it made her feel better. It made Francie feel better. The girl was thinking about others instead of just feeling sorry for herself. That was a very good thing.

The scrawny handyman was juggling an enormous sheet of plywood around the house. He returned to his van several times and soon was nailing plywood over the French doors, in place of the door shutters. It wasn't very attractive, Francie thought, wincing as the nails went into the beautiful old doorframe. But it would do.

The operation took over an hour. The handyman made a call to someone, seemingly describing his work. He took a photograph with his phone and sent it off. He smiled broadly to Francie, displaying his stained teeth. He set the broken shutters against the house, gathered up his tools, and gave the plywood a last, satisfied look.

In the front of the house Phoebe was placing a folded sheet of lined paper under a rock on the front step. She looked up at Francie. "What about the sweater? They'll need it in the cold."

"Put it with the note."

Phoebe spent a few minutes arranging the sweater just so and placing the note on top of it. She set the rock on top of it all and stood back to admire her handiwork.

"Do you think he'll see it—or she, if it's a homeless lady?"

"They probably will. Good job, Phoebe." Francie gave the handyman her address at Merle's for the bill and waved him off in a cloud of dust. After locking up the house again she put a hand on Phoebe's shoulder. "What about lunch? I think I saw a café in that last town we went through."

Phoebe looked up at Francie and grinned as she skipped to the car. "Sure."

Francie felt her heart lift a little. Maybe she'd get the hang of this parenting thing after all.

CHAPTER TWENTY-FIVE

Francie was down in Merle's wine cave the next day, taking photos of the body cast thing, trying to get a good shot of the unreadable signature tucked into the rough edge, when her phone rang.

"Dylan, hey. How are you?" They hadn't spoken since he left on Sunday night.

"Good. Where are you? You sound like you're in a barrel."

"Close. The wine cave. Remember that plaster thing Merle and I found? I'm taking photos of it to send off to the art appraiser in Paris."

"That's why I'm calling. I found someone in Toulouse who can come and take a look at it as soon as tomorrow."

"Great. So I can get out of this spidery, mousy basement?"

"Definitely. How is Phoebe doing?"

Francie wrapped the body cast back into its blankets and reattached the tape as she talked. "She's doing better. Yesterday we went over to the villa to get that door repaired and she was so sweet. At lunch afterward she jabbered the whole time." She paused on the stairs and whispered, "Don't tell anyone, but I think she likes me now." She glanced back at the wine cave. "Wait a second, I forgot to lock the door on the cave."

"So the break-in or whatever at the villa wasn't too terrible?"

"No." Francie was back upstairs, tipping the trapdoor closed with a bang. "Ouch, that was loud. Who would have thought I'd be so comfortable with trapdoors?"

"Is the weather nice? Outside, not in the basement."

She stepped into the garden. It was a cloudy afternoon. The breeze had definite bite to it. "About the same—chilly. The villa didn't look like anything was taken. There's nothing to steal. The real estate appraiser thought it was probably just some kids looking for a place to party. I see they're getting a nasty storm back home."

"Yeah, hey, I have to go when you start in about the weather."

"You started it." He laughed. She remembered a thought she'd had in the night. "Hey, have you seen Mathilde's full file there at Bozonnet?"

"Um, no, I guess not."

"See if you can get your hands on it. I was wondering who managed her money before Bozonnet."

"I'll try. So the appraiser's name is Clément Boudreau. He has your address. He says he can come take a look at the sculpture tomorrow."

Francie hung up and sat on a green chair in the garden. She pulled her sweater tighter. What did she have going tomorrow? Nothing. So now she would wait for the appraiser to call, or show up. If he had to drive up from Toulouse he wouldn't be there until midday at the earliest.

Merle called from inside the house. Albert had invited them to dinner tonight. A simple affair, he said. Although the old man was a decent cook, they had been asked to bring a dessert and a side dish, and now they must go to the market. Francie grabbed her jacket and set the market basket on her arm. Phoebe decided to stay home and read, which probably meant playing on her new tablet.

"Don't answer the door, honey," Merle called up the stairs. "Okay?"

"Okay."

"You're sure she's good to leave on her own?" Merle asked Francie.

"She's nine. Oh. *Only* nine, you mean?"

Upstairs Phoebe was stretched out on the bed, reading. "Change of plans, honey," Merle said. "We're getting treats after the market. Cocoa or ice cream or whatever you want. Put your shoes on."

DINNER AT ALBERT'S was not as elaborate as the Sunday meal, but it was not what any American would call "simple." Merle made her acclaimed duck fat potatoes again. Francie roasted asparagus spears. Albert baked a chicken with lemons and herbs. The dessert they brought was from the patisserie, a berry tart with layers of sweet cream filling on a buttery crust. Soon she wouldn't fit into her pants, Francie thought. Merle seemed to never gain an ounce, which was completely unfair.

As she lay in bed that night Francie wondered if Dylan would come back on the weekend again—or was it time to go home? She was getting a little bored here in rural France. The country house had potential, but what else was there to do there? She glanced over at Phoebe. She was asleep, curled with her back to Francie, her dark hair splayed across her pillow. She was doing better, that seemed evident. But she needed to go home.

They all did.

MERLE ANNOUNCED at breakfast that they should take a field trip to see the old château that sat on a nearby hilltop. It was reportedly in the family of the romantic poet Lord Byron.

"Is it falling down?" Phoebe asked over her bowl of cereal.

"A little. But mostly it's still very nice. You can see how people lived two hundred years ago." Phoebe's eyes bugged out. Merle looked at Francie, sipping espresso. "You'll come, right?"

"I have to wait for the art appraiser. I haven't heard when he's coming, so it probably means I'll wait all day and he'll show up at five."

"That's rude," Merle said. "But typical. Well, mademoiselle, we will just have to explore the old château on our own. Bring your tablet and you can take pictures of it for your dad."

· · ·

BEFORE THEY LEFT, Merle helped Francie push back the heavy cupboard, open the trapdoor, and retrieve the blanketed body cast from the wine cave. They set it on the dining room table where it looked like a latter-day mummy.

Eleven o'clock passed peacefully. Still no word from the art appraiser. Francie started in on yesterday's pots and pans. She swept the main room then moved on to the stairs and the loft. By then it was almost noon, and she was thinking about lunch, staring into the little refrigerator for some leftovers, when the knock on the front door made her jump.

The man standing outside was late middle age with black hair streaked with silver. He had a pleasant smile and wore funky glasses that she supposed must be considered arty in France, square with purple frames. He removed his black cap and gave her a little bow.

"Madame Bennett?" He stuck out a hand and she shook it. "Clément Boudreau. From the agency in Toulouse. Mister Hardy has sent me."

"Yes, please come in." *At least he speaks English,* she thought. She led him through to the dining table, not a great many steps in this tiny old *maison.* "We just brought it up from the basement. Shall I unwrap it?"

He set down a battered leather briefcase and extracted a camera, putting the strap around his neck. He had replaced his cap on his head, and now that she stood closer to him his hair seemed much too black for a man his age. The French could be so vain, she thought, then realized so could she.

"I will do it, Madame. Do not worry. This is my job, I will be extremely careful." He tugged at the duct tape from the blue blanket, allowing it to fall open against the table. "You do not know the provenance of the object?"

"Like where it's from?"

"*Oui.*"

"It's been in an old villa about an hour from here. How long, I don't know. At least twenty-five years. That's when the woman who used the house quit coming for summers and it was closed up."

He nodded thoughtfully, staring at the oilcloth. He laid a hand on the cast protectively. "Could you get me a glass of water, Madame? I feel the excitement of this find in my throat."

"Of course." Francie went to the kitchen and ran water into a glass. When she returned to the salon a large man in a shiny black suit, white shirt, and skinny tie stood next to the appraiser. She startled, juggling the glass.

"And who is this, Monsieur?"

The appraiser took the water glass. "My driver. His name is Antoine. It is all right that he comes inside? He has been parking the car."

Francie nodded in reply. Antoine was broad-shouldered and large-jawed like a bodybuilder. His jacket pulled tight against his biceps. She felt a tingle of apprehension that she tried to tamp down. "Can I help open the oilcloth?" *Let's get this over with.*

"I have it, Madame," Boudreau said in a gentle voice. "Never fear."

He peeled back the tablecloth and revealed the rough side of the plaster cast. "Ah. This is it?"

"Turn it carefully. The other side is—well, you'll see."

His eyes sparked with anticipation. He set his water glass down on the table, bent his knees, and carefully rotated the cast. The iridescent blue of the other side glowed against the oilcloth. Again Francie felt how beautiful this thing was—whatever it was—like a clamshell you open to find a glowing pearl inside.

Boudreau clucked. "It is the IKB."

"Excuse me?"

He said no more, saying something in French to the big guy who held the cast on edge. Boudreau snapped some photos with his old camera then nodded to Antoine to lower it. Carefully Boudreau pulled the oilcloth around it then rewrapped it with the blanket and tape.

"Do you know what it is?" Francie asked as he put his camera in his briefcase.

"I will research and return my assessment to Monsieur Hardy in Paris," he said. He picked up his water glass and raised it to his lips. Then, suddenly, he threw the water in Francie's face, making her yelp.

"What the hell?" she sputtered, dripping.

Boudreau and the driver had the cast halfway to the door before she cleared the water from her eyes. Antoine kicked open the door with a large boot. It crashed against the side of the house, shattering glass.

"Wait! What are you—? Stop right now! Are you kidding me? Stop!" Francie lunged toward Boudreau, who carried the end of the cast, grabbing him by the arm. In a quick move he backhanded her, sending her flying across the room onto her ass. Stunned, she shook her head to clear it and clambered to her feet. They were out the door before she could get up.

"Stop!" Francie ran into the street. The two men were shoving the plaster cast into the back seat of a beat-up black sedan. They jumped into the front seats. Antoine peeled out against the cobblestones, tires squealing. Francie ran after the car, yelling for them to stop. They skidded around the corner at the end of the street and disappeared.

"Dammit!" She let loose a few curses. Madame Suchet's sister, Ninon, stuck her head out of her door.

"Madame? *Ça va?*" Ninon inquired. Are you okay?

Francie bent over and put her hands on her knees, gasping for breath. "No, Madame. Everything is definitely not *ça va.*"

MERLE AND PHOEBE came home twenty minutes later. Merle made an angry comment outside about the front door, the subject of much abuse over the years. "What the hell happened to the front door?"

Francie sat on the horsehair sofa, head in hands. "They stole it."

"No, it's just broken—" Merle threw Phoebe's jacket onto the dining table. "Where's the plaster thing?"

"That's what I'm telling you, Merle. They stole it. Right in front of me."

"Oh, no." Merle sat next to her sister and put an arm around her shoulders. "Who were they?"

"They said they were art appraisers. One of them. The other one was supposedly his driver."

"Did you call the police?"

Francie nodded. "They may not have understood me."

"At least you got photos of it. Right?"

"Yeah. I took photos."

Merle retrieved her phone, ready to call the gendarmes again. Phoebe watched them, a frightened look on her face. Merle reached out to her. "It's okay, honey. It's just some art thing that got stolen. Nobody got hurt or anything."

"But what if we'd been here?" Phoebe whispered. "We could have helped."

Merle squeezed the girl's shoulder. "They probably planned it for when we weren't here. Because they know we're secret ninjas."

Phoebe gave a little smile. "But not Francie. You're not a ninja, are you?"

Francie sighed, again. "Nope. Never a ninja."

CHAPTER TWENTY-SIX

"Dylan."

Francie knew her voice sounded angry, rude even, but she couldn't help it.

"What's up?" he answered warily.

"That art appraiser. He was here."

"What did he say?"

"He stole it! The plaster cast. He threw a glass of water into my face and ran out the door with it."

Dylan swore under his breath. "That bastard. Are you all right?"

"I'm fine. Well, he pushed me across the room, but luckily I'm well padded where I landed. Who is he? How did you find him?" His anger had taken a little of the sting out of her own.

"He called me. I don't know how he got my name, or the information about the cast. He even knew where it was, in Malcouziac. I thought—I don't know what I thought. Maybe that you had contacted the agency."

Francie frowned into the garden, slumped under the nearly bare acacia tree. "But you—How did he know? How many people even know about the cast?"

He paused again, thinking. "I talked about it at the firm here. Maybe a handful of people know."

"You need to ask them who they told, Dylan. Now."

"Okay, okay. I will."

There was a commotion inside Merle's house. Alarmed, Francie stood up and walked to the kitchen window. Had the police arrived? Or more thieves? Then she heard the big laugh. Pascal was back. He could help with the police.

"I have to go talk to Pascal. Can you get Axelle to call me again?" He apologized again and said he'd try.

Francie stood inside the back door, gathering her thoughts. Pascal had to call the cops for them, explain the theft and the circumstances. They would listen to him. But how did Boudreau find out about the cast? And what had he called it—the I-K-B? Or was I-B-K? What the hell was that?

Merle saw her lingering in the kitchen. "Come here. Tell Pascal what happened."

They spent the next two hours explaining in detail to the gendarmes on the phone everything Francie could remember about Clément Boudreau, his driver, Antoine, and the incident. The car, their features, their speech, everything they said. When Pascal had finished he sat down next to Francie at the dining table. The sandwiches Merle made for lunch hadn't been touched.

"Try to remember something more about the automobile," he told her.

Francie had already told him it was old, a medium-sized sedan with faded black paint and a French license plate. The plate was blue, but then almost all of them were. The numbers were lost to her memory. Pascal nodded and stood up.

"I think I'll take a look around."

Merle frowned. "He won't still be nearby."

"You never know."

They watched him jingle his car keys and disappear down the street. Francie said, "I guess it's better than just sitting around here stewing about what an idiot you are."

Merle put a hand on her shoulder. "You did the right thing. How were you going to subdue two large men?"

"I guess I should have taken that ninja course."

Phoebe looked up from the sofa. "I can show you a few moves. I take karate."

Francie smiled. "Sure. I need to defend myself better." To Merle she asked, "Have you ever heard of something called I-K-B or I-B-K?"

"No, what is it?"

Francie moved to the stairs. "I'm going to find out."

Firing up her iPad and stretching out on her bed in the loft, Francie saw she had several emails. One was from Dylan, earlier this morning. He'd sent a photo of the guest book from the funeral home that had arranged Mathilde Fourcier's service in May. She clicked on the photo and enlarged it to read the spidery handwriting.

Not a large crowd, just twelve names, several couples. Maybe eighteen attendees in all. There was Lucien Daucourt and his wife. Blandine Baudet, the faithful friend. She'd come alone. The other names weren't familiar. She scanned the list for a "Ceci" or something similar, the name of the last caretaker. The last name on the list was Cecile Yacine. Was that her? She sent a quick email reply to Dylan. Could he try to find this Yacine woman?

Scanning the photograph again she took out her notebook and wrote down the list of attendees at the funeral service. Then she returned to her browser and entered "IKB."

The top four entries were a bank, an engineer, a protein, and—*bingo.* The fourth entry was the name of a color invented by a French artist, Yves Klein: International Klein Blue. That color, she realized, was the same vivid shade of blue on the inside of the plaster cast. More searching led her to body casts of the artist's friends done in the fifties and early sixties. Her heart rate jumped: *this was it.* Similar to the one that was stolen except in reverse, as if molded from a plaster life cast, they were male torsos from the top of the head to midthigh, painted blue. They were owned by museums and collectors around the world. They were famous.

No mention of any female casts by the artist. Maybe it was a copycat piece. Klein was well known in his time. Francie spent an hour reading up on Yves Klein. He had persuaded young women in Paris in the early sixties to paint their naked bodies in his blue paint and prance around in front of an audience and a chamber orchestra as they made impressions of their bodies on a large canvas tacked up on a wall. Or dragged each other across a canvas on the floor. *He must have been very charming,* she thought. He was definitely quite a showman.

How did you get a basic color like blue named after you? Apparently the blue paint used in the fifties lost a lot of its luster when mixed and thinned with linseed oil or when a fixative was brushed over the painting. So Klein invented his own blue paint, one that was so vibrant and special that it retained that special glow, and didn't need any fixative. It seemed like a publicity stunt to Francie—*International! Klein! Blue!* But he did invent some special medium to mix into the paint. Long after his death, IKB lives on, immortalizing his artistic— or marketing—genius.

Francie glanced through his artworks. The color was the sort of bright, cheery ultramarine blue that was hard to dislike. Didn't everyone love a good, bold blue? Klein was also into sea sponges, oddly, soaked in IKB.

Klein's replica of the Venus de Milo in IKB had been reproduced in large numbers after his death. Some auction prices made her eyes water. One sponge piece fetched over nine million euros at an auction. That didn't mean the plaster cast was worth that much, but without a doubt it was worth stealing, if it was by Klein. A big 'if.'

Who was that guy with his purple glasses? Francie fumed a bit after an online search for a Clément Boudreau in Toulouse came up empty. Of course it was a false name. She set aside her iPad and closed her eyes. She took a few deep breaths to let her anger dissipate. She'd been duped by an imposter, one her own boyfriend had sent to her.

THE CALL from Axelle came as they were getting ready for dinner, always a late affair in France. Pascal hadn't returned from his wild goose chase. The phone line from the prison crackled and popped for a good thirty seconds before Axelle came on the line.

"Axelle? Are you there?" Francie shouted.

"Where else would I be?" She sounded cranky as usual.

"I'm afraid I have some bad news. A sculpture that was in Mathilde's country house has been stolen by two men posing as art appraisers."

"A sculpture?"

"Were you told about it? We found it last week. I was showing it to these men—do you know anyone named Clément Boudreau? Supposedly from Toulouse?"

"No."

"I have no idea how he found out that I had moved the sculpture over to Merle's house. He must have been following us. Anyway I'm so sorry. We were conned by this guy. We're trying to get it back. It might be valuable. In fact I'm pretty sure it's by the French artist Yves Klein, but we'll have to wait for the appraisal. If we get it back."

Axelle sighed. "I see."

"Do you think your aunt knew this Yves Klein? He lived in Paris in the fifties and sixties." There was a long pause. Francie thought the line had been disconnected. "Hello?"

"What was this sculpture?" Axelle asked finally.

"A plaster cast of a woman's body, from the neck to mid-thigh, painted that bright blue that he was famous for—International Klein Blue. It had a little signature or marking on the back, but I couldn't read it."

Another long pause. Francie could hear her breathing and waited.

Her voice was a whisper. "I don't know if my aunt knew Yves Klein. But I did."

CHAPTER TWENTY-SEVEN

*a*xelle seemed reluctant to tell the story at first, but once she got started it spilled out of her. She had been young, barely in high school, when she began hanging around with art students and going to gallery openings. It was a grand time to be young in Paris, the early sixties. Her parents didn't approve, but she lied and went out with her friends in the evenings. At one gallery she and her friends met the young artist Yves Klein.

"I was a little in love with him," she said. "A little crazy, sure. I thought he was so handsome, and a creative genius."

After his big splash with the painted models he asked her to pose nude for him. She declined. He asked her to paint her body blue and press it into a canvas. She again declined. Then he asked if he could make a plaster cast of her body. She thought about it for two weeks then said yes. She couldn't say why she changed her mind. Immortality? Possibly. She got a girlfriend to go with her to his studio. She stripped down and lay still on a mat on the floor as Klein and her girlfriend slapped wet plaster of Paris on her. It took all day for the process and the drying.

"I was mortified at first. But I was also thrilled. It was a compliment that he admired my body so much that he wanted the world to see it, yes?" Someone talked nearby. "The crazy bitch who runs this place says I only have two minutes left."

"What happened to it?"

"A couple months later my parents found out. I think my friend slipped up. My mother and father marched over to Yves's studio and paid him to destroy it. I thought it had been crushed. It was never seen again, by anyone."

"How did Mathilde get it?"

"I have no idea. She must have heard about it through my parents. He never destroyed it. I can't believe it." She laughed like a schoolgirl. "My mother would be so mad. She was such an old stick—"

"Who was your friend, Axelle?"

"Who went with me to the studio? Blabla, of course. Blandine."

The line went dead.

Francie stared at the phone, this new information swirling in her head. Merle called them to the table. Pascal didn't make it home for dinner.

As they finished, wiping up gravy with slices of baguette, Francie was eager to talk to her sister, but Phoebe's presence stopped her. They'd talked about murder enough. Francie watched the girl's solemn face. She'd hardly spoken at dinner. Was she missing her father? Francie didn't know what to say or ask her. Was it better to pretend you didn't notice a child was depressed? That didn't seem right. Merle asked the girl to get into her pajamas, and she stomped up the stairs.

Francie grabbed a towel to dry the dishes as Merle washed. She whispered, "It was Axelle. The body cast."

Merle's eyes widened. "She told you that?" Francie nodded. "When was this?"

"The early sixties."

"She was so young."

"That's why her parents freaked out and told her to stay away from artists and museums."

"Did she tell them about it?"

"It was Blandine, her friend, the one who was murdered. Blandine went with her to get the plastering done."

Merle handed her a plate. "How did this fake appraiser find out about it?"

"We don't know. How did he know it was here at your house? How did he know Dylan? But it seems like it's somebody who knew Axelle and Blandine, right?"

"Someone they went to school with?"

"Or maybe was in the student protests with them?"

Phoebe appeared in the doorway in her pajamas. Merle asked her to brush her teeth, and she slipped into the bathroom. As Francie dried the last plate the front door opened. Pascal hollered into the house: "Francie, come quick. I think I found him."

Phoebe stepped out of the bathroom at his voice. "What? What's going on?"

Francie and Merle looked at each other, quickly.

"It's okay, Phoebe," Francie said. "I just need to go with Pascal to find the thing that got stolen."

"Come on," Pascal said, holding the door open. "Get your jacket. Hurry."

A minute later Francie struggled into her jacket as they ran down Rue de Poitiers. "Where are we going?" she gasped, trying to keep up with Pascal.

"My car is out here." He pointed to one of the arched portals of the village. They skidded down the hill to where his old green BMW sat, poorly parked by a tree. He unlocked it and had it going before they had their doors closed.

"I've been driving around, looking for that automobile," he said, swinging around a corner and heading away from the village. "I went all the way to Montauban and around to Cahors. Then, on the way back, I spy something funny going on."

"Something funny?"

"Two men, arguing, almost coming to blows, out in the middle of a wheat field. I pass by, trying not to stare, you know, but I think I see those purple glasses you mentioned on the smaller one."

"Was the other one bulky, like a thug?"

Pascal smiled. "Perhaps. So I drive on and wait for their argument to play out. They take so long I look around and find the car, hidden in some trees."

Francie watched the signs on the intersection, barely readable in the glow of the headlights. "Are we going to Mathilde's house? Near Miramont?"

"Yes, that direction." He glanced at her as he accelerated onto a bigger road. "You think they will go there? There is a connection?"

"That's where the plaster cast was hidden. I don't know why they'd go there now. It's locked up. What happened at the wheat field?"

"I left them to work on their problems. And pierced the tires of the car so they can't drive it. They are stranded."

Two minutes later they arrived at a junction. The sky was nearly black, a purple glow in the west. Trees grew close on one side of the road; the other side was a harvested wheat field, rows of golden stubble. No sign of arguing men, or anybody.

"Where are they?" Francie craned her neck to look into the field.

"They must be at the car." Pascal crept the car forward and pulled off the road. "Stay here." He opened his car door and gently closed it. Francie leaned over and locked his door.

The night was moonless and velvety dark, the last glimmers fading away. The starlight was bright out here in the country but did little to illuminate the woods where the shadows were deep under the trees. Pascal disappeared into the forest. Francie bit her nails for a moment and he was back. She unlocked his door as he ran up.

"The car is there, so they are on foot somewhere." He turned the key and pulled out onto the narrow road. "They can't be far."

"Maybe you shouldn't have come back for me. You could have caught them."

"I need you to identify them. And I will need to call the gendarmes when we spot them. Unless you have been practicing your ninja moves?"

Francie chuckled. "Did Phoebe tell you that?"

"She says she will be a black belt by the time she is twelve, and I believe her." Pascal turned on his high beams. "They will be on this road, I believe. Or that one." He pointed at the right fork in the road. "You pick."

"Left."

Pascal punched a number on his cell phone and spoke rapidly in French. Then he pocketed the phone. "I changed my mind. I call the gendarmes, just in case. It will take them some time to find us."

They crawled along the road, looking for movement in the ditches and fields. After five miles Pascal sighed and turned around. "Now we try to the right."

Back at the junction the right fork dropped down a hill, passed a vineyard and a couple low-slung farm buildings. At the bottom they crossed a creek and continued up to the top of the next hill. Pascal stopped the car on the top, the headlights shining into the night.

"Did we lose them?" Francie asked.

"I don't think so." He turned the car back around and killed the headlights. They began rolling down the hill.

"It's very dark. Is this safe?"

"Probably not. But I remember where the road goes."

Francie clutched the door handle, hoping Pascal had good night vision. As her eyes adjusted she could see a little more, the gravel on the edge of the asphalt, a row of bushes. They eased slowly back down the hill toward the creek, the brake lights behind them flashing on and off. She could make out the larger barn on the other side. Then—

"There!" She pointed at movement near the barn.

"You see him?" Pascal turned off the engine and let the car roll silently onto the verge on the side of the road.

"By the barn," she whispered. "Where did he go?"

They waited two beats, then three more, for him to make his move. "It is the big one, or both?" he asked.

"Just one, I think, but not sure which."

Pascal reached into a duffle in the back seat and came up with a handgun. Francie watched as he checked it for bullets, pulling back the slide with a metallic click.

"Oh," she said.

He shrugged. "Even wine cops need protection."

"Yes indeed."

They turned back to the night scene. "Ah. There he is."

A dark figure moved away from the barn, onto the stone bridge that crossed the creek at the bottom of the valley. He was moving toward them when he froze. He had seen them.

"Here we go." Pascal got out of the car. Francie watched as he raised his handgun toward the man and approached slowly. He called out something in French. It had the ring of "Stop, it's the cops" to Francie, but she wasn't sure what he said. At any rate it gave the man on the bridge pause. He didn't move.

Pascal was on his cell phone again, keeping the gun pointed at the man. He was at least twenty or thirty feet away from him. Francie couldn't identify the man in the dark, not at this distance. She opened her door silently and stepped out onto the grass.

Pascal saw her and called, "Get back in and turn on the headlights. And stay in the car."

She did as she was told, reaching over to the driver's side to pull the lever for the lights. Instantly the scene changed. A beam flickered off Pascal's gun. The man on the bridge blinked, stunned for a moment.

It was Clément Boudreau, he of the purple glasses. They reflected in the headlights' glare. He wore the same black hat and gray jacket. He was carrying a large bundle. The plaster cast, still wrapped in the blue blanket and secured with silver duct tape. "There it is," Francie whispered. So close.

He turned away from Pascal as if to run. Then he looked back, right at the gun. Pascal yelled at him again. Boudreau's head moved left and right, as if he was gauging his options. Run or stay, get shot or get arrested.

Without warning two patrol cars screamed up over the far hill and roared down past the grapevines toward the barn and the bridge, lights flashing. The gendarmes had the sense to turn off their sirens at least. They screeched to a stop next to each other. They left their headlights on and blue flashers going as they jumped from their cars, guns drawn.

Francie felt like she was watching a cops-and-robbers show through the windshield. She slid down the seat so she could barely see over the dash. This was really happening, three guns pulled on the so-called art appraiser caught in the beams in the middle of the bridge in the middle of nowhere in the middle of the night. The gendarmes in their navy uniforms set themselves up at the opposite end of the bridge, blocking his escape route.

Pascal yelled something and one of the cops returned to the patrol cars and turned off the blue flashing lights. It was a relief.

Pascal glanced back at Francie and waved his hand for her to come forward. She got out of the car again and inched slowly up behind him. Now it didn't seem like a television show at all. It seemed scary. It was dark and there were guns and bad guys.

She huddled behind Pascal's back. She felt like an idiot, a scared child. "Yes?"

"Is that the man who attacked you?"

"That's him. And he's carrying the Yves Klein thing."

"*Quoi?*"

"The plaster cast. I figured out it must be by the artist Yves Klein."

"I know that name. He is famous, yes?"

"Yes." Francie glanced over his shoulder. "What are you going to do?"

"Make him surrender. Go back inside the car now."

She backed away to the car. The policemen all stood silently, pointing their guns at Boudreau. He continued to look back and forth, over both shoulders, as if hatching a plan. He was doomed, they could all see that. He should just give up.

The gendarmes were shouting as Francie slipped back inside the car. Boudreau backed a few steps away from them. Pascal moved a few steps closer to him in response. The tension was getting to Francie. Why didn't he surrender?

Pascal was yelling now, and pointing at the ground with his gun, as if telling Boudreau to put the plaster cast down. The man tipped his head as he backed to the edge of the bridge. He turned his back to them and held the bundle over the creek in his outstretched arms.

"Oh, no," Francie gasped. "No, no, no." She jumped out of the car again. "Don't let him drop it, Pascal!"

Pascal shouted in French. The gendarmes yelled in French. Boudreau said something to them in a nasty voice. He turned back toward the gendarmes. Slowly the three cops all put their guns away. They took slow steps toward Boudreau and he barked at them. They stopped. He set the bundle on the ground and smirked at Pascal, muttering.

What was he doing? Negotiating his surrender?

Now the gendarmes were backing up, hands in the air. Boudreau spoke to Pascal, smiling in a cruel way, waving him forward, demonstrating how he wanted Pascal's hands too up in the air. Pascal raised his hands as he stepped closer to the bridge. As he got near, Boudreau bent, scooped up the bundle, and heaved it right into Pascal's face. It knocked Pascal sideways as he tried to catch it, giving Boudreau an opening. He ran past Pascal, jumped the low wall on the bridge, and disappeared down the creek bed into the night.

The two gendarmes fumbled their weapons, shouting. They bumped into each other, looking for the culprit in the darkness. Luckily no one got shot in the foot.

Francie watched all this as if in slow motion. The heft of the bundle, its unlikely weight, throwing Pascal off-balance. The two uniforms bumbling around, cursing each other, trying to get their guns out again. The bundle sailing through the air, hitting the side of Pascal's head, then his hands, then the bridge. She heard the *thunk* as it cracked, glancing off the stone wall of the bridge, tipped over the edge, and fell twenty feet onto the rocks below.

She stood at the end of the bridge, looking beyond the beams to the murky depths of the creek. The bundle was visible on the edge of the water, lying at a weird angle on stones, exactly like a broken torso.

"Are you okay?" she called to Pascal, who was rubbing his temple.

"Yes, fine."

"I'm going down to get it," she announced, pointing at the bundle. She had to know. She had been a coward with the guns, but now that the thief had fled her courage returned. She needed to retrieve Axelle's sculpture. Her beautiful sculpture.

She picked it up, the tape flapping. It was definitely broken, in pieces from the fall. It crunched and rattled as she carried it back up the slope to the road and laid it on the asphalt. Stripping off the tape, she pulled back the wrappings.

It was the body cast, there was no doubt. She'd had a weird hope that Boudreau had switched it, given them a ringer. But no. The plaster cast was in at least six large pieces, broken through at the waist, the arms, the legs. Blue crumbles mixed with white, a breast here, a shoulder there. She poked at the dismembered torso, turning over the white to blue, that famous, precious blue. She looked up at the stars for a moment and closed her eyes.

They had it back and it was ruined.

CHAPTER TWENTY-EIGHT

The moon finally rose, a sliver in the eastern sky, as Pascal and Francie returned to Malcouziac. As they unlocked the front door Merle leapt to her feet from the sofa.

"Thank god, you're back. What happened? I was so worried."

Francie carried what was now a sack of broken bits into the room and set it down on the dining table. Merle peered at the pile of blanket and tape. "Oh, no."

"Complete ruin," Francie said. "Thrown off a bridge. And the creep got away."

Pascal winced. He shrugged to Merle. "We almost had them both."

Francie snapped out of her funk. "Pascal got hit in the head. If not for him the thief would have been in the wind completely. Thanks for trying, Pascal." She glanced at her sister. "And he didn't shoot anybody."

Merle blinked. "With your—gun?"

He didn't answer, weaving past the women to the bathroom. Merle raised her eyebrows.

"He's a cop," Francie whispered. "The two gendarmes had guns too. But nobody fired. The phony appraiser jumped into a creek and ran away and they just let him. I don't blame them. It was dark."

"But this." Merle laid a hand on the broken plaster. "It's sad. It might have been worth a lot to Axelle."

"And the sentimental value," Francie agreed. She sighed. "It's over. Go to bed, Merle."

FRANCIE LAY in her bed in the loft, staring at the ceiling. She could hear Phoebe in her bed, snoring softly. The events of this evening replayed in her mind: the guns drawn, the headlights, the flashing blue lights, the square reflection of Boudreau's glasses. The plaster cast dropping to the riverbank, breaking into a million pieces. Or a hundred. It didn't matter how many; it was not going to be glued back together. It was shattered.

Axelle would still have her aunt's country house, or the proceeds from the sale of it. Had she been hoping for more? Had Francie given her some unexpected hope? She hadn't even told Axelle about the cast until it was stolen. All these years she'd thought it was destroyed, and now, finally, it was.

Francie buried her face in the pillow, trying to sleep. Something was missing. The reason why Axelle was framed for Blandine's murder —what was it? Was it the plaster cast? It could have been worth millions, and Blandine knew about it. Did she know where it was? Even Mathilde seemed to have forgotten about it.

The theft was meaningless now. Unless it was connected to Blandine's death. And how to make that connection?

She pounded the pillow three times and willed herself to sleep.

WHEN FRANCIE CAME down the stairs in the morning breakfast was finished. She'd finally drifted off sometime around three A.M. Phoebe sat at the table with the remains of her cocoa and a scattering of croissant crumbs. Merle was in the kitchen, Pascal was gone. Francie mumbled a "good morning" to Phoebe as she passed into the kitchen.

"Any coffee left?"

Merle poured Francie a cup from the new coffeemaker she'd

brought back from the US. Francie sipped coffee, watching Merle tidy the kitchen. "What's on today's agenda?"

"You told me the cleaners are going to start at Mathilde's today. Somebody needs to unlock the house for them."

"Oh, right. Did I mention what time?" Francie looked at her watch. Crap, it was already nine.

"Ten o'clock." Merle dried her hands. "You want me to go?"

"I'll do it. I just need to get dressed." Francie turned to go up the stairs with her coffee. Phoebe watched her, bright eyes conveying something. Francie paused, trying to read the child's face. "You want to come?"

Phoebe stood up eagerly. "I'll get my shoes."

As Francie came back down the stairs, dressed and hair brushed, Merle was waiting for her. "Okay if I come too? You seem to get all the fun."

Phoebe sat in the front seat where they hoped she would do better with her carsickness. The day was bright and as cloudless as the night had been. Phoebe rolled her window down and smiled as the autumn colors of the countryside whizzed by. Francie felt happy at the sight of the girl, relaxed and calm.

"Maybe we can tip that fountain back upright," Francie said. "Will you help, Phoebe?"

"Sure." The girl glanced at Francie. "I wonder if the homeless person got their sweater."

"What homeless person?" Merle asked.

"Tell her the story," Francie said to Phoebe.

Excitedly the girl relayed how she'd found a white hair on a rolled-up sweater inside the house. When they locked up she'd left it on the step for the homeless person, in case it got cold.

"With a note," she explained.

"What did the note say?"

"I just said I hoped they found a home somewhere. And maybe come see us in Malcouziac and we'd try to help them."

Francie frowned. "Can you spell Malcouziac?"

"Sure," Phoebe said. "It's not that hard. I won the spelling bee in third grade."

"Hmm." Merle said: "So this homeless person knows where we live."

"Right," Francie said. She glanced at Phoebe. "It was a nice thing to do. I hope they came back for their sweater too."

As soon as Francie parked the Citroën in the driveway, Phoebe disengaged her seat belt and raced to the front step. When the sisters arrived she turned to them, eyes wide: "It's gone! But here's my note." She pulled it out from under the rock. "It looks like it got rained on." She turned it over in her hands. "Look! It says: 'mercy.'"

Francie leaned in to read it. "*Merci*. That means thank you. Good job, Phoebe. You helped somebody stay warm."

The cleaning crew hadn't arrived yet. They were probably lost in the countryside. At ten thirty Francie got a call. It was the crew, speaking French. She handed the phone to her sister, who gave them directions to the house. Meanwhile they opened all the shutters and windows again. It was a perfect day to clean, sunny and brisk.

Merle stared at the plywood over the terrace doors in the dining room. "That's attractive."

"Someone kept breaking in."

"Someone who now knows where we live," Merle said. "I wonder who it was."

"Anyone could have read Phoebe's note."

Merle turned to her sister. "But this homeless person. Do you think it was the art appraiser?"

"Yes. Don't you?"

Merle nodded. "No one has ever had trouble finding me in Malcouziac. They just ask for that American lady. But I guess it doesn't matter now, does it?"

When the cleaners finally arrived, a crew of three women, Francie was glad her sister was with her to translate. How had she thought she could do this without Merle? She made a pact with herself to take French seriously before her next trip.

Outside Phoebe was swinging a stick around like a sword. Francie walked through the thistles to join her. "Show me those karate moves."

Phoebe smiled then made a fierce face. "Okay, watch this one." She took a fighting stance, fists clenched, then kicked a bunch of weeds with a high kick. She continued battering the thistles, making ninja noises and enjoying herself.

"Wow, you are great," Francie said, smiling. "I'm very impressed."

"Didn't you take karate when you were little?"

"Nope. Took some golf lessons though."

Phoebe stuck out her tongue. "That's not going to help when somebody attacks you."

Merle joined them. The three of them decided to tackle the fountain. They pulled down on the lip, jumping back as it crashed upright near their feet. Phoebe yelped a victorious ninja cry. Francie looked inside the bowl of the dry fountain. A huge crack streaked across the middle.

"Another broken thing," she said. "Oh, well."

"How long do we have to stay here?" Phoebe asked.

"We have to wait for the cleaners to finish."

Merle dusted off her jeans. "Let's go look around in the house. Maybe we missed something last time."

The crew was busy in the main salon, washing windows, mopping floors, and swatting cobwebs. The sisters and Phoebe decided to look in the cave again. Merle had brought a flashlight and led the way down through the trapdoor. Phoebe made spooky noises, obviously unafraid of the dark.

They did a thorough look around, behind the junk and firewood in the basement. They unlocked the wine cave and examined the cabinet where the plaster cast had been found. Nothing new, nothing interesting.

"Are we done?" Francie said. "It smells down here."

Back upstairs they looked around in the kitchen and dining room then headed up to the second floor. Phoebe raced from room to room, jumping and leaping like a ninja.

"Open the secret door," Merle said.

Phoebe stopped in her tracks. "Secret door?"

Francie smiled mysteriously. "Watch this." She stuck her fingernails in the crack and gently pulled open the door hidden in the paneling. Phoebe's mouth dropped open. "Cool, huh?"

Phoebe looked up the steps then ran up. Francie called out to be careful as the sisters followed her. At the top of the stairs Phoebe stood, arms akimbo, looking around at the junk. "Wow. This is awesome."

"The floor might not be too solid, so be extra careful where you step."

Phoebe walked gingerly to the far end of the attic and stopped by a broken dresser. She yanked on a drawer. Peering inside, she declared it empty.

"Maybe we should get the rest of those old photos," Merle said. "Which trunk was that?"

They opened one trunk and found the old wedding clothes. The next held the photographs. The sisters sat on the floor and sifted through them. Merle loved them and declared if Axelle didn't want them, she did.

Phoebe wrinkled her nose at the old clothes in the first trunk. "These are stinky."

"People like vintage clothes," Francie said. "They might be salvageable."

The new plan was hatched. They put the photographs in the trunk with the old clothes. It was a beautiful old steamer trunk, a faded rose with decorative pressed tin, with little drawers under the lid. It might have some value. Or Merle could use it for a coffee table.

The sisters each took a handle and they lifted it. "Oof. It's heavier than it looks," Merle said, side-walking toward the steps. "Let's slide it down."

With some awkwardness the sisters slid the trunk down the steps, one by one. The turn in the stairs was difficult, but finally they had it out. Phoebe didn't really want to stop exploring the attic, but Francie promised her lunch at the café where they'd eaten before. They struggled more with the trunk, down the main stairs, out the front door, and set it on the car's back seat as it was too big for the very small luggage space.

"There's seating the size of a grasshopper back there." Merle observed.

Francie smiled. "Luckily you are as big around as a cricket."

They told the cleaning crew they would be back in two hours to lock up and to do what they could on the main floor with the time left.

On the drive home later in the day Merle asked from her cramped spot in the back if Francie had told Dylan yet about the plaster cast. Phoebe had fallen asleep, after exploring for treasures, ninja weed whacking, and ice cream.

Francie had put off calling Dylan to confess the destruction of the Yves Klein piece. If only she and Pascal hadn't chased down that idiot. If only they hadn't made him so desperate. It would still have been lost to them, but at least it wouldn't be lost to the world. It wouldn't have helped Axelle, but it might have immortalized her as she'd once desired, maybe even made her so famous they would let her out of prison. Well, that was unlikely. You had to be practical.

Merle tapped her shoulder. "Don't worry. At least the old villa will bring in some money."

Francie squeezed the steering wheel, nodding. She didn't mention the email she'd read over lunch. Dylan had sent a copy of the real estate appraiser's report. In its present state of decrepitude—overgrown, abandoned for decades, without running water or a septic system, the electric lines torn out years before for "safety concerns"—Villa Pardoux was reckoned to be worth about forty thousand euros.

How much did a murder defense cost in France?

A well-known Parisian criminal attorney must charge a lot more than that.

CHAPTER TWENTY-NINE

PARIS

The visitors' room at the *maison d'arrêt* was nearly empty that Friday morning. The only people visiting prisoners were their lawyers, and so it was with Axelle Fourcier. PRISONER NUMBER 15,667, as it said on her wristband. *Surprising they don't tattoo it on your arm, like the Nazis,* she thought sourly, waiting on the hard chair for Monsieur Garnier.

He was only ten minutes late, early in France. She tried to smile at him but found her face refused. He was a tall, elegant man with a long nose and hands made for the piano. His dark graying hair was neatly trimmed and pressed into place. He had hard, black eyes that no doubt helped in his profession. He greeted her without touching—no handshake or cheek kiss even with one's *avocat*. It seemed very un-French.

He set his briefcase on the floor by his chair. "How are you today, Madame?" His manners and his French were impeccable, with an elite school accent. These cues came back to Axelle the longer she was in France: the class identifiers, the Paris accent.

"About as well as expected," she replied.

He nodded sympathetically. "Next week we have a meeting with the judge and the prosecutors to present evidence. If there is anything else you can add to what we have already discussed, please share it so I can tell the judge."

She frowned. "I told you I called Blandine on Saturday, right?"

"Yes. And we have the evidence of that on your mobile phone."

He'd already told her that was not helpful. It might even be used as evidence that she was trying to make contact with her friend and perhaps had gone to her house. "Can they tell where I was from my phone? Is that possible?"

"It shows you were in Paris. But not to say you were exactly at this or that address. Let's go over your activities on Sunday again."

There was not much to tell. She had walked through Luxembourg Gardens and stopped in at the Centre Pompidou to see the modern art but hadn't kept her ticket. She told him what restaurant she'd eaten in, alone, near her hotel. She'd gone to bed early.

"The desk clerk saw you arrive at the hotel?"

"I can't remember."

"Anyone you spoke to at the restaurant?"

She shook her head.

He asked a few more questions then backtracked to Saturday. She had done nothing that day, she said, because she was ill. She left out that she was severely hungover. He asked about Monday. She told him, again, about meeting her lawyer, Miss Bennett, about the estate, then her friend Xavier at Musée de l'Orangerie, and lunch at the bistro, and him walking her back to her hotel. Then she had gone to Blandine's and found the police barricades and heard the awful news.

"Did you speak to this Xavier about Madame Baudet?"

"We were all in school together. In the same class. I mentioned her, of course. We all protested together in sixty-eight." She said that proudly but that went right past Garnier. He scribbled something in his notebook.

"Perhaps he can give you an alibi. What is the name?"

"Xavier Voclain."

"Voclain," he repeated, frowning. "Is this person related to the man who came to visit you?"

"A relative—" She stopped herself. Xavier had asked her to use his brother's name and now she was hesitant to admit that to her lawyer. She blinked up into his hard eyes. "He—"

"He what, Madame?"

A chill passed over her. What had Xavier said? He had a record with the police. For what exactly? Was it just from 1968? Should she tell her lawyer? She swallowed hard and her mind adjusted. Perhaps, just perhaps, Xavier wasn't entirely truthful.

"He asked me to give a false name. His brother's name."

"Gregoire Voclain was a false name?"

"That's his brother." She shook her head. "Xavier told me he had a criminal record. I thought it was just from the protests when we were in school. It seemed innocent to use his brother's name."

The lawyer pressed his lips tightly. "Spell his name. His age?" She guessed at it then told him what high school they had attended, in what year they graduated. "His address?" She didn't know. "Phone number?" It was on her mobile phone.

Garnier stood up abruptly, slamming his notebook closed. "I must go. *Bonne journée.*"

And a good day to you too, sir, she thought, clenching her teeth. She felt stupid about Xavier and his false name. But maybe he was telling the truth. That he had been in the protests—that much was true. He could have been injured by the cops. The cops beat so many that day, and gassed thousands. Maybe he lied just so he could get in to see her, because he cared. Maybe he just had a few run-ins with the *keufs* over the years. He couldn't have gotten a state bureaucrat's job with a serious record.

A matron took her back to her cell. Her roommate was an African woman who was very tidy and meek, so deferential to Axelle that it made her cringe. She looked up from her bunk as Axelle entered and whispered, *"Bonjour,* Madame.*"*

Axelle turned back to the matron. "I need to make a phone call. Please. It's an emergency."

LUCIEN DAUCOURT WAS HANGING up his white coat in his medical office at seven that night when the call came to his personal mobile phone. It had been another busy week and he was ready to relax with his wife. He pulled the phone from the pocket of his suit coat, still on the hanger on the back of the door where he left it each morning. The number was blocked. He was ready to decline the call when he saw that other blocked number calls had come through, three times since the morning.

"Oui?" he said gruffly.

"Hold please for Madame Fourcier," a voice said. Music came onto the line. A nice touch for a prison. Lucien shrugged into his suit jacket and locked his office door. In the reception area everyone had gone home but his office manager. He waved at her with his phone under his chin and stepped out into the corridor. How long did you wait for a call from a prisoner?

He had time to reflect on his cousin's fate, arrested for murder just when everything seemed to be going so well for her. Except, of course, her signing over the elegant apartment to him and losing the Rothko to the government. He and Severine had celebrated that Friday night with Crémant de Bourgogne, an expensive bubbly she adored. By Tuesday, when he heard of the death of the woman and Axelle's arrest, he felt a mild shame about that.

Still, he hadn't bothered to visit her in prison. But what could he do? He hardly knew the woman, and from what he had seen she had a mean streak. She was taller than he was, and powerful despite her age. He could see her snapping in anger, lashing out. His commiseration with her situation would hardly be helpful, or welcome. So why was she calling him now?

He was in his car, ready to head home, when Axelle finally got on the line.

"Lucien? Is that you?"

"Allo. Ça va? How are you, Axelle? I'm sorry to hear about your situation."

"I'm sure," she said sarcastically. "But listen, I need a little information. Can you help me?"

Her request wasn't terribly onerous. Severine would be incensed that Axelle had reached out to him. His wife was not a fan of his cousin, but that was neither here nor there. He wasn't heartless, was he? If he was charged with murder, rightly or unfairly, wouldn't he want someone to help?

"I'll see what I can do at home," he said. "Can I call you?"

"I'll call you tomorrow." And she was gone.

CHAPTER THIRTY

DORDOGNE

*W*ord came in the morning that Mathilde's old house, Villa Pardoux, was the scene of another break-in. The gendarmes in the area had seen it and called the real estate agent whose number was on the new sign in the yard. They in turn called the lawyer handling the estate, who eventually called Francie. Could she make another inspection, see what had happened, and change the locks?

It nearly noon and she had nothing to do anyway. Two quiet nights had passed since she'd been at the villa. Merle had laid out a tea party for Phoebe on the rescued steamer trunk, now placed in front of the settee. They hadn't gotten around to sorting the photographs or vintage clothes, but it made a great coffee table.

Talking to that stuck-up Élodie Maitre from Bozonnet wasn't fun. But Francie could hardly refuse; they were supposedly still paying her to manage whatever needed doing at the villa. Dylan was no longer working on the estate. She had talked to him for an hour last night, telling him finally about the botched recovery of the plaster cast. He wasn't mad; in fact he had no real interest in the cast, but still she felt responsible for the destruction of the artist's work. They made plans to go to Paris, she and Phoebe, in a few days. It was time to wrap things up, with or without an amazing body cast possibly by an iconic French artist.

Francie sat down next to Phoebe and picked up her teacup. "Want to go for a drive over to the old house again? I have to check out another break-in."

Phoebe's eyes sparkled. "Is it the homeless man?"

"I don't know, honey." She hoped not since that was probably that bastard Boudreau.

Merle came in from the kitchen. "You're not going over there by yourself, are you?"

Francie stood up. "You think it's him?"

"Yes." Merle frowned. "Wait for Pascal."

"When is he coming back?"

"This evening. Wait until tomorrow."

"I told them I'd go today. It'll be fine. Just a quick check and call somebody to fix whatever needs fixing. Do you want to go?"

Reluctantly—except for Phoebe—they made the trip through the fields and hills and vineyards, back to Villa Pardoux. They stopped in the largest village along the route to buy new padlocks. When they pulled into the weedy driveway Phoebe was out of the car like a shot again, racing to the front door.

"It's broken! Look," she cried.

The door shutters had been splintered by what looked like an axe. Inside them the main door had a pane of glass broken and sat open.

"How are we going to fix that?" Merle said, disgusted. "It took me ages to find new door shutters for my place."

"We'll just have to call someone. I've got that handyman's number."

Merle and Phoebe stepped tentatively into the dark house. Merle flicked on her flashlight. Francie stayed outside, waiting for the service to pick up. When they did she stumbled through her French again, trying to explain they needed new door shutters. Nailed up plywood wouldn't work. They needed to be able to enter the house.

"I'll leave the new padlocks in a cabinet in the kitchen." That was a tricky one to translate into her bad French, but she felt like she'd gotten it communicated. "Also a pane of glass in the door, a small one, must be replaced. I can measure it for you. And can you change locks? Yes, then, please change the main door lock and mail the keys to the real estate agent." She read off the name and address from the sign.

When that was accomplished Francie sighed and looked around the yard. The weeds had been flattened by car tires, presumably by the new real estate agent. She had hoped he would find someone to clean up the yard, but it looked as dead and unappealing as ever. It might take years to sell this place. She turned to go inside when the man appeared around the corner of the house. He stopped, squinting at her.

"Miss Bennett. We meet again."

Francie froze, fear coursing through her, striking her speechless. Clément Boudreau, or whatever his real name was, stepped closer and she backed away. Finally she croaked, "Get away from me."

"But you have something that belongs to me. It would not be right for you to steal it, now would it?"

"You broke it, you jerk. You threw it into the creek and it broke in a million pieces."

"That was unfortunate."

"No shit. Now, get out of here." She glanced at the house. "Merle! Come out here!"

"Where is it? Do you know? Maybe you are too stupid to know what you have."

"Merle! Now!"

The door opened and Merle stood in the doorway, shielding Phoebe behind her. "What's going on here?"

"It's him. The guy who attacked me and stole the sculpture."

Merle stepped out on the stoop. "Why come back, Monsieur? What is it you want?"

Phoebe peeked around Merle. "Hey, he's wearing the sweater."

Francie smiled. "Are you—whatever your name really is—Are you homeless? Or just an ordinary thief, looking for things to steal."

Boudreau had stopped about five paces from Francie, with Merle still on the front stoop with Phoebe. Francie took a step backward.

"You've got white hair," Phoebe piped up. "We found your hair! You're old!"

He moved closer to Francie, quickly. "Let's go inside and find the sculpture." He grabbed for her arm. She pulled away, lost her balance, and stepped sideways. He grabbed for her again, catching her before she could fall. "Move."

"Let go of her," Merle ordered, to no avail. Francie squirmed, grunting and cursing. His grip was surprisingly strong for an old man.

Suddenly Phoebe was in action, jumping forward, kicking wildly, hitting Boudreau in the kneecap then following with another swift kick to the groin. He startled, wincing, and dropped Francie's arm. Phoebe growled in fierce attack mode, ready for more, but Francie had put her left foot behind his right one as Merle shoved him backward off his feet. He fell hard on the packed gravel, falling back and hitting his head.

While he lay stunned, Merle grabbed both Francie and Phoebe and ran for the car. They threw themselves inside and locked the doors. Francie fumbled with the keys and started the engine, reversing in a hail of gravel that sprayed Boudreau as he rose to his feet. He shook a fist at them, shouting, but they weren't listening.

Merle was laughing, high-fiving with Phoebe. The girl was yelling, "Take that! And that!" Francie steered wildly around corners, hunched over the wheel, saying, "Oh, shit, oh, shit," in endless loops. She drove until they reached the village with the café where they had eaten lunch. She stopped the car and collapsed over the wheel.

Merle and Phoebe were still in high spirits. They regaled each other with recaps of the kicking and tripping as Francie gulped for air. Finally she looked up at their smiling faces.

"What—the hell—was that?"

"That was little Phoebe taking down a grown man!" Merle said.

"With the help of you two. I saw that trick. Our teacher tried to show us how to do it ourselves, but it works better with two people."

"Our father, Jack, taught us that one. We used to practice it while we were jumping on our beds."

Francie got out of the car and gulped the cool breeze. She opened the back door. She definitely wasn't completely over her adventures of that other summer, when she felt so vulnerable and helpless.

"You drive. I need to lie down."

As she drove home Merle told Phoebe the story of Francie's bravery that summer, when she'd been kidnapped by some bad Italians looking for a dog. She was tied to a bed in a barn, Merle told Phoebe, leaving off some of the more horrendous parts like the barn being set on fire. "She was so brave. She ran right out at the end and saved herself."

Phoebe looked over the seat back. "I bet that was really cool."

Francie lay flat on the back seat, arm over her eyes. "Not as cool as you, little ninja. Not as cool as you."

As THEY PARKED the rental car in the lot outside the village walls, Francie decided it was time to call the police. She made Merle talk to them, tell them they had seen the man who stole the artwork, and give them directions to Villa Pardoux. She told them he had broken into the house and attacked Francie. Once again they had to admit they didn't know his real name.

"Can't the cops figure out who he is?" Phoebe asked as they walked home. "We can be witnesses! We'll go to the thing where the guys hold up numbers and you choose one."

"The lineup," Merle said. "That would be kind of fun."

"Before that they have to catch the guy," Francie said morosely. "That's twice now he's slipped away from us. Although technically I guess we slipped away from him this time."

"We kicked away!" Phoebe cried, demonstrating her skills on thin air. "We won't let bad guys get us. Not like that mean man who got my mom. I would have kicked him so hard. Then tripped him and kicked him in the nuts!"

The sisters exchanged glances. "Did your mom get attacked?" Francie asked.

"Yeah, but it was only a few bruises and her purse got stolen." Phoebe seemed nonchalant about it. "That's why she has wine every night. She says her nerves are shot."

"I understand that," Francie said. "I feel a little shaky myself."

Merle threw an arm over her shoulders. "Luckily I have wine."

"What are nerves exactly?" Phoebe asked.

"Electric energy in your body," Merle said. "I think she means she feels upset or worried."

Phoebe listened, nodded, and ran ahead to the front door of the house, rattling the padlock. "At least *your* house is still locked up," she called back to them.

"Oh, good," Francie muttered. "We don't have to kick anyone in the nuts."

THAT EVENING Pascal was still at the dinner table, finishing his wine, as the knock came at the door. The sisters had told him the story at dinner, and Phoebe had demonstrated her technique on the attacker, in high spirits. He had cancelled his undercover work for the week after the theft of the plaster cast. Tonight he retrieved his gun from his car and brought it into the house after hearing the story, but he hesitated now about going upstairs to get it. Merle stuck her head out of the kitchen.

"Are you going to get that?"

He wiped his mouth. The door shutters were padlocked. He spoke through them, asking who was there. "Gendarme," came the answer. He unlocked the shutters. A young policeman in navy blue tipped his hat to Pascal and asked for Francie. Pascal let him in, looked up and down the street, and relocked the front door behind him. The story of the thief at the villa had enraged him. Why had the women gone there again? But he kept it to himself. He couldn't protect them everywhere, every minute, and the girl had proved quite a powerful adversary. He smiled, thinking about her karate moves in the garden.

If only they had waited for him. But Merle said Francie was set on going. She could be quite stubborn. One would have thought the theft of the art object would have made her cautious.

Pascal called for her. Merle knocked on the bathroom door. Francie emerged in her jeans and college sweatshirt, her hair pulled back from her face.

"What is it?" she asked the gendarme. "*Parlez-vous anglais?*"

He shook his head. Pascal told him he would translate and took out his police identification card to show the gendarme. He glanced at it, at Pascal, and returned his attention to Francie.

"Madame, I am here about the assault. We have a photograph for you to look at, to see if you can identify the man." The gendarme reached into an envelope and pulled out a photograph printed on computer paper. He handed it to Francie.

She looked at it for a long moment and handed it to Pascal. He raised his eyebrows at her with a slight nod.

"That's him," she said. "Both assaults. He stole a valuable sculpture too. We reported it."

"Who is he?" Pascal said. "I can identify him as the thief as well. I saw him later that day."

"His name is Xavier Voclain. He is known to the Police Nationale. We got a tip from another case. Thank you, Madame. Monsieur." He tipped his hat again and was gone.

Francie sat down on the settee. "Will they get him now? Please tell me they'll get him."

"Now that they have a name, yes. He will be found," Pascal assured her.

Merle sat down by Francie. "Okay?"

Francie nodded. "I just wish I was a ninja."

CHAPTER THIRTY-ONE

*L*ater that evening Francie sat in the garden, a thin blanket pulled around her. The stars were popping out overhead. Dylan called from his office in Paris. "What happened? Your text was so cryptic."

"Well, let me first say that your daughter is awesome. Whoever got her those karate lessons was genius. She knows her stuff."

"Ooo-kay. What did she do?"

Francie gave him the short version about Phoebe kicking the thief, leaving out the part about being so scared she almost passed out. Why had she gotten so panicked after the attack was over? She needed to think about that more.

She told him the cops had identified the man who attacked her and stole the sculpture. "His name is Xavier Voclain. Somebody gave them a tip, he said. They had his photo."

"Who is he?"

"I don't know. Can you look him up online? I'm mildly curious."

The tapping of computer keys. "I'm searching. Spell the last name." She made a guess, as the gendarme hadn't spelled it. "I'm sorry you had to go through that again."

"I seem to be a magnet for bad guys."

"Well, I'm attracted to you."

She smiled. "And good guys. Listen, I need to tell you something Phoebe mentioned. You probably know this, but she said Rebecca was mugged and her purse was stolen. That's why she—quote—has to drink wine every night—unquote."

"She was mugged? When was this?"

"I don't know. But maybe she started Phoebe on karate so she could defend herself in a similar situation. It is working, let me tell you. She is fierce." Francie looked up at some birds flying overhead and thought of flying home. She was actually getting homesick for her tiny apartment. "Find anything on Xavier?"

"Ah—I ran his criminal record. Wow. It's four pages, all sorts of petty crimes: shoplifting, pickpocketing, car theft—not so petty— assault and battery, robbery. He's been an active boy. It goes back twenty years, possibly further."

"Pascal assures me they will find him now."

"They must be familiar with his haunts. Did he hurt you?"

She pulled up her sleeve and looked at the mark made by his grip. "Not really. Hey, are you thinking of going home soon?"

"I was thinking Wednesday. Does that work for you, or are you going to stay with your sister?"

"I'm ready to head back. I'll bring Phoebe up to Paris."

It was decided they would take the train on Monday, have a day to play tourist, and fly out on Wednesday. Dylan would arrange it. He wasn't looking forward to calling Rebecca to tell her.

"Ask her about the mugging. Maybe it wasn't that bad. Or maybe it was worse. You should know."

They said goodbye. Francie sat back in the little green chair, shivering as a breeze blew in. She should really get her coat but wasn't quite ready to move. She closed her eyes, trying to calm the panic from the day that still lived in her chest. That old man, that angry face, the way he sneered at her—she tried to get angry instead, a sure way to kill the anxiety. Then the words he said rang in her head.

Maybe you are too stupid to know what you have.

Let's go inside and find the sculpture.

But he knew the sculpture was in bits, ruined. Was there something encrypted on the plaster, some clue? Or some *other* sculpture? This Xavier had been in the house multiple times and he hadn't found it. Maybe it was tiny, because there were no hiding places in that house Francie and Merle hadn't searched. They'd looked in the wine cave, the cabinet there, the kitchen, the dining room's built-in cupboards, the attic.

Everywhere.

Maybe she *was* too stupid to know what she had. Or maybe she didn't have anything. Maybe he was just blowing smoke.

Merle stuck her head out the back door. "Phoebe wants to ride her bicycle around the village. Want to come?"

The evening was perfect for a brisk walk. The sisters paused in the middle of the village, watching Phoebe ride circles around the dry fountain in the center of the plaza. Francie felt better, less anxious, after the exercise and fresh air. Merle reminded her she was always saying she would join a gym and that it would be good for stress. Francie rolled her eyes. Merle was always so *sensible*.

They walked back to the house. Francie told her sister they would be leaving on Monday. Merle hugged her arm and said that made her sad. But Francie had a law practice to manage, and she understood.

They watched Phoebe run up the stairs to get ready for bed. "She is doing so well," Merle said.

"Weirdly I think the attack was a blessing in disguise," Francie said. "It gave her such a boost of confidence."

"It's been fun having a kid here again. I miss my little guy." Her "little guy" was now nineteen, in college, and over six feet tall.

"We've been getting along pretty well, don't you think?" Francie asked. "Phoebe and me."

Merle went to the kitchen to put water on for tea. "Are you kidding? You're like best friends now. She attacked a guy for you."

Francie sat down on the settee and smiled. Maybe it would work, this stepparent thing. She realized she wanted it to work, for Phoebe's sake and Dylan's sake, but most of all for her own sake. Her life was so centered on work-work-work, and now there was more. Or at least the possibility of more. She would look back on this time in France with Phoebe (and Dylan, of course) with a rush of fondness, no—of love. She loved this time together. She loved Phoebe. It brought a tear to her eye. She really cared for that little ninja.

Merle brought out a teapot and two cups on a tray and set it on the steamer trunk. She poured them each a cup of weak herbal tea, the way they liked it. They sat back in their chairs, warming their hands, content.

"We should look at those old clothes before you go," Merle said.

"Now?"

"Do you want to wait until morning?"

"I'm too wound up to sleep. Let's get it over with."

Merle moved the tray to the dining table. Francie unlatched the trunk and opened it wide. The little drawers set into the lid were on their sides. She pulled one open, thinking of her theory about the tiny object. Was it tucked into a drawer?

"This must have been used sitting on its end. See the hooks for hangers up here?" Merle pointed to a metal piece attached to one end of the lower section. "Should we upend it?"

"Let's get the clothes out first," Francie said. "They'll all fall in a pile if you do that." She continued opening the tiny drawers. They must have been used for jewelry and gloves and unmentionables on long journeys.

Merle picked up a lace dress, the one that looked like a wedding gown. It was yellowed and torn. She laid it across the chair and reached for another, a pale pink flapper dress with lots of beads. "I love this."

"Keep it."

"I think I will." Merle draped it on a dining chair and examined the intricate beadwork. "It needs some repairs, but not too many."

Francie finished with the drawers. They were empty except for dead moths, no treasures to be had. She dug into the clothing. A man's suit with a cutaway jacket had many holes in it. Below it she felt something hard. She pushed back two other suits and a pair of silk hose.

The color screamed out at her and she stepped back.

"Merle. It's the—the IKB. The blue," she whispered.

In the bottom of the trunk was another body cast, this one the reverse of the plaster, the outer contours of the young woman's body like in life. Made, obviously, from the plaster cast and painted that iconic blue.

"What the—" Merle gasped.

"He told me. The thief told me there was another sculpture. He said I was too stupid to know what I had. But how did he know?"

Merle kneeled down by the trunk and felt the sculpture. "What's it made of?"

Francie kneeled beside her. She knocked lightly on the piece. "Something like plastic, I think."

"Did he make this? That artist?"

"I guess. I don't think Axelle knew. She said her parents paid him to destroy the plaster cast a couple months after it was made. Plenty of time to make a cast of the cast."

"Should we—can we pick it up?" Merle asked.

Gently they each took an end and lifted the cast out of the trunk and set it on the dining table to examine it. It was not terribly heavy, the material it was made from just a half inch thick. Francie took some photos of it, anxious now that it might somehow be stolen like the other one. They found a tiny initial that appeared to be "YK." The sculpture felt delicate and pure, a true-to-life rendition of a young female body, all in brilliant International Klein Blue, from her swan-like neck to her belly button to her pubes. There was no prurient nature to it, no sexiness, just a young woman, as she was. They exclaimed on its beauty, and Axelle's nubile perfection.

Then they put it back in the trunk and covered it with the mildewed suits and tattered dresses. Francie insisted Merle keep the flapper dress for herself. The rest went back in the trunk to conceal the sculpture.

"We can't tell anyone," Francie said. "Not a soul."

Merle nodded. "I looked up Klein online. It must be worth a fortune. Will you take it to Paris?"

"In the trunk?"

"We'll think of something. Does he know? The thief? That there was another one?"

"I think he does. That's why he went back to the villa." Francie rubbed her face nervously. "Is Pascal coming back tonight?"

Merle looked at her watch. "Soon, I hope."

CHAPTER THIRTY-TWO

*M*erle called Pascal and asked him to come home. He was nearby in a bar, talking to locals, his best sources for gossip about fraud, he said. He returned to the house with a worried look on his face. The sisters showed him the newly discovered sculpture in the trunk. He immediately began to speculate about the thief returning and suggested he stay up all night to keep watch. Merle argued they could take turns. He agreed, as he was tired from the long day. He thought a break-in was unlikely, but he would be upstairs at the ready when the women took a shift.

He took the first watch. Probably the thief, being an old man, would make an attempt early rather than late, if indeed he knew they had the sculpture. Pascal had his gun at his side, sitting at the dining table, reading the case file for the vineyard owner he was checking out for possible fraud. He made notes from his visit there today, the harvest trucks nearly done carting off the grapes. When he finished with that he made himself an espresso and logged onto the internet on his phone, looking at celebrity sites and movie stars until his eyes dried out.

At two A.M. he woke Francie, shaking her gently. She bolted

upright, making the sound of a wounded cat. "Sorry," he whispered. "It is time."

This rotating watch made Francie think of old Westerns, someone always keeping an eye out for outlaws or Indians. Was it ridiculous? Maybe. Was it paranoid? Not necessarily. And there was no way they could all sleep through this night. Not while sitting on the Yves Klein.

She pulled on her robe and slippers and tiptoed down the stairs. The room was chilly. She turned up the electric heater in the salon and made herself a cup of tea. As she waited for the water to boil she gazed out the kitchen window. The garden was bathed in moonlight even though the moon was still just a fingernail. Silvery leaves shimmered against the back wall. Vines trailed in a crazy pattern against the stone. She would miss Merle's garden. She always would miss it, every time she left. There was something so secure and calm about it.

Tea in hand, she turned on her iPad and read the news from the US. She'd been so cut off all these weeks, which had been great. She had to read old stories to know what the new ones were talking about.

Time ticked by slowly. Once she thought she heard something on the street. Her adrenaline spiked, on alert. Then the quiet returned. Maybe a cat had knocked over a garbage can. She got up and did the rounds of the windows. The shutters were secure in the front and sides. She couldn't see out, but everything seemed okay. She opened the back door and peered around the garden, then relocked the door.

At three thirty she was sure she was being overly anxious. Maybe the *policiers* had already caught Xavier Voclain. Surely they had. Did he have another car? Did he fix his flat tires? Was he on foot, on a bus, on a train? The questions went round and round.

Just fifteen minutes more. She sighed, trying to keep her eyes off her watch. She rubbed her face hard and gave herself a little slap on the cheek to stay awake. She was settling back on the sofa when she heard it. In the garden. Definitely *something*.

She went to the kitchen door. The upper portion had small windowpanes. She could see the hulking pissoir that Merle had glammed up for her laundry. The new tree she'd planted, a little fruit tree, some kind of apple. The garden gate, closed and locked. She craned her neck to look in the corner of the garden, next to the house by the pear trees, when the face appeared at the door, inches from hers, up close.

And very scary.

The thug, Antoine, was right at the door, rattling the knob. She jumped back, gasping. He shouted, pulled his fist back, and smashed through a windowpane. Blood spurted from his knuckles as glass scattered on the tile floor.

"Pascal!"

Francie ran to the stairs. "Pascal! Come quick!" The thud of footsteps reassured her. "Your gun!"

Antoine stood in the kitchen, legs apart, shaking his bloody fist and swearing. Francie backed past the stairs, to the edge of the big dish cupboard. Pascal was dressed but in his socks, pounding down the stairs. "He's in the kitchen!" she cried.

The two men collided at the bottom of the stairs. Pascal was a tall, strong man, but Antoine was huge, wide, with a head like a melon. He tried to head-butt Pascal as they struggled. Pascal had the gun in his hand, but Antoine held his arm straight up, pointing it at the ceiling. There was grunting and swinging and shoving. Chairs overturned. Antoine stepped hard on Pascal's stockinged foot, which made Pascal grunt in pain and jam his knee into the man's groin. But they were still in a stalemate until Antoine swung Pascal around and dropped him against the wooden back of the settee.

The gun squirted out of Pascal's hand and skated across the wood planks toward Francie. The men were breathing hard, staring at each other. Francie reached for the pistol instinctively. She held it with both hands, pointed at Antoine.

"*Arrêtez!*" she yelled, glad she remembered some French——stop!—— in the heat of the moment. "*Laissez-faire l'homme.*" That was wrong, but who cared.

Pascal and the thug didn't pay attention to her, focused on their fight. They grunted, at another standoff. Antoine reached down, grabbing Pascal's shirt and pulling him to his feet so they could grapple some more. Pascal landed a solid punch on the man's jaw. Antoine only flinched. He was more strength than finesse and missed his return punch, catching air with his bloody hand. Then he was angry, swearing as he picked up Pascal again like a rag doll and tossed him over the sofa. He hit the corner of the steamer trunk hard and rolled onto the floor.

"I will shoot you," Francie declared. "Is it loaded, Pascal?"

"Yes, but—"

Antoine turned on her like a bulldozer changing direction. He took two strides. On the second step, Francie pointed to his legs and fired.

The sound of the gunshot was deafening in the small room. Francie thought she'd missed her target, the man's kneecap. They all paused as the sound faded, looking at Antoine's leg. She had hit him in the thigh. A bloody hole in his pants told the story. The recoil from the pistol had thrown her back against the wall. Antoine had a strange, pissed-off look on his big, ugly face. He touched his bloody leg then looked at her and growled like a bear again.

It wasn't stopping him. She couldn't believe it. He gathered himself and took another step toward her. Francie pointed the gun at his other leg, a little lower, and fired again.

He was closer this time and her aim was better. He howled, collapsing on the floor, holding his knee. Pascal was back on his feet. He gave Antoine a kick in the kidneys for good measure then held out his hand.

"The gun, Francie." She handed it over silently. "*Merci.*"

CHAPTER THIRTY-THREE

"*P*ascal! Oh, my god."

Merle stood barefoot on the stairs, staring in horror at the man bleeding on the floor.

"Get a sheet or towel, Merle. *Vite*," Pascal said, putting the gun in the back of his pants. He had called the emergency number already and asked for police and an ambulance. "It could be a while before the medics come."

Francie stood frozen, watching the big man writhe and moan. She didn't want to move, to step close to him. There was a spatter of blood on her slippers.

She had a shot a man, twice.

She hadn't killed him—thank god—but she hadn't hesitated either. She just shot him in the kneecaps. It was difficult to believe she was capable of it, but the evidence was undeniable. She could still feel the pistol in her hand, the weight and lethality of it.

Merle ran down the stairs with a gray sheet. Pascal kneeled and began wrapping it around the man's knee. He had a wound in the other leg, but this one, the second bullet hole, was the one bleeding. A dark puddle of blood wet the wood floor, growing by the minute.

Merle looked up the stairs then back to Francie. "Go check on Phoebe. She's upset."

Francie backed away from the wounded man, skirting Pascal and Merle to get to the stairs. *I'm upset. Someone should comfort me.* As she stepped up the stairs she realized she was wrong. She wasn't shaking. She wasn't panicked. And she wasn't upset about shooting that guy. He deserved it. She was only upset that he had broken into the house and tried to hurt her. But she had put a stop to that.

She was sort of *righteous,* a real badass.

Phoebe cowered on her bed, arms around her knees, crying. Francie ran to her, took her in her arms, and tried to soothe her. She rubbed the girl's head and back. "It's okay now. It's over."

After a fresh batch of crying Phoebe gulped and looked up at Francie. "Did Pascal shoot somebody? Is he dead?"

"No, he's alive. He'll be fine. It was me, not Pascal. He dropped the gun and I picked it up. I got the guy in the kneecap like you told me."

Phoebe blinked away her tears. "What?"

"The vulnerable place, the kneecap. He might have a limp, but he'll be okay."

"Is it the homeless man? Did you shoot the old homeless man?" Her voice rose in hysteria.

Francie hugged her again. "No, sweetie. It was another guy."

She sat with Phoebe on the edge of the bed, holding her hands, reassuring her that everything would be fine. Then the sirens started blaring. An urgent battering on the front door. That would be the police. The wounded man groaned and thrashed. There were loud bursts of French, terse orders. Then Pascal's voice, low and calm.

Francie wanted to go downstairs, but Phoebe needed her. She tried to get the girl to lie down again, but what were the chances any of them would sleep more tonight? Phoebe insisted on sitting up, putting an arm around Francie's waist and cuddling tight. "I'm sorry this happened, Phoebe." *Your father is going to kill me.*

"Did he break in?"

"He smashed a pane of glass in the back door. He must have jumped over the wall."

"So Pascal—I mean, *you* had no choice, right?"

"I certainly saw it that way." She hoped the gendarmes would see it the same way. When would they ask her to come down and explain? It was self-defense. A giant thug against a small woman. They would understand, wouldn't they?

She closed her eyes and the scene replayed in her head. The struggle with Pascal, the brute tossing him over the sofa. The gun skittering across the old plank floor, spinning. Her hand, picking it up. It felt so right in her hand, so natural. The warm grip. The man turning on her, his awful scowl, his primitive growls. She shivered.

More yelling and loud Frenchmen from downstairs. What the hell was going on? Had the man recovered? Finally Merle appeared at the top of the stairs. She walked over and sat on Francie's bed. She looked pale, and there was blood on her hands.

"Pascal told them he shot him," Merle whispered. "So just go along with that. He's a cop, so it will be all right."

Francie frowned. In some small, stupid way she wanted credit for the shooting. She had saved the fricking day, right? Then she thought: that's ridiculous. She should be ashamed of shooting another human. It went against everything she believed in, peace and non-violence and the belief in legal justice. But sometimes, well—sometimes they deserved it. He brought it on himself. It was self-defense. She remembered her fear last winter when the young lawyer surprised her in the parking lot on a dark night. She felt afraid, powerless. Something had changed in her. She felt different now, stronger.

"Be practical," Merle urged, watching her face. "I think he's also not cool with somebody else using his police weapon. He could get in trouble."

Pascal taking the blame made sense. He would smooth things over as he always did.

"Okay. That's fine," Francie said.

"He's lying to the police?" Phoebe said, her eyes widening.

"Just this once," Merle said. "For Francie, so she doesn't have to go make a statement at the police station and all that."

Phoebe's eyes flashed. "But it's a lie. Lying is wrong. My dad always says so."

"You're right," Francie said. "It is. But sometimes grown-ups lie for a good reason."

"Like helping you?"

"Right." Francie mouthed "thank you" to Merle.

"But you had no choice. You said you had to shoot him," Phoebe said.

"True." Francie rubbed her back. This line of reasoning wasn't going to help. Not now.

Finally another siren announced the arrival of the ambulance. Merle went to the window overlooking the street. Red light bounced around the room. "Every one of our neighbors is out in the street. All five of them."

"Big excitement for old Rue de Poitiers," Francie said.

"Who is that guy, Francie? Do you know him?" Merle asked.

"The appraiser called him Antoine. He was the driver the day they stole the sculpture. Boudreau's sidekick."

"So Boudreau told him the other sculpture was here. But how did they know about a second body cast? Did Axelle say anything?"

"She thought the plaster one was destroyed years ago. She never mentioned a second one." But Boudreau—Voclain actually—had known about it. From somebody.

Merle walked back to the bed and sat again. Downstairs the commotion rose: groaning and cursing and shouting. Phoebe rested her head on Francie's shoulder, eyes closed, calm now. Merle reached out her fist to Francie and whispered, "Case of courage . . ."

Francie smiled, tapping her fist onto Merle's. This might be the first time she believed in this Bennett sister motto in her whole life. A shiver went up her spine.

"Bucket of freaking balls."

BY DAWN the *policiers* and the medics were gone. They had taken Pascal's statement on the spot and dragged Antoine off to the hospital. Later that day they were told his name was really Lucas Laflèche, wanted by the Police Nationale in connection with numerous home invasions and burglaries.

The sisters stared at the dark red stain on the wood floor that evening. Francie had already thrown her clothes into her suitcase for the trip to Paris tomorrow, wrapping them around the body cast. Xavier Voclain was still at large; she was taking no chances.

"It may never come out," Merle said, crossing her arms and frowning at the spot.

"Sorry," Francie said. She'd already apologized for the shooting, the front door being broken, the back door glass, a cracked planter in the garden, and everything else. "I seem to attract messes."

"A bloodstain is a new wrinkle, but it's not the first time someone broke in here," Merle said, throwing an arm over Francie's shoulders. "Hopefully the last though."

"God, yes."

Phoebe came in from the garden, pushing her bicycle across the kitchen. "You can leave that here," Francie said. "For when you come again."

"I want to give it to that girl," Phoebe said, rounding the sofa and heading for the front door. "The one around the corner. She doesn't have a bike."

"We'll go with you," the sisters said in unison. They looked at each other, laughed, and said, "Jinx."

Phoebe made one last ride down the cobblestones of Rue de Poitiers in the twilight. Madame Suchet waved from her stoop. She'd been over at midday with a tart and a need for details about the action in the night. Her sister stood at her half door and gave them a nod. Francie suggested going by Albert's house one last time. Phoebe turned right and right again, rounding the block, high on her pedals, hair flying.

"She seems no worse for all the violence," Merle said.

"In some ways she seems stronger." Francie's inner voice said: *And so do you.*

"The French countryside agrees with her, for all its troublemakers."

"It agrees with all of us."

By the time they reached Albert's he was on his front step, talking animatedly to Phoebe. She didn't wait for them, mounting her bicycle again, waving to the old man, and heading back to the corner.

"Thanks, Albert," Francie called, turning back to run after the girl. "See you again!"

"Come back soon," the old priest called.

EARLY MONDAY MORNING Francie drove her rental car, that little black Citroën, with Phoebe in the front seat and the luggage in the back seat, to the train station in Bergerac. Merle and Pascal had hugged them and said goodbye from their front door. Pascal gave Phoebe a squeeze and said, "*Á bientôt,* Frenchie. See you soon."

Repairs were underway behind them, a man working on the broken door. Inside a glass repairman was replacing the windowpane in the kitchen door. Francie knew her sister and Pascal would have plenty to distract them from their departure.

Phoebe watched the fields and traffic and sky in silence as Francie drove. At the train station there were delays as they turned in the car, but soon they had boarded and were on the way back to Bordeaux, then Paris.

Phoebe couldn't seem to get enough of the countryside this time, her eyes glued to the stone villages with orange tile roofs and old men and mothers with babies at train stations and the yellow leaves of autumn. She pointed at white cows and blackbirds and steeples. Finally she turned to Francie and sighed.

"That was fun, wasn't it," she said with a contented look.

"Yes," Francie replied, a little surprised. "Yes, it was."

CHAPTER THIRTY-FOUR
PARIS

The first thing that Phoebe said to her father, before "hello" or "how are you" or "I missed you," was, at high volume: "Francie shot a man in the kneecaps!"

The day before had been so busy with visits from the gendarmes, cleaning up blood, and packing dirty laundry around art objects that Francie hadn't called Dylan. Now, seeing his face, she regretted it. She should have warned him.

"We had an intruder," she said. "I'm sorry. Can we talk in the bedroom?"

They walked around the suitcases in the hallway, leaving Phoebe playing a game on her tablet in the salon. Francie sat on the bed while he paced the floor, an angry, hurt look on his face that she didn't like. "I should have called you, I'm so sorry." She explained about the new sculpture found in the steamer trunk, about Antoine breaking into the house, the heavy for Xavier Voclain.

She dialed into detective mode: "The one thing I don't understand is where Voclain got his information. How did he know about you? Plus he knew about both the plaster cast and this new one. No one else did. I think they were following us, but it doesn't add up."

"Where is it? Did you leave it down there?"

"It's in my bag." She rolled her suitcase into the bedroom and set it carefully on its back on the floor. Unzipping it, she pushed aside her clothes to reveal the pillowcase they'd placed around the resin cast. She pulled down the top of the case to reveal the intense blue color.

"International Klein Blue, I assume," Dylan said.

"Worth a small fortune," Francie whispered. "I didn't tell Phoebe about it because I didn't want her to blurt it out somewhere. We've got to keep it on the down low." She covered it again and zipped her bag. "At least until I talk to Axelle."

"Wait. Back up." He held up his hands. "You shot a man?"

"It was Xavier's sidekick on the day he stole the plaster cast. A big guy, like a boxer. He broke into the house Saturday night. Actually it was about five the next morning. Pascal came downstairs with his gun. They struggled and the gun fell on the floor. I picked it up."

"And—? Fired?"

"He came at me. He was huge, Dylan, like a tank. He threw Pascal across the room."

"Is he dead?"

"I only shot him in the legs."

"So he's alive?"

"They patched him up. He's already confessed to the theft of the plaster cast. And gave the cops information about Voclain, where he's hiding. They may have found him by now."

Francie felt her anxiety ratchet up again. With Voclain possibly still running around the Dordogne she was on edge, even far away in Paris. Her sense of righteousness from after the shooting was gone. Now she was second-guessing herself. If Dylan thought she was a crazy hothead, she didn't know what she'd do. But what could she have done to avoid shooting that bastard?

"Don't be mad. Please. After the first attack, where Phoebe kicked the guy, I was a mess, unlike your daughter. I just collapsed into a soggy pile. But something changed after that. I hated being that person. I found out I could stand up for myself, be brave. Do what had to be done. Be, well, not a ninja, but strong. I never want to be a soggy pile of fear again."

He crossed his arms, his face still set in anger. What was he thinking?

She took a deep breath. "Dylan, I've never shot a gun before—ever. And I hope to never shoot one again. It was self-defense. Pure instinct. And Phoebe didn't see any of it."

He looked at her, examining her face. He rubbed his chin. "She seems okay."

"She is, I think. Merle thinks she seems unfazed by it all. Maybe even more confident after she kicked that old guy in the, um, well, you ask her. I think we're alike, Phoebe and me. Neither of us like being a victim."

He relaxed and sat beside her on the bed. "I talked to Rebecca. She did get mugged back in the spring. She was hurt a little but mostly so rattled that she had to take time off work. That's probably why she got fired. She didn't want to tell me about it, afraid it would affect custody."

Francie frowned. She didn't even know what Rebecca did for a living. "Is she better now?"

"She finally started counseling. Had to face her demons, she said. The break, the time alone, helped her, I think. Pushed her to find somebody to talk to."

"I'm glad. You know what Phoebe told me on the train? 'Well, that was fun, wasn't it.'"

He smiled. "Thank you for taking her to the country. I know you took her as a favor and couldn't have predicted all this. I don't know what I would have done with her here in Paris."

Dylan hugged her tightly. Francie felt her anxiety drain away. They would be okay. She so wanted them all to be okay. She was surprised when Dylan wiped tears off her cheeks.

"I'm sorry about all of it. I never—" She sniffed as a few more tears fell.

"Planned on getting attacked? Of course you didn't. Are you all right?"

She nodded. "I just want to talk to Axelle."

Dylan got up and went to his briefcase, sitting on the floor. "I found something. In Mathilde's file. I finally got my hands on the full file, going back to the nineties, when she brought her business to us."

Francie blinked, clearing her vision. "Really?"

He pulled a single, wrinkled sheet of stationery from his briefcase and held it out. "Credit Suisse handled her money. One person in particular."

THE JAIL where Axelle was being held wasn't the worst place of incarceration in Paris, but it had little to recommend it that sunny Tuesday morning. The walls were old and crusty, the guards foreboding. Francie waited in the visitors' anteroom at the *maison d'arrêt,* the short-stay portion of the huge penitentiary, standing against a wall, looking at her battered fingernails. It was early; she'd only had a *café crème* on the way. She was to meet Axelle's attorney here. Dylan had gotten through to Marcel Garnier last night. She still wasn't sure if she would be allowed to speak to Axelle. If not, at least the attorney could ask her some questions.

The chairs in the waiting room were worn. Half the room was full of visitors, young and old, most with worried expressions. They all had a chance to examine the chipped paint and scuffed floor in silence.

Garnier finally arrived twenty minutes later. He wore a gray suit with a red tie and white shirt, very lawyerly. "Monsieur Garnier?" She introduced herself.

"Oh, yes." He looked rushed but paused to examine her. "What is it you want with Madame Fourcier?"

"I have something that belongs to her."

"And? You are giving it back?"

"I need instructions."

The attorney squinted at her, shrugged, and led the way down a corridor, where they were signed in and patted down for weapons. It was less invasive than the prison she'd visited in the spring, but it was still a prison. She wasn't allowed to take her coat or purse inside.

In the visiting room, a dreary place with mold and bad vibes, Axelle looked smaller, as if life inside prison had shrunk her, taken away some of her lifeblood. She was pale, her hair ragged. She had a cut on her nose that had scabbed over. She saw Francie and straight-ened, surprised.

"Miss Bennett. Monsieur Garnier. *Bonjour*," she said tentatively, her guard up.

They sat down opposite her at the small, scuffed table, dragging over an extra chair. The attorney began telling her some procedural matters related to her case. He seemed optimistic that new evidence would soon come to light if she was patient. Then Axelle turned to Francie.

"Why are you here?"

"I just got back from the southwest, from my sister's in the Dordogne." She paused. "I saw Villa Pardoux. It's a lovely place. I hope you get to see it again someday."

"I very much doubt it. You're selling it, right? So that Monsieur here doesn't have to forgo his truffles and wine?"

Garnier winced. Francie continued, "It's been listed with an agent. So you know, it's been broken into a few times. I wouldn't put a lot of hope on getting a big payday out of it."

Axelle frowned. "Naturally. Because the republic continues to toy with my fate. So much for your truffles."

Garnier said, "Do not concern yourself with that, Madame."

"Oh, you're not going to bill me?"

He gave her a funny smile and turned to Francie. "Are you finished, Madame?"

Francie ignored him. "Axelle, there is another *objet d'art*. A cast made from the original plaster cast—does that make sense? It's your, um, the torso again, but lifelike, not in reverse. Made out of some-thing lightweight, plastic or resin." She glanced at Garnier. "It's blue."

"What?" Axelle cried.

Francie nodded, letting her figure it out for herself. She didn't want to go into details in front of the attorney. At this point she didn't trust anyone. "One of the thieves has been caught. The driver for Xavier Voclain."

"Voclain?" Garnier asked sharply. "The man who visited madame?"

"He visited you?" Francie asked. "Do you know him?"

Axelle looked embarrassed. "He and I went to school together. We were in the protests together."

"We have informed the police of his visits to madame. We are aware," Garnier said.

"That he is a habitual criminal? Did you know that, Axelle?"

"I didn't know his history or what he was doing. He gave me a string of lies."

"Someone tipped off the police to him." Francie raised her eyebrows in question.

Axelle looked away, silent. Garnier said, "As I said, I mentioned his name to the authorities, but not in relation to your business in the provinces, Madame. I was not aware of that."

So it *was* Axelle. Francie leaned in. "Did he know about the sculpture from you? Did you tell him?"

Axelle shook her head. "So many years have passed. Perhaps."

"Could you and Blandine and Xavier have talked about it? Back in the sixties?"

Axelle's eyes widened. "It's possible," she muttered, staring at Francie. "I was very upset when my parents found out and demanded it be crushed."

"You said Blandine went with you to Yves Klein's studio," Francie continued, trying to put it all together. "You left Paris but could she have known what really happened to the sculptures, that they survived? She kept up with your family. Could she have asked Mathilde about the sculptures, at your parents' funerals maybe? Or maybe gone back to Klein's studio for some reason? Could she have been killed because of what she knew?"

Garnier crossed his arms. "Explain please, Madame."

"Before Bozonnet took over Mathilde's finances she used a bank trust department. That bank was Credit Suisse. Blandine's husband was Stephan Baudet. He was older than Blandine by at least ten years. He worked in the trust department of Credit Suisse. By the time he passed away in 1996, he had been head of the trust department there for ten years."

Axelle frowned at her. "So?"

"One of his oldest clients was your aunt, Mathilde Fourcier. She said in a letter to Bozonnet that she'd been with Credit Suisse for nearly thirty years. That would be around the time Blandine got married. She may even have recommended her husband to Mathilde. But Blandine definitely had plenty of opportunities to visit Mathilde with him over the years. To talk to her about her assets, her art collection, and the past. To exchange confidences even. That is how she kept up with you and your family. And probably how she got your phone number. You wondered about that, didn't you?"

Axelle glanced at her lawyer. Francie continued.

"Xavier Voclain found out you were in Paris again. How did that happen? Did you have contact with him?"

Axelle's eyes twitched. "No. Yes." She covered her mouth then composed herself. "He saw me in a bistro with Blandine that first night we met. He seemed familiar but I didn't recognize him. Then, out of nowhere, or so it seemed, he found me in that bar. I should have wondered how it could be."

Francie nodded. "Okay. He follows you around Paris. He remembers the Klein cast from way back. He knows they're valuable. Did he ask about them when you met?"

"I drank a lot of wine that night, I'm ashamed to say. There are things I don't remember."

"All right. Maybe he asks you. Or maybe he doesn't want to tip you off, or he realizes you think they've been destroyed. Either way he visits Blandine to get the information. He threatens her. She tells him what—that your aunt kept them? And what about the country house? Now that she's dead, it's time to find the casts?"

"I may have mentioned the villa," Axelle said quietly. "We talked about the art in Mathilde's apartment, the surprise for me, and the pleasure it gave her."

"He broke into the apartment, you believe?" Garnier asked Francie.

"He must have thought the paintings would still be there. When he got in and saw that they were gone, he figured he had no chance for them. But the sculptures were still a secret. He had to get the information about them from someone. He felt desperate. He had just missed stealing a Rothko and a Matisse. And a Roy. Millions of euros' worth of art. He took a candlestick and some other things to implicate someone else and cover his tracks. Later, after he used them, he put them in your hotel room."

"He knew my hotel," Axelle murmured. "I showed him." She put a hand on her forehead, aghast at her own ignorance.

They sat silently for a moment, running scenarios in their heads. Francie looked for a flaw in her story and assumed Garnier would be looking too. She looked at him questioningly.

"It's a theory. Where is this Voclain now?" the lawyer asked.

"He's somewhere in the Aquitaine. But his driver has confessed about his own part in the theft of the plaster cast. He's told the police where Voclain is probably hiding. He's cooperating with the police."

"They will find him," Axelle said.

"Soon," Francie agreed.

"And when they do they will investigate him for this death, Madame. I will make sure of that." Garnier straightened and actually smiled. "Their case is very weak. This is excellent news."

"Axelle." Francie leaned closer to her. "I have the second cast, the one made out of resin. They tried to steal it too, but we didn't let that happen. What do you want me to do with it? It belongs to you."

"Where is it?"

"In my possession. It's safe right now, but I'm flying back to the US tomorrow."

"Do you want to put it into an auction? Perhaps with your aunt's other artworks?" Garnier asked.

"No. Not with the others. Those I split with Lucien. This one is special—I wish I could see it."

"When you are free," Garnier said.

"It's beautiful, Axelle," Francie said. "One of a kind. Should I find another auction house for it? Or an art gallery? It needs to be properly mounted and preserved. And kept safe of course."

Axelle blinked hard, biting her lip, baffled by the questions. She looked like she might cry.

Garnier leaned in. "Do not worry, Madame. I will help you. We have a secure vault at the firm. I will take care of it until you are free. Then you make decisions for yourself. Is this good?"

Her hand on her cheek, overcome with emotion and fast-moving events, Axelle nodded. *"Merci,* Monsieur.*"*

As they exited through the waiting room Francie turned to the attorney. "This vault—it's very secure?"

"It is, Madame. We have several priceless works of art in there. An early Picasso." He raised his eyebrows.

"All right. I'll bring it by this afternoon." He gave her his business card. "I'll need a receipt and proof of insurance up to thirty million dollars US."

He looked down his thin nose and tried not to smile.

"Bien sûr, Madame. But of course."

EPILOGUE

At noon that day, their last in Paris, Francie met Dylan and Phoebe at an elegant ice cream emporium on Île Saint-Louis, where they explored the exotic flavors in lieu of a proper lunch. Phoebe giggled at the extravagance and ordered three different kinds. Dylan and Francie held hands under the table like they had in law school.

Francie whispered to Dylan about what had transpired with Axelle Fourcier at the prison. Phoebe's eyes sparked between them, listening hard, but the ice cream was too enticing. "Let's try to forget all that, for one day," Francie told him.

They took a *bateau-mouche,* a touristy excursion boat, down the Seine to the Eiffel Tower and battled the crowds on the steps for an hour. The view stretched for miles, the skies an endless French blue, as if showing off and reminding them of the iconic color. Francie took photos of father and daughter with the skyline behind them. They went to the Rodin Museum and the Picasso Museum, the smaller ones that were easier on the girl, and, truth be told, her father. Francie looked for works by Yves Klein, but neither museum was the right sort of place.

She left them outside the Louvre in late afternoon, discussing the merits of one more museum, and took off for the apartment to transfer the sculpture. She taxied across the city to the law offices of Garnier Frères with the precious cargo packed in her suitcase. Eyebrows raised when Francie withdrew it from her wadded-up underwear and placed it in the vault. She took several photographs to memorialize the event. Monsieur Garnier handed her the proof of insurance and the receipt without comment.

They flew out at noon the next day. Phoebe was in high spirits until they got on the airplane. She was nauseous until she fell asleep, her head in Dylan's lap and her feet in Francie's. Her mother met them at the airport. Phoebe ran into her arms and held her tight.

Rebecca was a lovely person, as it turned out. A redhead, as reported, tall, athletic, and very pretty. She looked nervous as she shook Francie's hand and thanked her for taking care of her daughter. No one had told her about the events of the last few weeks—the murder, the attack, the shooting, the theft, or how Phoebe had fought off a creep with her own two feet. That would make a good story, but they would let Phoebe do the honors.

They declined the offer of a ride home with Rebecca, letting her have Phoebe to herself. Dylan and Francie got in a cab, silent as they reconnected with the landscape of their home. Big American cars, sprawling suburbs, oversized houses. Autumn was in full swing, with trees in their splendor and pumpkins on porches.

"Stay with me tonight," Francie said as Greenwich came into view. She took his hand.

"You've never asked me before," he said.

"Things are different now."

He laced his fingers through hers and brought them to his lips. "Yes, they are."

XAVIER VOCLAIN WAS RUN to ground later that week, hiding in a barn ten miles from Villa Pardoux. A sweep of the countryside took much time and manpower from the Police Nationale, and they weren't very gentle with him. He was transferred to Paris to stand charges in the investigation of the death of Blandine Baudet. A single fingerprint was found in her house that matched his. More evidence would no doubt come to light, but it was a start. After a lengthy stay in a notorious prison Voclain went on trial for the murder of Madame Baudet. Lucas Laflèche testified against him, and told the court he heard Xavier threaten Blandine with violence. She told Xavier about the sculptures as a way to get him to leave her home. It didn't work, unfortunately. The big man's limp was remarked on by several people in the courtroom. Voclain was found guilty and given a sentence that would see him into his twilight years.

It would take a full three weeks from the time Francie Bennett visited her in prison before Axelle Fourcier was released from custody. With Voclain in the hands of the police, charged with murder, her charges were finally dropped. Francie got the news from Dylan and gave a yelp in her office, sitting behind her partner's desk, wearing a new, bright blue suit.

A few days later Axelle wrote Francie a long text. She had seen the resin cast of her torso in International Klein Blue and was breathless. It took her back to times and places and people she didn't want to recall. It reminded her of her vanity with Xavier, falling for his insidious French charm. Of poor Blandine, who didn't deserve a violent death because of their friendship. Of Paris in the bad, old days. And the harshness of her parents, who never tried to understand her, who rejected her and would destroy the artistic record of their only child for prudishness or the sake of their own reputations. As beautiful as it was, she hated the feelings that came over her, the memories that she'd worked hard to bury.

She may have forgotten for a while, but Axelle knew who she was now. She was no longer particularly French. And she was old. It was fine. She accepted it. Her young, supple body was a foreign land to her, forgotten and so very far away.

 It speaks a different language, of hope and youth. It holds promises that have faded and died. It lived a life now gone, as surely as the mist evaporates with the rising sun.

To look at it confuses me, confounds me.

Too long I have ignored the past, hoping it would die a quiet death with no intervention from me. Now I realize it is I who must act. I must accept it all and move on."

IN THE MONTHS TO COME, after she returned to her cottage in Oklahoma and moved her boxes of books halfway across the continent to her house on the ocean, Axelle Fourcier arranged for the cast of her very young, very blue torso to be mounted on a sumptuous gold panel, similar to the other Klein body casts.

In Paris the cast was carefully cleaned, restored, and preserved, and put in an art auction in late spring. The auctioneers named it simply "Axelle" and ensured its validity with a certified letter of authenticity from the owner and model. To her shock it sold for nearly forty million euros— a ridiculous amount even for bourgeois, elitist collectors who had more money than sense. But it was unique, the auction book said, the only female life-mold body cast by Yves Klein ever seen. He was a French hero, an icon of *nouveau réalisme* and the Pop Art movement of which France had only a handful. The new owner planned to lend it to the Musée d'Art Moderne in Klein's hometown of Nice.

A trust was set up anonymously for the grandchildren of Blandine Baudet, two boys and three girls. Five million euros was set in it, one million for each, to grow until they reached university age. Villa Pardoux was sold for a very small price to an enterprising Australian couple, eager to restore the house to its majesty.

Lucien and Severine Daucourt moved into the vast ninth arrondissement apartment and squabbled constantly about the state of the plumbing. When they sold off the remains of Mathilde's furniture a woman named Ceci bought a bed and an armoire. She explained she had lived there with Mathilde and wanted to remember her. The Daucourts didn't react to the sale of the Yves Klein piece, despite massive publicity. Perhaps no one told them it belonged to Axelle. Perhaps they were privately bitter. The other artworks were bought by museums or auctioned in Paris. Severine complained at length about the split of proceeds and the onerous taxes, but no one expected anything different from her.

Late that year Axelle Fourcier painted her house by the sea an intense ultramarine blue, a color so brilliant it hurt the eyes and sensibilities of the good folk on the neighborhood board. She listened politely, smiled, and carried on. One board member was a French Canadian widower with a shock of white hair and a PhD. When the cold, wet winter had passed, the two of them began taking walks together on the beach just before sunset, often with a glass of French wine in hand while they discussed history and politics and sea turtles.

She had to pinch her arm at least once daily to remind herself this was real. This was her beach. This was her ocean. This was her life.

And she was happy at last.

Bisous, tantine. Repose en paix.

~

ACKNOWLEDGMENTS

There is very little I like better than to learn about a fabulous artist I've never known. I hope discovering Yves Klein, if you didn't know about him like me or Francie, has been fun. In the past I have used fictional artists, like in my Jackson Hole mystery, *Painted Truth*.

But Yves Klein is very real, and his legacy and monumental conceptual *nouveau réalisme* pieces are revered in France and around the world. He made three life casts of friends, painted them in IKB, and mounted them on gold panels. A Klein retrospective in the UK was held at Blenheim Palace in 2018, an odd juxtaposition of Victorian and Pop Art. The casts— sometimes called "relief portraits" —that Klein made have been used repeatedly after his death but his value and reputation have remained high. There have been as yet no female life casts by Klein found— except in fiction.

Thanks to everyone who helped with the book. Your support, whether I mention you by name or not, has been so important to me. Thanks to Laura Dragonette for editing, to Katy Munger for cheerleading and more, to my family, always there for me. To Kipp who remarked: 'Another book? That was quick!' (It wasn't.) To Helen, my indefatigable French travel mate who helped me navigate the backroads of Aquitaine.

To my readers who clamored for more of the sisters, without you I wouldn't be writing at all! I can't thank you enough. Come join us, if you want, at the Girl Talk Facebook page, or subscribe to the newsletter.

Find me on your favorite social network— check my website for links at lisemcclendon.com.

ABOUT THE AUTHOR

LISE MCCLENDON is the author of numerous novels of crime and suspense. Her bestselling Bennett Sisters Mysteries is now in its ninth installment. When not writing about foreign lands and delicious food and dastardly criminals, Lise lives in Montana with her husband. She enjoys fly fishing, hiking, picking raspberries in the summer, and cross-country skiing in the winter. She has served on the national boards of directors of Mystery Writers of America and the International Association of Crime Writers/North America, as well as the faculty of the Jackson Hole Writers Conference. She loves to hear from readers.

Join her newsletter here
copy/paste: https://mailchi.mp/lisemcclendon/landing

Or connect on the social interwebs by searching for "Lise McClendon"

THE BENNETT SISTERS MYSTERIES

Blackbird Fly

The Girl in the Empty Dress

Give Him the Ooh-la-la

Things We Said Today

The Frenchman

Blame it on Paris

The Bennett Sisters French Cookbook

A Bolt from the Blue

Go for it!

Get the Box Set of the first 4 books

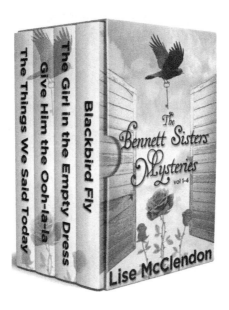

Box set fanatic?!

Explore all the box sets on Amazon

ALSO BY LISE MCCLENDON

The Bluejay Shaman

Painted Truth

Nordic Nights

Blue Wolf

One O'clock Jump

Sweet and Lowdown

All Your Pretty Dreams

❧

as Rory Tate

Jump Cut

PLAN X

❧

as Thalia Filbert

Beat Slay Love

❧

Printed in Great Britain
by Amazon

17631782R00159